THE ALICE AND JERRY BOOKS
READING FOUNDATION SERIES
SINGING WHEELS

MABEL O'DONNELL
Elementary Supervisor, Aurora, Illinois

Illustrated by
Florence and Margaret Hoopes

ROW, PETERSON AND COMPANY

NEW YORK CITY   EVANSTON, ILLINOIS   SAN FRANCISCO

Contents

STAGECOACH DAYS

Here Comes the Stage! 5
Wilder's Inn 14
All Aboard! Stage Going! 24
An Exciting Adventure 35
Hastings Mills 43

LOG CABIN DAYS

Getting Acquainted 53
The Smithy 61
Other Places to Go 67
The Old Harness Shop 75
Home 84
Off for the Big Woods 93
All Work and No Play 104
Cabins on the Hill 116
The Screech Owl 129
Secrets Astir 135
Indigo Blue 146
Fine Feathers 160
Bringing Home the Deer 167

Copyright, 1940. Row, Peterson and Company
Registered in U. S. Patent Office. Printed in the U. S. A.
International and Imperial Copyright secured
All rights reserved for all countries, including the right of translation
1912

Log Cabin Days (Continued)

Waubonsie	174
Fox Fire	179
Butchering Time	188
Pigeon Pie	199
"Yankee-Doodle"	206
"Whipping the Cat"	228
The Wolf Hunt	244

Snowbound

School Days	253
Reading, Writing, and Arithmetic	267
Spelldown	279
Whittling	294
The Christmas Clock	299
Tinkerer	310
Merry Christmas	317
Frozen River	326

Spring's in the Air

Sap's Running	341
Sugaring Off	349
Bee Tree	354
The House on the Hill	363

Stagecoach Days

Here Comes the Stage!

High up on the driver's seat of the big brown stagecoach Lightning Joe sat and blew his bugle loud and long. His left hand held the reins with which he drove the four swift horses. His right hand held the bugle to his lips.

The boy who sat among the bags and trunks on top of the coach leaned eagerly forward. "Don't forget your promise, Lightning Joe," he shouted. "When we get to Hastings Mills, it's my turn to blow the bugle. Don't forget!"

Lightning Joe had no time to answer. At the sound of the bugle the horses, which had been going at a fast trot, raced swiftly forward.

LUGGAGE

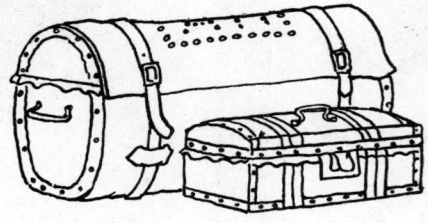 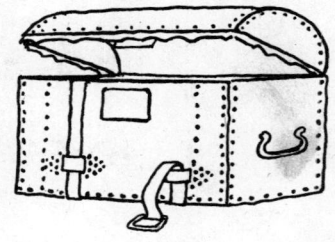

If it had not been for the railing round the driver's seat, Lightning Joe would surely have tumbled from the coach and landed on the hard, rocky road.

Forward over every bump in the road went the flying horses. What did they care for bumps? The bugle call meant that the stage station, or stopping place, was not far ahead. There, other horses would be waiting to carry the heavy coach farther on its way. The tired horses, which had been pulling the stage for three long hours, would have a good dinner and a well-earned rest. No wonder they pulled with all their might!

Up and down over all the bumps went the two small front wheels and the two large back wheels of the stage. Forward and back between the wheels rocked the coach, for all the world like a big rocking chair. Forward and back it rocked on thick leather straps which were fastened beneath the coach and which served in place of springs.

The yellow dust of the road rose like a cloud beneath the horses' feet. All at once, through the thick veil of dust, Lightning Joe saw a deep hollow at the side of the road. Could the wheels of the stage miss the hollow? If not, ten chances to one the coach would turn over. But no stage was going to upset with Lightning Joe on the box.

"Gentlemen, lean to the left!" he yelled. He dropped the bugle onto the seat beside him, took hold of the reins with both hands, and pulled the horses sharply to the left.

Among the travelers on the coach all was confusion. Tom Hastings, the thin, sandy-haired, long-legged boy on top of the coach, leaned to the left in a hurry. The three men who sat inside the coach did likewise. But Mrs. Ann Eastman, the only woman among the travelers, was so much alarmed at the thought of the coach turning over, that she dropped the bonnet box which held her best Sunday bonnet. Then she sat and held on to the edge of the seat with all her might, trying to remember which was her left side and which was her right.

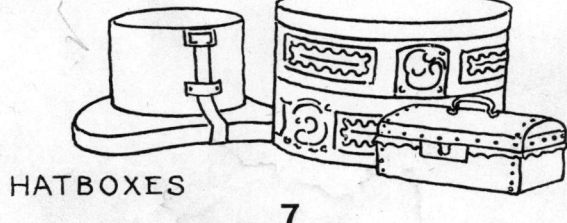
HATBOXES

Down over the very edge of the hollow went the right front wheel. For a minute the coach rocked forward as if it were about to stand on its head. Everyone held his breath, even the driver. Down over the edge went the back wheel, and the coach leaned as far to the right as it could without turning over.

But the horses, with the thoughts of a good dinner in their heads, raced so swiftly that the wheels were out of the hollow before the coach had time to upset. In another second the danger was over.

"Saved by a hair! Just by a hair!" yelled Tom. "Now I know why Grandpa said you were the best stage driver from the east to the west!"

"I've never had a stage turn over yet, son, and I'm not beginning now," chuckled Lightning Joe. The proud smile on his face was a sure sign that he was pleased with himself.

The inside of the coach buzzed with talk about the narrow escape.

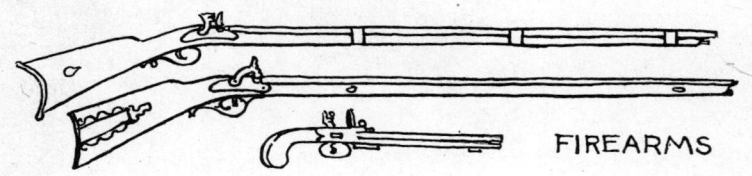

FIREARMS

"Sakes alive! My heart stopped beating!" sighed Mrs. Ann Eastman, as she settled back in her seat, smoothed down her flowered calico skirt, and tied the strings of her second-best bonnet.

"With anyone else on the box we would have gone over sure," said Mr. Tom Brooks, leaning from the open window to shake the dust from his high beaver hat. "Lightning Joe is the best driver that ever came out of New York State."

"He may be a good driver," said Mr. Forest Eastman, looking at his wife, "but the rocking of this coach is enough to kill any man, woman, or child who rides in it. I declare, my back is broken. My dear, I can never forgive myself for choosing this way of coming west."

"Come now, man," replied Mr. Andrew King. "A stagecoach is not an easy way of travel, but it is a fast one. We have come well onto twenty miles since early morning."

"We'll be dead by the end of the journey," insisted Mr. Forest Eastman. "What good is twenty miles to a dead man?"

Then once more came the long, loud call of the bugle. From his seat on top of the coach, Tom saw ahead of him the gray log cabins of a little town. Barefooted boys shouting, "Here comes the stage!" raced down the road to meet the coach.

"Look, Lightning Joe! The whole town is out! How long are we going to stop? Long enough for you to show me how to use my gun? Maybe I could shoot a bear!" shouted Tom.

"Perhaps a deer would do as well," smiled Lightning Joe, pointing with his bugle to the woods at the left of the road. There, standing in the sunshine, was a big deer. It stood for a second as if watching the hurrying coach. Then it disappeared into the shadows of the wood.

"Oh, Lightning Joe!" cried Tom. "I like this new country! Wolves and bears and deer and everything! A few more stations and I'll be home. The first thing I'll do is to shoot a bear. Did you ever shoot a bear? Did you ever see such a good gun as mine? Don't you think my Uncle Will was great to give it to me? I'm going to save my first bearskin just for him."

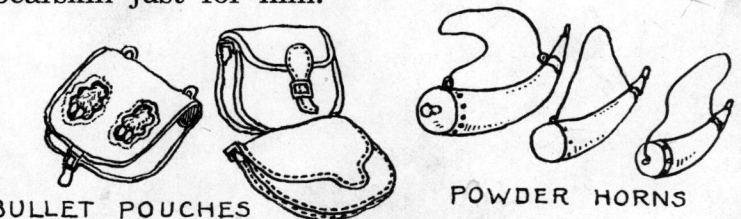

BULLET POUCHES   POWDER HORNS

Tom turned to pick up his gun from the safe hiding place which Lightning Joe had chosen for it among the trunks and bags. He hoped it was not too heavy. He hoped it was not too big. The wood of the handle was smooth and shiny. Tom loved that gun. How he wished that someone would show him how to load and use it!

But Lightning Joe had no time now to look at guns or to listen to a boy's chatter. He was pulling

his tired horses to a stop under the big sign which said "Wilder's Inn."

The <u>dusty</u> street of the little town was filled with people. At the first sound of the bugle they had left their work and had crowded from the log cabins into the road. Now they were waving their hands in welcome as they awaited the coming of the coach.

Already, in front of the inn, four fresh horses were pawing the ground in their eagerness to be off. No time to lose! Before the coach had come to a stop, men were at work changing the horses.

Wilder's Inn

The friendly, excited crowd gathered closely about the coach.

"Welcome, strangers!" "What news from the East?" "Any traveler here from Maryland?" "Any letters?" called one friendly voice and then another.

"What news of the journey?" "Come in!" "Dinner is waiting!" called another voice and still another.

Of course, the coming of the coach was as exciting as a holiday. How else could anyone in Wilder's Corners hope to find out what was going on in the big world except from travelers on their way to the West?

Maybe there was a friend among the travelers on the coach. Stranger things than that had sometimes happened. Perhaps there was a letter for someone in Wilder's Corners in the brown leather bag fastened tightly about Lightning Joe's waist.

WOMEN'S CLOTHES

But even if there were no letters, it was worth leaving one's work to see people rich enough to ride in a stagecoach. It was worth leaving one's work to hear what was happening back East in the big world where everyone in Wilder's Corners had once lived. Yes, the coming of the stage was reason enough for a holiday.

Today astonishing things began to happen almost at once. Down from the top of the stage climbed a boy all dressed in "store-bought clothes." He even had a "store" cap on his head! And there were shoes on his feet, and it wasn't even Sunday!

Barefooted boys crowded round Tom, and barefooted girls looked at him from under their sunbonnets. Think of it! A boy rich enough to ride on a stage and to dress in "store clothes"! They had never had anything but homemade clothes in all their lives, and they never wore shoes except in winter and sometimes on Sunday.

MEN'S CLOTHES

"Where are your ma and pa?" asked one boy, braver than the rest.

"There they be!" cried another, as he pointed to the open door of the coach. Mr. Tom Brooks had let down the steps from the inside of the coach and was helping Mrs. Ann Eastman to alight. Then the fathers and mothers saw Mrs. Ann Eastman's flowered calico dress and bonnet box and Mr. Tom Brooks's high beaver hat and flowered waistcoat. Their eyes were as big as the eyes of the boys and girls had been when they saw Tom.

"They're not my ma and pa!" cried Tom. "My pa is out West at Hastings Mills, and my ma is, too. They came west more than a year ago. They brought my sister Sally and my brother Jim with them. I had to stay with my grandpa and grandma and go to school. But my ma got lonesome for me. So now Lightning Joe is taking me home. He's a friend of my pa's."

Then all at once Tom stopped talking. He remembered that he was hungry, more hungry than he had ever been in his life before. He didn't want to kill a bear. He wanted to eat one. He started on the run for the open door of the inn.

The first thing Tom's eye lighted upon was the log table in front of the fireplace. He had never dreamed that one table could hold so many good things to eat.

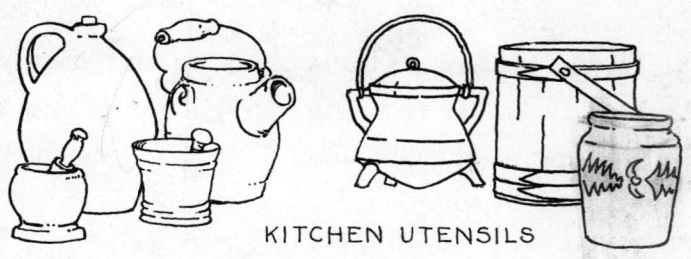
KITCHEN UTENSILS

At one end was a blue bowl piled high with a mountain of snowy, white potatoes. A hole in the top of the potato mountain was filled with butter which overflowed and ran down on all sides. At the other end of the table two fat roast chickens pointed their drumsticks into the air. Tom could see the good brown dressing coming out from inside the chickens.

Here and there in other bowls were hills of baked beans with juicy bits of meat on top.

There were loaves of bread still warm from the oven, dishes of cheese, bowls of applesauce, and jars of jelly. Best of all were the pies — golden-brown pies—apple, pumpkin, and good-smelling pies of all kinds. Tom didn't count them, but he was sure there must be a dozen.

The innkeeper's wife was on her knees, taking more pies from the oven at the side of the fireplace. She was short and fat, with a merry twinkle in her brown eyes. Her cheeks were red from the heat, as red as the buttons down the front of her blue calico dress.

"Hungry, son?" she asked, smiling up at Tom. "What is keeping the rest of the travelers? Don't tell me that the first roasting chickens of the year will get cold waiting for them! I'm the only woman in Wilder's Corners too busy to run out to meet the coach. But I know Lightning Joe. If dinner is not ready and waiting, he will carry you off before you have time for even a bite."

Before he had time for even a bite! Even a bite of that good chicken! Tom couldn't stand that. He just couldn't! Why, he was all hollow inside, he was so hungry.

Now, I guess the innkeeper's wife liked to cook for travelers, hungry travelers. All she had to do was to look at Tom's face to know that he was about the hungriest traveler who had ever stopped at Wilder's Inn. Anyway, she must have liked boys, because what do you suppose she did? She cut off a drumstick, a big brown drumstick.

KITCHEN UTENSILS

"Don't say a word," whispered the innkeeper's wife, as she handed the drumstick to Tom.

The meat was rich and juicy. It fell right off the bone into Tom's mouth. Tom had never, never tasted anything so good before.

"Come now," said the innkeeper's wife. "Let's see what is keeping the rest of the travelers. Something out of the ordinary must be happening to keep them from their good dinner."

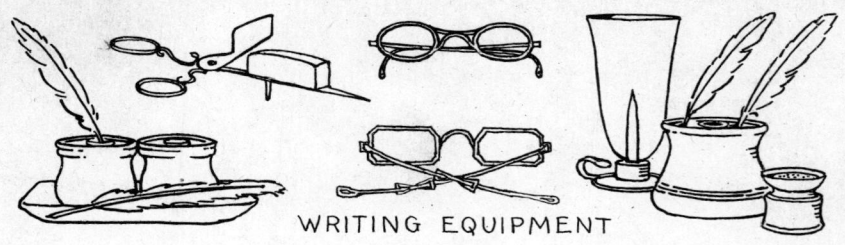

WRITING EQUIPMENT

Something out of the ordinary was happening. Excited cries of, "Don't tell us you lost it!" "Was it for me?" came through the open door of the inn. By the time Tom and the innkeeper's wife got to the door, Lightning Joe had taken a letter from his bag and was waving it high overhead.

"Who is the luckiest lady in town?" he called, and his whole face wrinkled up into one big smile. "Mrs. Mary Wilder is, I reckon, because here is a letter from her ma."

Of course, you know who Mrs. Mary Wilder was. The innkeeper's wife! Lightning Joe handed her a letter big and fat and overflowing with news. It was all sealed with a big splash of red sealing wax in which there was a picture of flowers and trees and even a bird or two.

When Mrs. Mary Wilder saw that letter, she thought she was the luckiest, and she knew she was the happiest woman in the land.

Then all the travelers piled into the inn and sat on log benches on each side of the table. That is, all but Lightning Joe went inside. He couldn't leave his seat until the day's work was over. So he called to the innkeeper to bring him his dinner, and he ate it sitting high up on the box.

Of course, the older travelers had to be served first. Tom thought it would never be his turn. But when his turn did come, he didn't have to answer questions the way the other travelers did. When a boy was at table, he was supposed to be seen and not heard. For once, Tom was glad about that. He didn't say a word. He ate chicken and potatoes, beans and cheese, and applesauce and jelly. Then he started all over again.

All the barefooted boys and girls looked at him and wished that they could be Tom and ride on a stagecoach. But when Tom heard them talking about a boy named Sam Race, who had killed a wolf all by himself, Tom wished as hard as he could that he were Sam Race. Boys and girls are that way. They are always wishing that they could be someone they can't be.

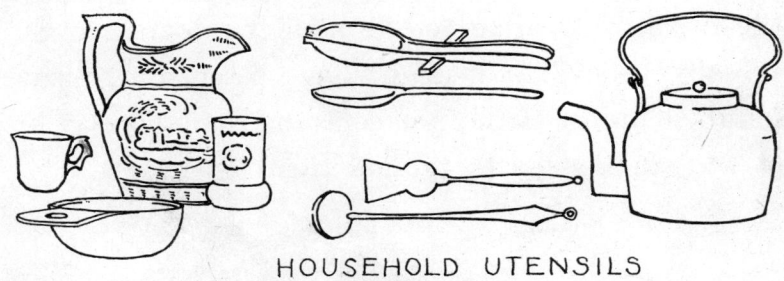

HOUSEHOLD UTENSILS

All Aboard! Stage Going!

Tom had just finished two pieces of pie and was about to start on another. All at once the long, loud call of the bugle made every traveler jump to his feet in a hurry.

"All aboard! Stage going!" someone called.

And then everything was confusion. Every traveler knew that Lightning Joe would not wait a minute, not a minute for any one of them. All the travelers tried to get through the door at once. I really believe they might have forgotten to pay for their dinner if the innkeeper had not been right at the stage steps to remind them.

Tom and his gun were up among the bags and trunks again like a flash. But Mrs. Ann Eastman was in such a hurry to get back to her seat that her skirt caught on the door of the coach. Then she had to back out, turn sideways, and begin all over again.

"Good-by! Good-by!" called the travelers.

"Good-by! Good-by!" called every man, woman, and child in Wilder's Corners. They waved their hands until the big brown coach disappeared in a cloud of yellow dust.

Before long, the first wild dash of the horses was over, and they settled down to a steady trot. Lightning Joe did not hurry the horses now. There was a long stretch of road ahead, and he did not want to tire them at the very outset.

The travelers on the inside of the coach took their naps in between bumps, and Tom and Lightning Joe were left to themselves to talk things over.

As far as Tom could see to the north, south, east, and west, stretched the rolling prairie. The long grass had turned yellow and brown beneath the hot autumn sun. Blue and yellow flowers growing everywhere made gay spots of color. The hot breeze of the early afternoon rippled the long grass until it rose and fell like waves on the seashore.

"Buffalo trails," said Lightning Joe, with his eye on the road ahead of him. "I reckon you don't know about them, son. Buffalo made this road we are traveling on. Great herds of them used to wander across these prairies, beating down grass and bushes and even small trees as they went. The herds went back and forth from the north to the east and south, and no one knows why they did it. Every herd that passed made the paths deeper and wider."

BUFFALO

COW   CALF   BULL

The minute Lightning Joe had begun to talk, Tom had leaned far over the railing round the top of the coach. His eyes were big with interest in Lightning Joe's story. Lightning Joe pulled in the horses, moved over a little more to the right, and made room for Tom on the box beside him.

"Then came the Indians," Lightning Joe went on, "and their trails followed the buffalo trails. You see, son, buffalo are wise. Their trails always lead to the easiest fording places in the rivers and the easiest passes in the hills or forests. No wonder the Indians followed where the buffalo led. And now the white man's road follows the Indian trails."

"And the buffalo — where are they?" asked Tom.

"The herds that are left have been driven far to the westward," answered Lightning Joe.

"To the west where we are going?" asked Tom, almost holding his breath in his excitement.

"No, much farther west than we are going," replied Lightning Joe. "You may see deer and bears and wolves, and even a wildcat or two. But I doubt that you will ever see buffalo wandering these prairies again. But remember, son, they made the first roads."

While Lightning Joe was talking, two men on horseback, their saddlebags full to overflowing, appeared in the road in front of the coach. They called a gay "Hello" as the stage passed by. Farther on, the coach passed a man walking, his pack on his back.

"There are ways and ways of going west, son," said Lightning Joe. "Walking is the hard way and the slow way, and it takes a brave heart."

Tom did not say anything. He was having a pleasant daydream. In his daydream a great herd of buffalo thundered across the prairie. Tom was Tom no longer. He was an Indian chief and had just killed the leader of the herd.

"Gentlemen, get out and walk!" The loud call of Lightning Joe wakened Tom from his daydream. Ahead of him he could see a long, long hill which stretched on and up as if it would never end.

From the inside of the coach came grumbling and more grumbling. Why should travelers walk when there were horses to pull them? But Lightning Joe was "king of the stage." It was enough to expect the horses to do to pull the heavy coach up the hill. When Lightning Joe told travelers to walk, he meant "Walk."

Before many minutes Tom and the other men travelers were toiling up the hill in the hot afternoon sun. But Mrs. Ann Eastman sat all by herself in the coach and was glad she was a woman.

The top of the hill at last! While the tired horses rested from their climb, the tired travelers returned to their places in the coach. From his seat high up on the box Tom could see storm clouds gathering in the west — dark clouds that looked like thunderheads.

For a time the road lay straight before them, with the endless prairie on all sides. Then, far ahead, Tom could see something white rolling from side to side. As the coach drew nearer, he saw that the something was a covered wagon — two, three covered wagons traveling together. Each wagon was pulled by four slow-moving oxen.

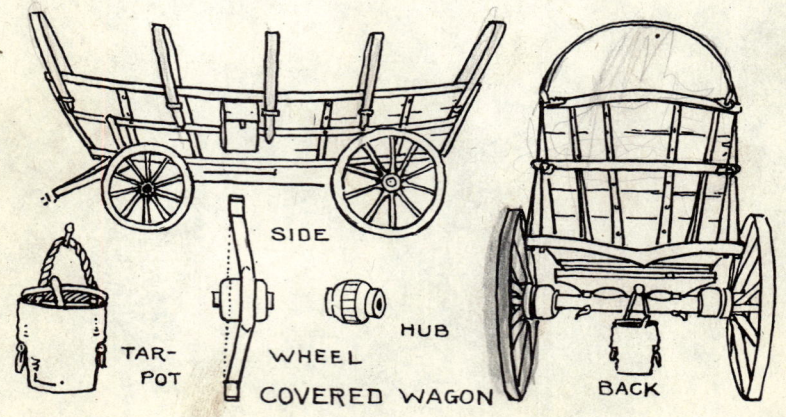

"There must be people in those wagons. Where do you think they are going?" asked Tom, as if he really believed Lightning Joe would be able to tell him.

"Settlers on their way to new homes in the West," replied Lightning Joe. "That's all I know."

Tom pointed to a cow tied by a rope to the back of one of the wagons. She was trying her best to put her nose into the feedbox.

Lightning Joe began to chuckle. "I've heard tell," he said, "that all you need to do is milk the cow and put the cream into a pail. The jolting of the wagon will churn the cream into butter as sure as you live."

"Do you believe that story? Do you?" asked Tom. But Lightning Joe just chuckled and said nothing.

"They can't travel very fast," Tom went on.

"Only as fast as a cow or an ox can trot, son, and that isn't very fast. Twelve or fourteen miles a day," said Lightning Joe.

"Look! Look! There is a boy driving one of the wagons, and he isn't a bit bigger than I am, not a bit!" shouted Tom. "There he is! There he is, walking along by the side of that big brown ox."

Sure enough, there was a barefooted boy walking along by the side of the ox that was closest to the wagon on the left side. He had an ox whip in his hand. There was a man sitting on the "lazy board," or seat, which came out from the left side of the wagon.

"That is his pa, I reckon, that man on the 'lazy board,'" said Lightning Joe, with a twinkle in his eye. "The boy may be driving the wagon, but his pa is keeping his eye on him."

As the stage passed by, Tom saw that the front seats of the wagons were crowded with women and children. One woman had her baby in her arms.

All the travelers in the coach waved and called "Hello," and all the people in the covered wagons waved their hands and called "Hello" in return.

"Where are you going?" asked Lightning Joe.

"Somewhere west where the land is good," called back the man on the "lazy board."

"Come to Hastings Mills!" shouted Tom to the barefooted boy. "That's where I'm going. Hastings Mills! Do you hear?"

The boy looked up with a wide grin on his freckled face. "Hastings Mills! Sure, I'll remember! Hastings Mills!"

"Do you think they will come? Do you, Lightning Joe?" asked Tom, as the stage left the covered wagons far behind.

"Maybe so," answered Lightning Joe. "If their road takes them to Hastings Mills, they might stop there. It is a good place to make a home."

That was all Lightning Joe needed to say. From that minute on, Tom was sure that he would see the boy again. He took the next few minutes to tell all the things that were going to happen when the freckled-faced boy and he hunted bears together.

But there was little time now to talk about bears. In the excitement of meeting the covered wagons, Lightning Joe had forgotten the storm clouds gathering in the west. The loud roll of thunder and a few drops of rain made him crack his whip high above the horses' backs and hurry the animals forward.

An Exciting Adventure

There was a worried look on Lightning Joe's face as he watched the clouds and the road ahead.

In another few minutes the rain was beating down. Lightning Joe drew in his horses long enough to pull his oilskin cloak closely about him. Tom pulled the oilskin covering over the bags and trunks on top of the coach and then crawled down among the bags out of the rain. All the while, he could hear the grumbling of the travelers within the coach as they began to fasten the leather coverings over the open windows.

For a long time the horses hurried on through the driving rain. The yellow dust of the road began to turn to mud — thick, sticky mud which slowed down the hurrying horses.

Now the coach was coming to a long, gently sloping hill. Tom, looking out from under the oilskin covering, could see a long stretch of woodland at the foot, a sure sign that they were coming to the river bottoms. He knew better than to talk to Lightning Joe now.

As the stage reached the woodland, Tom could see the gray waters of the river just ahead.

Now the road changed to a corduroy road made of logs placed side by side. When the road had first been made, the places between the logs had been filled with earth to make the road as smooth as possible. But the rains had washed the earth away.

As the heavy coach moved forward over the corduroy road, the jolting of the wheels threw Mrs. Ann Eastman from her seat and landed her on the floor of the coach. From then on, the travelers held on to their seats with all their might as the stage rose and fell from log to log. Every minute they were sure that some of the logs of the corduroy road would slip or break and that the stage would be stuck in the mud. But Lightning Joe guided the horses and the coach safely forward.

Now, close to the bank, Tom could see two stones which marked the fording place. In another minute the water was swirling about the wheels of the heavy coach as the stage started to ford the river. Would they make it? The river looked wider and deeper the farther they went. Even the rains of the afternoon might have deepened the river to the point where it was dangerous to cross. Down, down went the wheels farther and farther into the water. Then slowly, with the horses pulling with all their might, the great wheels began to rise from the water.

It was only when the danger was over that Tom heard someone calling a loud "Hello." He looked about him in surprise. There, fastened to a tree not far up the west bank of the river, was a flatboat.

On one end of the boat was a log cabin. On the other end was a log shelter for the animals. Two men and a woman stood in the open door of the cabin, waving and calling "Hello." In the animal shelter Tom could see a cow, a pig, two horses, and even some chickens.

"Hello! Hello!" called Tom, waving with all his might. But Lightning Joe was too busy and the other travelers were too much frightened even to answer.

Now the coach was out of the river and was splashing along over the corduroy road through the woodland on the west bank. In a few more minutes the stage would reach the higher land. Then all the danger of being stuck in the mud would be over.

All at once one of the horses stumbled and almost fell. As the horse stumbled, Lightning Joe gave a sudden pull on the reins. The great back wheel of the coach slipped from the edge of the corduroy road down into the mud at the right of the road. Down, down sank the wheel, deeper and deeper into the thick mud.

"Gentlemen, get out and push!" called Lightning Joe. The sharp ring to his voice showed how alarmed he was.

RIVER BOATS

Out from the stage piled Mr. King and Mr. Brooks and Mr. Eastman, and down from the top climbed Tom. In a minute their shiny boots were covered with mud. Mud reached halfway to their knees and splashed as high as the long tails on Mr. Brooks's coat. Before many minutes had passed, the men were wet through with the driving rain.

"Hello, the boat!" called Lightning Joe.

But the men on the boat had been watching the stage and were already on their way to help.

"Be thankful that only one wheel has slipped," said Mr. Eastman, as he helped place the small trunk of a fallen tree under the rear axle of the coach. By using the tree trunk as a lever, the men might be able to lift the wheel from the mud.

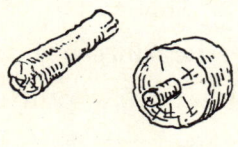

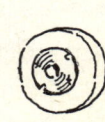

STORY OF THE WHEEL

Three men pulled up on the wheel, and two men and Tom pushed from the back of the coach. At last, with Lightning Joe guiding the horses from his seat on the box, and with the horses pulling with all their might, the wheel was back on the

40

road once more. The travelers, wet to the skin and covered with mud, returned to their places in the coach.

"Thanks, strangers!" said Lightning Joe to the two men from the boat. "Where are you off to?"

"To the mouth of the river," answered one of the men. "We have heard that there is rich land there for the asking. Our boat grounded on a rock a week ago. We have been all this time mending the hole in the bottom. Now we are waiting for the autumn rains to deepen the water and carry us safely over the fording place."

"You won't have long to wait. Good luck, strangers!" called Lightning Joe.

Now the stage left the bottom lands of the river valley behind and climbed slowly to higher ground. For a time it continued on its way through the rain and mud. Then once more came the long, loud call of the bugle, and once more Tom saw ahead of him the gray log cabins of a town.

This time there were no people in the streets, but the four fresh horses were ready and waiting. From the doors and windows of every cabin friendly voices called, "Welcome, strangers!"

The men travelers hurried into the inn to dry their wet clothes in front of the fireplace. Their clothes had just begun to steam a bit when the loud voice of Lightning Joe called, "All aboard! Stage going!" Out they piled into the rain again and back to their places in the coach.

FLOWERS THAT GROW ON THE PRAIRIE

Hastings Mills

No sooner had the stage started on its way than a break in the clouds to the west showed that the rain was over. A few more minutes and the sun was sparkling on the wide stretches of wet prairie. A cool breeze blew the clouds away.

Time went on. The great blue sky overhead, the unending prairie, and the everlasting clop-clop of the horses' feet gave Tom a lonesome feeling. Soon it would be night again. Would the stagecoach journey never be over? Would he never see his ma and pa again? The road ahead looked as if it would never end.

"Tell me about Hastings Mills!" he called to Lightning Joe.

"Lonesome, son?" asked Lightning Joe, with a kindly twinkle in his brown eyes. Once more he pulled in the horses, moved over, and made room for Tom on the box beside him.

"Not lonesome! Just want to know," said Tom.

"Well, suppose I tell you just how it is going to look. Then we will see if you know it when we get there. How will that be? Over there," said Lightning Joe, pointing to the north, "will be the Big Woods. That is what they call them, the Big Woods. And they are big woods. Hundreds of trees reaching right down to the riverbank!

"In that riverbank there is a cave where the Indians used to hide," Lightning Joe continued. "Get your pa to tell you about that."

Indians! A cave! That was enough to make any boy forget about being lonesome.

"Are there Indians there now?" cried Tom. A shiver of excitement ran up and down his backbone.

"Not now, son!" replied Lightning Joe. "A few, maybe, but the Indians, like the buffalo, have gone farther west. But there are deer and bears and wolves in those woods. Wild turkeys, too, and rabbits so thick you can step on them. Why, those woods are plum full of animals waiting for you and Jenny."

"Jenny! Who is Jenny?" asked Tom in surprise.

"Oh, I forgot!" said Lightning Joe. "When I was a boy, I always called my gun Jenny. Seems like she shot better when I gave her a name."

"Then my gun is going to be Jenny, too," said Tom, as he lifted the oilskin covering to see if his gun was safe in its hiding place.

"Right there in front of you going north and south will be the river," Lightning Joe continued, pointing straight ahead of him. "I've heard tell that there are more fish in that river than you can shake a stick at. On every rock sticking up out of the water, a big turtle will be sunning himself. I guess that is why the river is called the Big Turtle and why the inn is called Turtle Rock Inn. But best of all is the big wooded island in the middle of the river."

"Oh, I know all about that island," cried Tom. "My pa wrote me a letter about it. If you want to build a sawmill, Lightning Joe, be sure you have an island. You see, you have to have a big mill wheel to work your saws. You have to have a millrace to get water to turn the wheel. And you have to build a dam before you can have a millrace. But if you have an island, you need to build the dam only from the shore to the island, and not away across the river. Don't you see how that is?"

"I reckon I do," said Lightning Joe. "So right on the riverbank will be your pa's mill with a sign which says 'Hastings Mills.'"

"That's the name of the town, too," said Tom. "My pa is a great man. You have to be great to have a town called after you."

"Right across the road will be the inn and the blacksmith shop," Lightning Joe continued.

"I'll find out how to shoe a horse. That's the first thing I'll do," said Tom.

Lightning Joe went on talking. "Right next to Mr. White's blacksmith shop is Mr. Carter's store. Mr. Carter sells everything from dress goods to wagons. Next to his store is Mr. Harding's harness shop. Then there are the cabins where the Whites, and the Hardings, and the Carters, and your ma and pa, and the other families live. There are boys and girls in most of the cabins. And that is all there is to the town."

"My pa's cabin is the best! Isn't it?" asked Tom.

"I reckon you're wrong about that," answered Lightning Joe. "But there is one thing I forgot to tell you about. Over on the west bank of the river there is another mill — a gristmill for grinding flour. Mr. Gray owns that. He had to have a mill wheel, too, and so he built the rest of the dam. Do you know what your pa says? He says that with a sawmill to saw lumber for houses, a gristmill to grind flour for bread, rich farm land and woods, and a stage road to bring people from the East, Hastings Mills will be a big city someday."

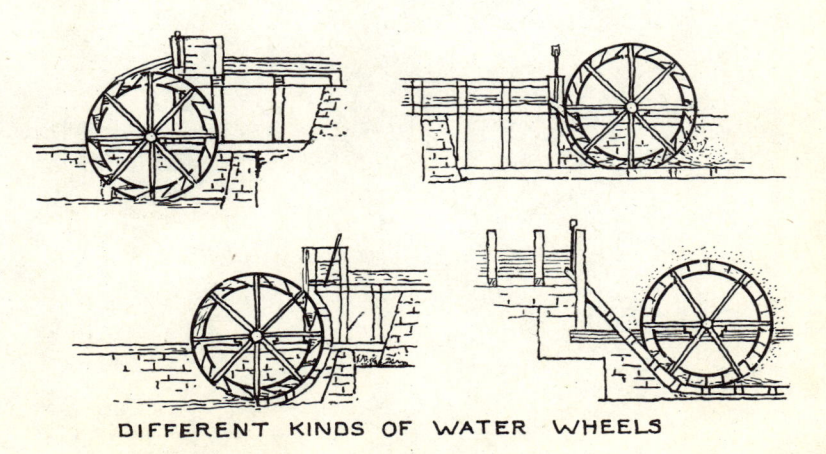

DIFFERENT KINDS OF WATER WHEELS

"My pa is right!" said Tom, slapping his knee the way he had seen his grandpa do. "And the next settlers will be the people in those covered wagons. You just wait and see."

I don't know how long Tom and Lightning Joe talked. But I do know that it was ten o'clock that night when the stage made its last stop. There were not beds enough in the inn, and so Tom and Lightning Joe rolled up in blankets in front of the fireplace. Before sunup the next morning they were again on their way.

It was pleasant riding over the prairie in the early morning. Before long the sun shone warm upon Tom's back. He could hear the call of the prairie chickens and the song of the meadow lark as it rose from its nest in the long grass. Once Lightning Joe pointed to a red fox racing away with a prairie chicken for his breakfast.

Time went on. About noon Tom noticed a telltale twinkle in Lightning Joe's eyes. The coach had come to the top of a long hill which sloped gently down into a river valley below.

Tom straightened up and gave one look. To the north, woods! Right in front of him, a river! A wooded island in the very center! And the log cabins of a town!

"Lightning Joe! I guessed it!" he cried. "Now will you keep your promise?"

Of course Lightning Joe handed Tom the bugle. But Tom was so excited that he didn't have any breath, and he couldn't blow a note. How Lightning Joe chuckled when that happened!

"Take a long breath and then try," he said.

This time Tom blew the bugle loud and long, just the way his grandpa had taught him to do. All the people in the town came running from their houses. Barefooted boys calling, "Here comes the stage!" raced down the road to meet the coach. Only this time there was a man among them. The man was Pa, and he was shouting at the top of his voice, "Tom! Tom, my boy, how are you?"

"Look, Lightning Joe!" cried Tom. "The whole town is out, and there's my pa."

The next minute the coach drew up in front of Turtle Rock Inn, and Tom and Jenny jumped down into Pa's strong arms. In a few minutes Ma was hugging Tom as if she would never let him go.

"Tommy, Tommy, you have grown a foot," she said, and she was laughing and crying at the same time. Tom's brother Jim held on to Tom's coat-tails, but Sally, his sister, just looked at him from under her sunbonnet as if he were a stranger.

The other travelers, who were going farther west, hurried into the inn for their dinner. Tom didn't. He hurried home with Ma and Pa. What did Ma and Pa care about news today? Tom was home, and that was the best news in all the world.

Just as the stage was about to leave Turtle Rock Inn, Lightning Joe heard a voice calling, "Good-by, Lightning Joe, good-by!" He looked around. There was a barefooted boy in blue jeans and a hickory shirt, waving to him from the door of a cabin. It was Tom.

Of course it was Tom. Of course he was barefooted. Of course he was dressed in blue jeans and a hickory shirt. He wanted to see and do things. And you can't see and do things all dressed up in "store-bought clothes" with shoes on your feet. Anybody knows that.

SWINGING SIGNS

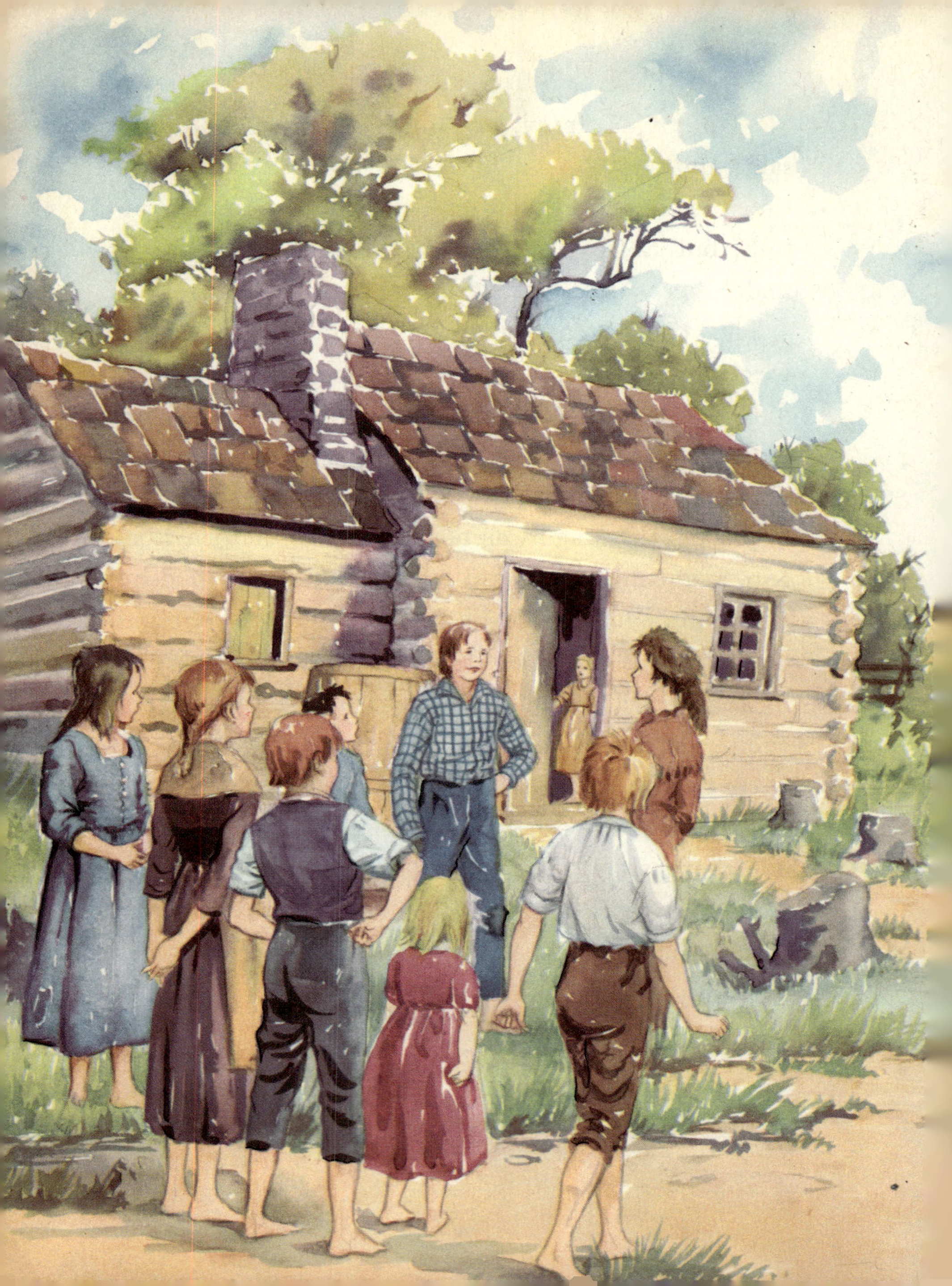

Log Cabin Days

Getting Acquainted

Tom had not been in Hastings Mills more than a few hours before he knew everyone and everyone knew him.

No sooner had the bugle sounded the call, "All aboard! Stage going!" than every boy and girl left the inn and found some reason for walking by the Hastings cabin. Of course they did. They wanted to look the new boy over.

There were half a dozen boys about as old as Tom, but the one who interested Tom the minute his eye lighted upon him was Sam White, the blacksmith's son. Sam was skinny and long-legged, just like Tom. He had a big grin and a freckled face. On his head was a fur cap with a fox's tail hanging down behind. Now, it was a warm day in early autumn, and Sam didn't need that cap, not a bit. But Tom didn't think about that. He just thought about the tail.

"Hello! Where did you get that cap? Did you shoot that fox? Did you?" asked Tom all in one breath.

"Sure, I shot him! Do you want to go hunting with my big brother and me?" asked Sam. He shook his head to make the tail wave and tickled the face of the boy next to him. "Come on over sometime. You can see my pa shoe a horse."

From that minute on, Tom had a satisfied feeling. Even if the boy in the covered wagon didn't come, Tom had found a friend. When Tom had a chance to go hunting in the Big Woods, he knew who was going with him.

Not one of the barefooted boys and girls could stay more than a few minutes, not even Sam.

There was work waiting for every one of them, and there was trouble in store for those who did not hurry. Already their mothers and fathers were calling to remind them. Even Sally, Tom's nine-year-old sister, had her knitting to do, and seven-year-old Jim had the wood box to fill and water to bring from the spring on the riverbank. Only Tom could do as he pleased.

"Come now," begged Ma, smiling up at Pa. "Give him today to get acquainted. There will be plenty of time for work tomorrow."

"Very well," answered Pa, in a voice which showed that he meant what he was saying. "But beginning tomorrow, young man, there will be plenty of work for a strong fellow like you."

Tom never forgot that first long afternoon of getting acquainted. Hastings Mills was the most interesting place in the world. There were so many things to see and do, and everything was so different and so exciting!

Of course, the first thing Tom wanted to see was his pa's mill. He dashed across the road and stood for a long time on the riverbank, listening to the rush of the water through the millrace and watching the great wheel turn round and round.

55

He stood on one foot and then the other while Pa told how he had made the dam by dropping stones and logs into the water.

Tom wished that he could have been out on a flatboat in the middle of the river, dropping logs to make a dam.

"Never mind, son," said Pa. "There is a bridge to be built before the snow flies. You'll be right on hand for that, I reckon."

Pa had not finished talking before Tom dashed into the mill. His eyes were big with surprise as he watched the upright saw move up and down through the hole in the floor of the mill. He helped to push the wooden car which carried the logs up to the saw and back again. He listened to the z-z-z-ing sound as the saw cut through the great logs.

Once Tom crowded so close to the saw's big teeth that Pa had to pull him back again.

"I declare! You are as bad as the Indians," said Pa. "When we first built this mill, they thought the saw was magic. They piled into the mill, and nothing we could do would get them out again. For a good many days we were never sure what we were sawing — wood or Indians."

You can imagine what Tom said then.

"Indians! Are there Indians around here? When will I see an Indian? When will I?" he begged.

"Most any day now," Pa replied. "The government bought their lands and moved them west to the great river about six months ago. But some of them will be going south for the winter. One or two will be sure to pass through Hastings Mills."

Tom wished that the government had waited a while before buying those lands. He would have forgotten about the saw and started out to look for an Indian, but just at that minute he heard a loud voice calling, "Haw, Bright! Haw, Flash! Don't you know your own names?"

Tom rushed out into the mill yard, and there he saw two great cream-colored oxen pulling an oxcart loaded with logs. By their side walked a little dark-haired, dark-eyed man no taller than the oxen he was driving.

"Welcome, stranger," called the little dark man, with a friendly grin in Tom's direction. "When do you reckon you're coming to work? We can't get along much longer without your help."

"He'll be with you in the morning, Frenchy," said Pa, who had followed Tom from the mill. "He won't be worth his salt for a long time to come, but I leave it to you to break him in."

Not worth his salt? Why, Tom could cut logs! He knew he could. He was ready to begin at once.

"Better wait until tomorrow," grinned Frenchy, as if he found Tom very amusing. "A few days toiling with me in the woods and you'll start grumbling. You'll never want to work again."

Then, while Pa helped unload the logs, Tom found out all there was to know about Frenchy. He was an old French trapper, and the best woodsman in these parts, so Pa said. When he was not working for Pa, Frenchy was trapping animals in the Big Woods and selling the furs for money. Of course he caught bears. Once he even caught a wildcat. Of course Tom could go with him someday when he went trapping in the Big Woods.

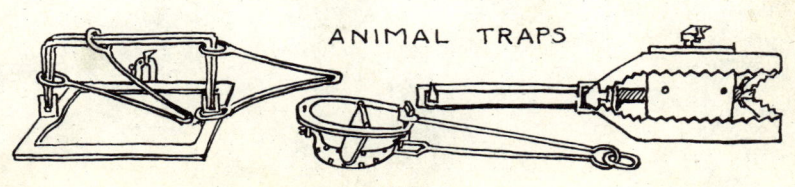

ANIMAL TRAPS

But when Tom suggested that Frenchy and he might go trapping today, Pa put an end to that idea in a hurry.

"Get it into your head, son, that there is work to be done around here. Why do you think we are piling these logs? We're doing it so that settlers passing through Hastings Mills will find logs for houses all cut and waiting for them. That will be one more reason for stopping here and going no farther west. Hastings Mills is going to be a big town someday if I can do anything about it."

Tom suddenly remembered that he hadn't told Pa about the covered wagons. Pa and Frenchy were as interested as could be. They made up their minds to be on the lookout for strangers.

The Smithy

There was no doubt in Tom's mind as to where he wanted to go next. Just as the first stage horse that had been left at Hastings Mills was ready for his last shoe, the blacksmith looked up and saw Tom in the door of the smithy.

Tom was sure he had never before seen such a big man as Mr. White. "Six feet four in his stocking feet," Grandpa used to say about a man back East. Tom believed Mr. White was even taller than that.

"Come in! Come in!" called the blacksmith. His voice was as big as he was himself. "So you're the boy who made this horse lose a shoe bringing you to town."

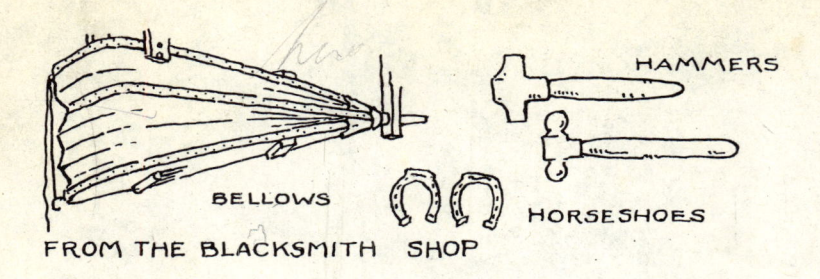

BELLOWS   HAMMERS   HORSESHOES
FROM THE BLACKSMITH SHOP

Tom looked curiously about the smithy, and the blacksmith went on talking. "You're thin and long-legged just like my Sam. Just the way I was, too, when I was no older than you. And look at me now! I reckon you might turn into a blacksmith yourself someday. Would you like that?"

I wish you could have seen the delighted look on Tom's face. If he could be a blacksmith, he certainly would. He watched every move Mr. White made as he nailed on the horse's shoe.

When that was done, Tom had to look into every nook and corner of the smithy. He could hardly believe it when he saw all the tools made out of iron. "There is not a thing made out of iron that the people in Hastings Mills need and that I can't make for them," said Mr. White proudly.

Tom could not keep his eyes away from the great forge. How could a fire be so hot? But, hot as it was, Mr. White was always adding some charcoal to make it even hotter. He gave Tom a piece of

TOOLS   ANVIL

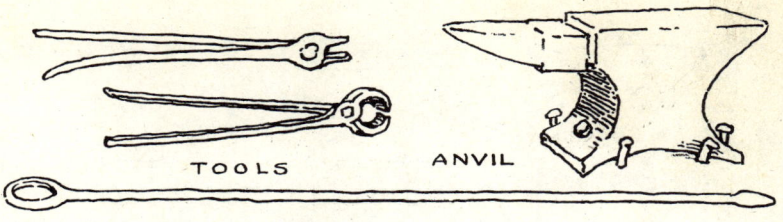

FROM THE BLACKSMITH SHOP

iron and one of his tools which looked like a big pair of pincers. Tom held the iron over the forge until it became red-hot and his own face became almost as red. Then he tried to shape the hot iron on the anvil. He soon found out that it takes more than a day to become a good blacksmith. When he tried to lift the big hammer, he found out, too, why Mr. White needed to be six feet four in his stocking feet and just as strong as he was tall.

The thing which interested Tom more than anything else was the big leather bellows which hung over the great forge. The bellows reminded Tom of a great fan. There was a leather strap fastened to the underside of the bellows. As the blacksmith pulled on the strap, the bellows opened and closed and blew air down a long pipe and under the fire. This made the fire burn hotter and brighter. Tom could pull that strap and blow the bellows, but it took the strong arm of the blacksmith to make it blow evenly and well.

BRICKMAKING   MOLDS   TOOLS

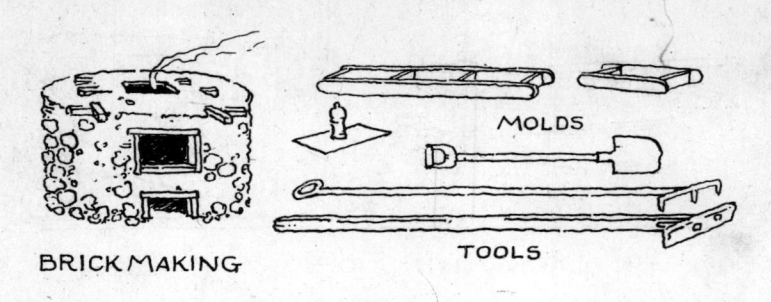

All this time Tom had a question he wanted to ask Mr. White. The better acquainted they became, the nearer Tom came to asking the question. At last, out it popped. "Where is Sam? I know him. He was over at my house."

"So you know Sam," chuckled the blacksmith. "He's been over to your house. I might have known it. He is out on the hillside near the Big Woods, making bricks with his big brother Joe."

"Bricks! How could Sam make bricks?" asked Tom.

"Out of clay, to be sure," replied Mr. White. "There is fine clay for brickmaking on that hillside. You see, Tom, you make a mold. A mold is just a box shaped like a brick, with no bottom in it. You fill the mold with wet clay and let it dry. Then out comes the clay brick, and you bake it in the brick oven. Where do you think we got the bricks in this forge? Sam helped make them, and Joe baked them.

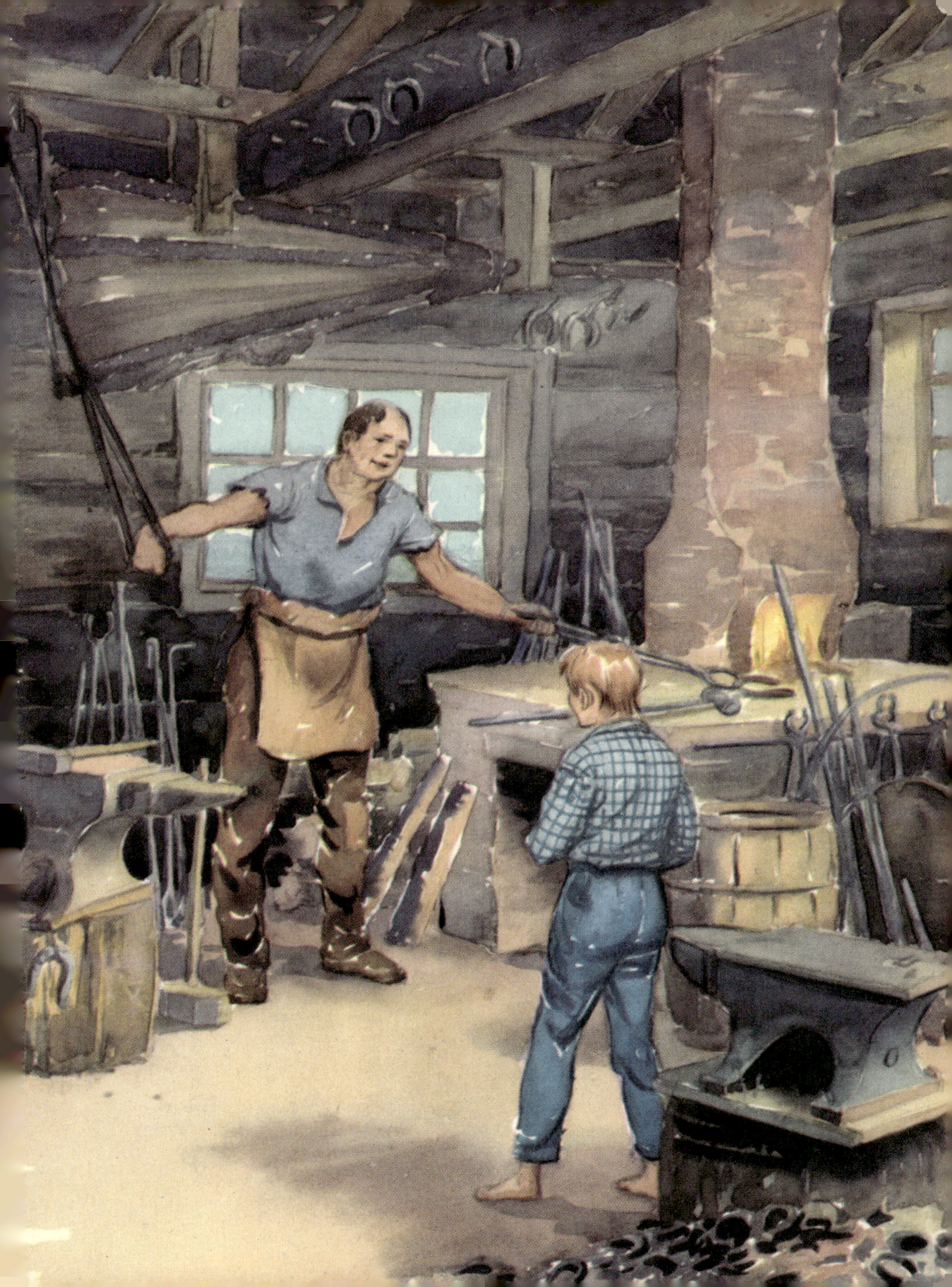

"Maybe you would like to know something else Joe is doing," the blacksmith went on. "He's making plaster. He has a hot fire of logs out on that hillside, and in among the logs are some pieces of limestone. When the fire burns down, he will blow away the wood ashes. What do you think will be left of the stones? Nothing but powder — lime powder. Later he'll add horsehair and sand and water to the lime powder and stir them all together. Then he'll have plaster. See the plaster between these bricks. That's how it was made. That's how the plaster in between the logs in your pa's cabin was made, too. Now what do you think about that?"

What did he think about that? Tom just looked wide-eyed at Mr. White. Sam could make bricks, and Joe could make plaster. What could Tom do? Nothing! But tomorrow he could. Tomorrow he would be a woodcutter, just like Frenchy.

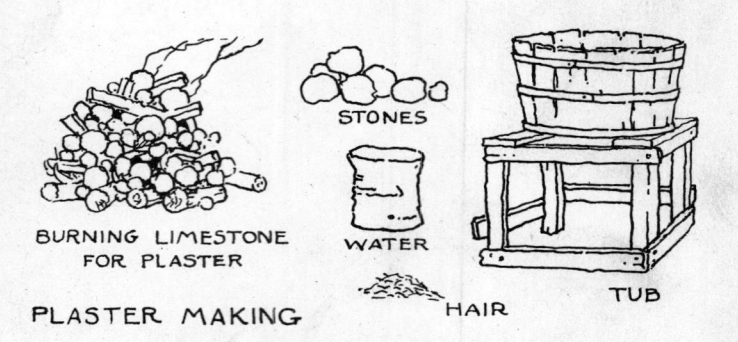

BURNING LIMESTONE FOR PLASTER

STONES

WATER

HAIR

TUB

PLASTER MAKING

Other Places to Go

Suddenly Mr. White remembered that there were three more stage horses which needed shoes.

"It wouldn't surprise me a bit if Sam would like to see you. I reckon he might even let you make a brick or two," he said in a hurry.

Out of the door of the smithy dashed Tom. I am sure he would have made for the Big Woods and the hillside, but just at that minute his eye lighted upon a flatboat made of logs. The boat was tied to a tree on the riverbank, and on the boat were two long poles for poling it across the river.

There was no one around to tell Tom not to go. Before many minutes had passed, he was out on the river, poling for dear life. Sure enough! On every rock sticking up out of the water, a big turtle was sunning itself. In the sparkling blue water beneath, Tom could see more fish than he could ever hope to count. Lightning Joe was right again. There were more fish in that river than you could shake a stick at.

Tom poled the boat around the end of the wooded island and over to the other bank.

There Tom saw another mill. Only this time the mill wheel was turning great millstones which ground the wheat and corn into flour. Tom hurried into the mill and stood watching the miller.

Men and boys on horseback, with bags of grain strapped to their saddles, rode up to the door of the mill. As they waited their turn for the miller to grind their grain, they talked to Tom. There were two men who were so proud of the mill that they could talk of nothing else.

"Why, we even helped Mr. Gray haul the first millstones," they declared. "Those first stones were nothing but two big stones from the riverbank a few miles from here. Mr. Gray smoothed them down and rounded them off, and they served their day. But these stones that you see! They came by oxcart all the way across country from Maryland. It took weeks to get them here, but here they are. There's nothing like them in these parts. People come from miles around to have their grain ground at this mill. And do you know what is happening? People are beginning to talk about moving closer to Hastings Mills to be near the mill that grinds the wheat that makes their bread. If this keeps up, the town will begin to grow before long. There is no doubt about that."

Tom listened to the talk, but his eyes were fixed on the millstones. One by one the bags were filled with the grist, or ground grain, and one by one the men and boys left the mill and started on their way again. Each in his turn left a small bag of grain with the miller to pay for the grinding.

There is no telling how long Tom would have stayed there, but all at once he felt someone tapping him lightly on the shoulder. It was Mr. Lake, one of the men who had talked so much about the millstones.

"Will you take me across the river, lad?" he asked. "It will save me a trip downstream to the fording place. I must trade some of my grist for sugar and other things which we need at home."

Mr. Lake rode his horse onto the boat. Then, because his arms were stronger, he poled the boat across the river.

"I'm surprised that smart men like your pa and Mr. Gray haven't figured out some way to build a bridge," he said, as they rounded the island. "A gristmill on one side of the river, and stores on the other! There is simply no sense in that."

"Never you mind! There will be a bridge here before snow flies," answered Tom.

If Mr. Lake was going to Mr. Carter's general store, Tom was going, too. They walked up to the door of the store together. Then, as if he were rooted to the spot, Tom stood still, overcome with surprise. He had never seen so many things in one place in all his life.

All along the walls were shelves overflowing with bright-colored calicoes — beautiful reds and blues and browns, with flowers and leaves of another color to make the calico look more beautiful. One shelf held women's bonnets and a man's high beaver hat. On another shelf were candle molds, and on another a few dishes and some iron kettles. On still another were knives — all kinds of knives, from hunting knives to jackknives.

Hanging on the walls were blankets, and rugs of bear and buffalo skin. The log counter was piled high with hammer heads, axheads, and guns. On the floor were barrels and kegs and wooden pails, and over in one corner were some barrel churns for buttermaking. In the middle of the floor was a round iron stove with a wood box behind it.

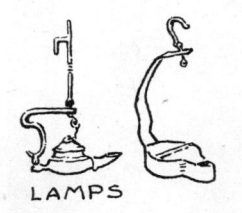

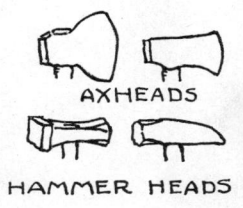

LAMPS   CANDLE MOLD   AXHEADS   HAMMER HEADS

The storekeeper knew Mr. Lake and came right out from behind the counter to welcome him. He was as short as the blacksmith was tall. He had smiling eyes, a big, hearty laugh, and brown, bushy whiskers which went out and in as he talked. He was just the kind of man that was meant to be a storekeeper.

"So your pack train got here at last," said Mr. Lake, looking about him at the well-filled shelves.

"It arrived day before yesterday," answered Mr. Carter, "all the way from New York State. Sixteen horses, each with a pack as heavy as he could carry. The train was four weeks on the way, and a week late in arriving. But we can forget that now. There is enough dry goods and all other kinds of goods in this store to last all winter."

He looked up and noticed Tom in the doorway. "Come in, son," he called in a hearty way that made Tom know that he was more than welcome. "So there's one more man by the name of Hastings in these parts now."

Tom just grinned, walked slowly to the center of the store, and began to look into every barrel and keg and pail. Salt in this barrel, flour in that! Candy in this pail, coffee beans in that! Nails in this keg, shot in that — round, gray shot that made him think of Jenny!

Was it possible for anybody to want anything that Mr. Carter didn't have in this store? Was that why it was called a general store? Tom was thinking hard, trying to figure out this question. He must have been thinking with his mouth open because all at once Mr. Carter popped a long stick of red-and-white peppermint candy into the corner of Tom's mouth.

"Now don't expect this every time you come into my store," chuckled Mr. Carter, and Tom grinned as wide a grin as the candy would allow. Tom stayed until Mr. Lake had traded his grist for sugar, nails, a hammer head, and a piece of blue cloth. Then, with a smile and a gay "Good-by," Tom left the store.

KETTLES

CHURNS

COFFEE GRINDER

SAUSAGE GUN

MEAT CHOPPER

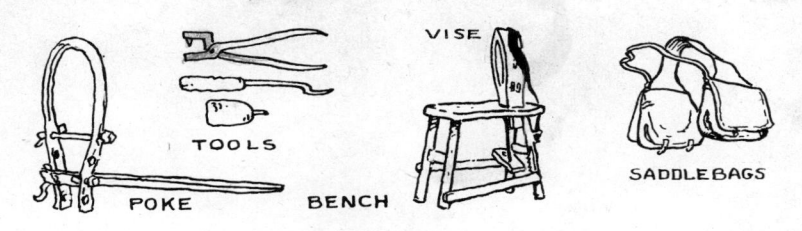

The Old Harness Shop

Tom wondered what Ma and Sally and Jim were doing, and so he decided to go home and see. Just then, he saw Pa going in at the door of the harness shop. Tom dashed pell-mell after him.

It seemed dark inside the harness shop, for there was only one window. There was a good smell of wood and leather in the air. Hanging all around the walls were saddlebags and pieces of leather. On the log workbench were a saddle or two and bits of broken harness.

Mr. Harding was sitting on a stool made from a sawed-off tree trunk. He was putting the finishing touches on a small ox yoke. He was older than anyone Tom had yet met. The skin of his hands and face and neck was wrinkled and almost as brown as the leather saddlebags which hung around him. But the thing that caught Tom's eye at once was the hat on his head, for sticking out of the hatband were three letters sealed with splashes of sealing wax. Pa saw Tom's eye fixed on the hat.

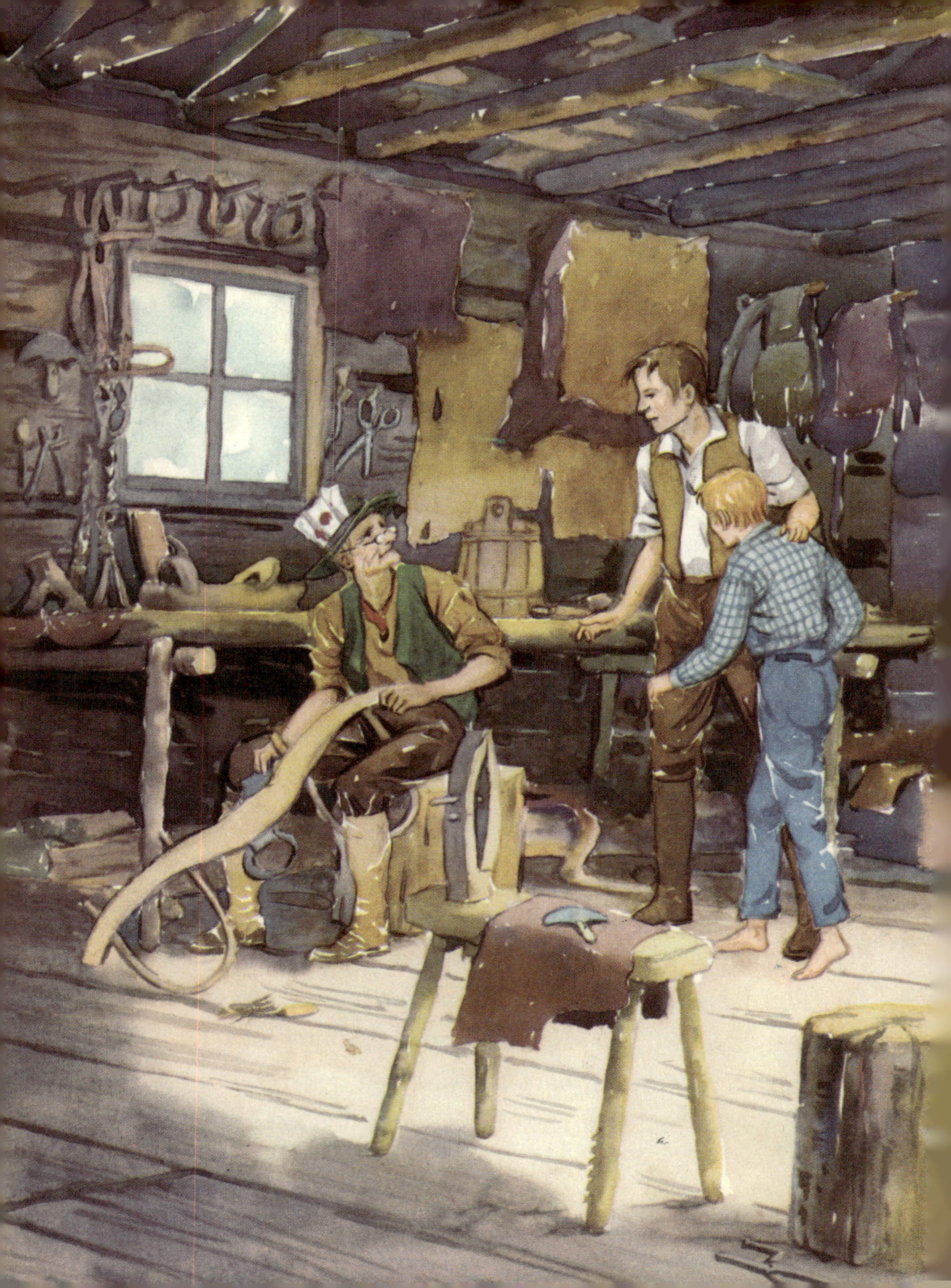

"How do you like our post office, son?" asked Pa, as an amused smile spread over his face.

Mr. Harding looked up with a pleasant, "Upon my word! Hello, Tom! Welcome home to Hastings Mills!"

Tom was too much astonished to say "Hello." "Post office!" were the only words that would come out.

"Yes, post office," Pa replied. "When Lightning Joe has letters for settlers in the country round about, he knows what to do with them. He puts them right in this hat. Every settler that comes riding into town stops here first to see what the hat holds for him. And the hat never comes off the postmaster's head until the last letter finds its owner."

"But what does he do at night?" asked Tom.

"Upon my word, I sleep in it! I declare I do! Don't you believe me?" laughed Mr. Harding.

"And what if the settlers don't come to town?" Tom went on.

"Well, then," said Pa, "someday when Mr. Harding is in a good temper and feeling lazy, he gets on his old horse and rides out over the prairie and takes the letter where it belongs."

"When I can find my way around, maybe I can do that for him," said Tom.

"Yes, you can," answered Mr. Harding. "That will be a big help to an old man like me."

"Oh, no you can't!" said Pa. "There will be work enough for you, hauling logs."

"That settles it," chuckled Mr. Harding, with a knowing look in Tom's direction. "And now, why do you think I am making this yoke?"

Why was he making that yoke? Tom hadn't an idea. But when Pa looked at the old harness maker and the old harness maker looked at Pa, Tom knew there was a secret somewhere.

"Too small for big oxen," Mr. Harding said, holding up the finished yoke. "It must be for a pair of yearling calves. A boy would like them."

Tom flashed one astonished look at Pa and another at the old harness maker. A boy would like them! "What is he talking about, Pa?" he cried. "What is he talking about?"

Pa pushed open the back door of the shop. There, standing quietly in the sunshine, was a pair of yearling calves. Their coats were red and shiny, and their horns were not yet fully grown. On the forehead of one calf was a patch of white.

"They are your calves, son," said Pa. "I've been gentling them and getting them ready for you. Already they have outgrown their first yoke. I brought them with me to save Mr. Harding a trip to our barn to fit the new one. These calves can pull a small oxcart already. If you do not load them too heavily, they will work well for you. Come and speak to them."

Tom never quite knew all that happened in the next few minutes. He remembered speaking softly to the calves. He remembered rubbing the bumpy places on their heads where their horns grew, while they looked at him with soft eyes and felt him all over with their wet noses. He remembered their names, Red and Patch. He remembered taking off the old yoke and putting on the new with the old harness maker's help. The yokes were too heavy for him to lift all by himself.

Then he was on his way home with Pa, leading his own yearling calves by a rope fastened to the iron ring which hung down from the yoke.

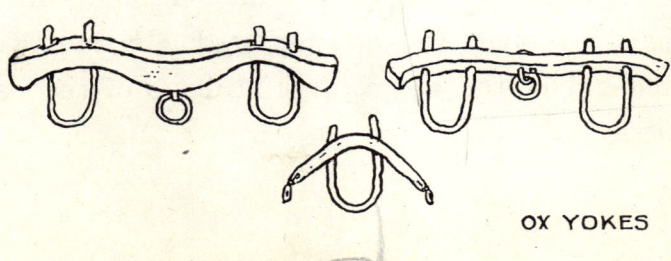

OX YOKES

"Hello, Tom! Are those your calves?" called two boys who appeared suddenly from somewhere and started to walk along with him.

Tom nodded his head and paid no more attention. He was so happy and so contented walking along with Pa that he did not care at that minute whether there was another boy in the whole world.

When Pa and Tom reached home, they let down the gate in the crooked rail fence and led the calves to their own stall in the log barn behind the cabin. The cows had already been milked, and all the animals had been fed and watered. Pa and Tom walked out of the warm, dark stillness of the barn together.

Then, like a flash, Tom remembered something Grandpa had said. There ahead of Tom was the little gray log cabin with the rain barrel by the back door. This was his home, and Pa's and Ma's, and Sally's and Jim's. A real log cabin! This was new, wild country, and Pa had been the first man to settle here. His pa was a pioneer. That's what Grandpa had called him, a real pioneer.

"Yes, Tom," said Pa in reply to Tom's eager questioning. "I guess that's what we are, Ma and you and I and the rest of us — pioneers. We have opened up new country and have built new homes. But the people who follow will turn these rich prairies into farm lands, and towns will spring up in the valley of the Big Turtle. We won't be pioneers long."

Pa put one hand on Tom's shoulder. With the other he pointed to the long, gently sloping hillside to the eastward down which Tom had driven with Lightning Joe that morning. There was a thoughtful, faraway look in Pa's eyes, as if he were dreaming a dream which he hoped might come true.

"All that hillside is ours, Tom," he said. "Bought from the government for only twenty dollars. Before another year comes round, the cabins will begin to climb the hill. And there on the very top, there by the two big maples, will be our house, a frame house built from lumber sawed in our own mill. The first frame house in Hastings Mills! I tell you, son, we will have such a house-raising as has never been seen in these parts before."

Something of Pa's excitement caught hold of Tom. "And people will come from all the country round to help with the house-raising! And they will stay one day and maybe two! And they will sing a song for the new house! Is that the way it is going to be?"

Just as quickly as it had come, the thoughtful, faraway look left Pa's eyes. "Yes, that is the way it will be, son. But don't forget! It takes hard work to make dreams come true, and there is work aplenty for all of us."

And then Pa lifted the leather latchstring, the door of the cabin opened on its leather hinges, and Pa and Tom were at home once more. Tom stood quietly in the doorway and looked around.

The glow of the sunset was shining through the front door of the cabin. There was Ma in her brown calico dress and blue apron, busy at her spinning wheel. Jim was sitting on a log stool at her feet while Ma taught him his A B C's. Sally, on another stool, was busy with her patchwork and singing softly as she worked.

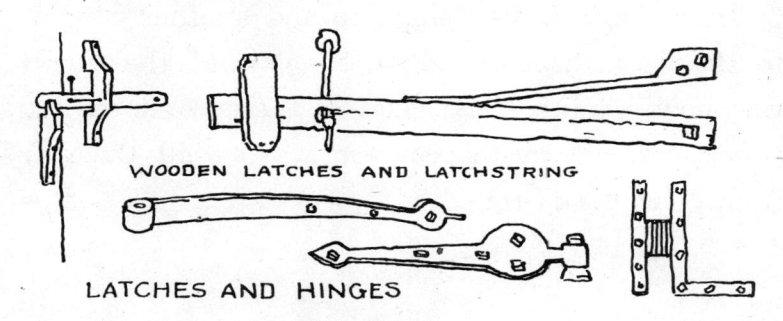

WOODEN LATCHES AND LATCHSTRING

LATCHES AND HINGES

Home

That morning Tom had been too much excited to notice what a pleasant and comfortable place the cabin really was. There was a big room and a little room, with a door in the wall between. The rest of the wall was taken up with the great fireplace made of cobblestones plastered together.

In the big room there was a front door and a back door. There was a window to the east to catch the first light of the rising sun and another window to the west through which the glow of the sunset was now coming. The glass in these windows had come with Pa in the covered wagons all the way from New York State.

The little room was where Ma and Pa slept, and pushed back under their big bed was the trundle bed where Jim slept. There was a window in the little room, but this window had no glass. It was like a little door high up on the wall and opened on leather hinges.

A good smell of meat cooking came from the big iron kettle hanging over the fire in the fireplace. On the puncheon floor of smoothed-off logs, were two bright-colored rugs which Ma had made by braiding long pieces of cloth together. Over in one corner of the big room was Sally's bed, and leaning against the wall by the fireplace was a log ladder which led up through a square hole to the attic where Tom was to sleep.

Then there were the tables and chairs which Pa had made, Ma's spinning wheel and loom, and the chest which Ma had insisted on bringing from the East. She couldn't keep house without that chest. Right above the chest the Christmas clock was ticking merrily. The clock had come from a country far across the sea, and it had been in the Hastings family for ever and ever so long. Even Pa would not think of moving west and leaving that clock behind him.

Tom filled the wooden pail from the rain barrel by the back door. Then Pa and he splashed water over their faces and necks and arms until they were clean and rosy.

The next thing Tom knew, he was sitting at the table, eating prairie chicken and corn bread and a big piece of pumpkin pie. Then, while Sally helped Ma with the dishes and Jim sat on a stool by the fireplace and looked on, Pa showed Tom how to load Jenny.

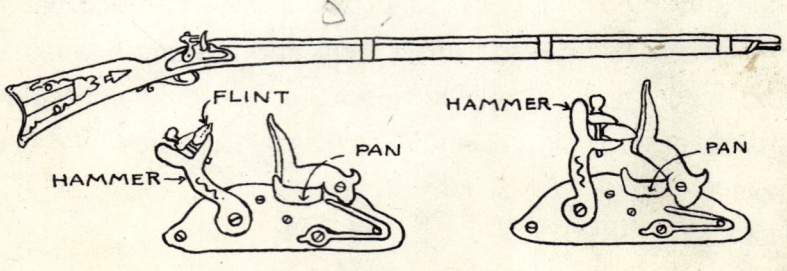

FLINTLOCK GUN

"Suppose we load my gun first," said Pa. "Then later you can load Jenny all by yourself."

First Pa unfastened his powder horn from the leather strap which reached over his left shoulder and hung down under his right arm. Pa's powder horn was nothing but a hollowed-out cow horn. There was a big piece of wood in the big end and a little piece of wood in the pointed end to keep the powder from falling out. Tom took out the piece of wood from the pointed end. Pa showed him just how much gunpowder to use, and Tom dropped the powder down the barrel of the gun. Then he shook the gun to be sure that all the powder reached the bottom.

Next Pa handed Tom his leather bullet pouch. Tom took out a bullet and the tin patch box in which Pa kept his patches. The patches were little pieces of greased cloth. Tom put the bullet on one of the patches. Then Pa showed him how he used the ramrod to push the bullet and the cloth down the barrel of the gun.

Now Tom was ready to load Jenny. Carefully he dropped the powder down the barrel of the gun. Carefully he put the bullet on the greased patch and used the ramrod, just as Pa had told him to do.

Last of all, Pa lifted the hammer and showed Tom the little pan on the side of the gun under the hammer. All Tom would need to do when the time came to use Jenny was to put some powder into the pan. Then Jenny would be loaded.

By this time it was growing dark, and Ma had lighted the candles. It was too late to think of trying Jenny that night. But maybe Tom could put her on the floor by the side of his bed. It gives you a safe feeling to have your gun close at hand.

But Ma and Pa thought otherwise. In the end Jenny found a safe resting place on the two wooden pegs on the wall above the front door.

Ma sat in her rocking chair before the fire, mending the holes in Jim's blue jeans and hickory shirt and putting another button on Sally's calico dress. Jim and Sally were safe in bed. On the other side of the fire Pa and Tom were busily at work softening the leather in Pa's high boots by rubbing them with bear grease. The warm glow of the firelight was shining on Pa's face as he sat and talked to Tom.

Of course, Tom must learn to shoot Jenny. Every man in a new, wild country must learn to use a gun. He must be able to kill wolves before they have a chance to kill him. He must be able to kill the foxes which rob his barnyard. He must kill deer so that he may have meat to eat.

"Yes, a man needs to be a sure shot," Pa explained, "but he doesn't kill just for the sake of killing, son. He always has a reason."

Shooting was no easy matter. It would be weeks before Tom could be trusted to load Jenny all by himself, and it would be years before he was a sure shot. But Pa would teach him, and Frenchy would, and Sam's big brother Joe. Tom would soon find out that Jenny was heavy and hard for a boy to handle. He didn't need to get it into his head that he could go around wasting powder and bullets whenever he wanted to. Bullets were too hard to make, and powder was too hard to get.

So now Tom was to listen to Pa and mind what Pa was saying. He was never to take Jenny out by himself, never until Pa said so. And if Pa ever caught him at it, there would be a "pile" of trouble in store for him. Pa's eyes wandered over to the south wall of the cabin. Tom's eyes followed Pa's.

There, hanging on a wooden peg on the wall, was a leather strap. Tom knew what Pa meant. Yes, he knew just what Pa meant.

"And now to bed," said Ma, putting aside her work and rising from her chair. Then she stood and smiled down at Tom, and Tom from his seat on the log stool smiled back at Ma.

"It's good to have you at home, Tommy. We've missed you so much," said Ma.

Pa put aside his boots and opened the door to see what the weather was going to be tomorrow. The stars were shining brightly, and in through the door came the faraway sound of fiddle music.

"It's the blacksmith," whispered Pa, as Ma and Tom came to stand beside him in the doorway. Then, before they knew it, Ma's feet were dancing, and Tom and Pa were humming softly,

"A penny for a spool of thread,
A penny for a needle,
That's the way the money goes,
Pop! goes the weasel."

And then Tom was climbing the ladder. All the time he was climbing, he was thinking how funny it must be to see a big blacksmith, six feet four in his stocking feet, playing a little brown fiddle.

Tom crawled into bed and lay there looking out through a crack between the logs. The round moon was coming up behind the two big maples on the hillside where the house-raising was to be.

He looked down into the garden, and there, just outside the crooked rail fence, a deer was standing with one forefoot lifted. Tom wished he had Jenny! Oh, how he wished he had Jenny!

Then, like a flash, he remembered what Pa had said. "After all, there must be some reason for killing." Just at that minute Jack, the watchdog, barked loudly, and the deer raced away over the prairie.

For a time Tom lay still, turning over in his head all the surprising things which had happened and which were going to happen. And then he was asleep, so sound asleep that he never even heard the big gray wolf which pointed its nose and howled at the moon.

Off for the Big Woods

Tom sat up in bed with a start. Pa was calling in a voice that meant no fooling, "Get up, Tom! Time for work!" Like a flash Tom remembered. There were yearling calves in the barn and trees to be cut in the Big Woods. He was into his blue jeans and hickory shirt and down the ladder before Pa had a chance to call a second time.

Pa and Tom went out to the barn together. The sun was just coming up, and the dew on the long grass was beginning to sparkle in the sunshine. Smoke was coming from every chimney. Here and there a cow, already milked, was following its crooked path to the prairie. The day of work for Hastings Mills had already begun.

The autumn chill in the air made Tom shiver, and the warm darkness of the barn seemed very pleasant. There were the big oxen, Bright and Flash, pawing the ground in their eagerness for their breakfast. There were the yearlings, pushing their wet noses through the log bars of their stall to welcome Tom. There was Pa's big gray horse, and there were the cows.

Tom worked fast, almost as fast as Pa. While Pa was busy with the feeding, Tom brought bucket after bucket of water from the barrel by the back door. Then together they cleaned the stalls and spread fresh bedding for the animals.

Next Tom sat down on the log milking stool, put his wooden milk pail between his feet, and began to milk Brownie. She was to be his cow because she was old and gentle and easy to milk. Tom's hands were not strong enough for a hard milker like Bluebell, even though he had been helping Grandpa milk for more than a year.

"Listen, Tom," said Pa, as the cows followed one another through the gate in the crooked rail fence. "You must learn the sound of your own bells. Then, when you go with Jack to bring home the cows, you will waste no time in finding them."

Tom stood listening to the tinkle of the cowbells and wishing that he could follow the bells for a long, wild day of discovery on the prairie. Anything might happen to a boy on a day like that. Another second and he remembered! There was work to be done. Minding cows was child's play. Jim could do that. Even cows could sense danger. They would not wander far, so Pa said. They were safe enough on the prairie in the daytime. Only at night, when wild animals were about, must they seek the safe shelter of the barn.

Now Pa and Tom were on their way back to the house with the milk pails. Breakfast was ready — juicy salt pork, corn bread, and great cups of sweet, warm milk.

Before breakfast was over, Frenchy's cheery whistle could be heard as he walked up from his cabin on the riverbank. With him was his son Pierre, who knew all there was to know about yearling calves. He was little and dark, just like Frenchy, and older than Tom by four years. Tom and he were to work together, and both today and during the weeks to come, Pierre was to keep his eyes on Tom and the calves. Tom wasn't sure he liked that idea, but he said nothing to Pierre.

Following right behind Frenchy were two other men, Indian Jack and a man named Charlie. Indian Jack was half Indian and half white. Pa said he was a half-breed.

Now the yoke was on the necks of the two big oxen. Bright and Flash walked out of the barn and stood quietly while they were hitched to the great oxcart which stood at the corner of the barn. Then Frenchy, Indian Jack, and Charlie loaded the great crosscut saws and the axes onto the cart and were off for the Big Woods.

Pa, on his way to the mill, lingered for a minute to watch the boys. Tom and Pierre lifted the small yoke and placed it gently over the soft necks of Red and Patch. Pierre showed Tom how to fit the bows under the necks of the oxen and push them up through the holes in the yoke and fasten them. All the time Red and Patch were watching the boys with their big, soft eyes, and Tom and Pierre were talking quietly.

Pierre filled his pockets with carrots from the wooden pail by the barn door, and Tom did, also. Then, holding a carrot in front of the nose of each of the calves, the boys led Red and Patch from the barn.

By the time the yearlings were hitched to the small oxcart which stood by the crooked rail fence, Tom was excited. He was so excited that he ran back and forth from the calves' heads to the rear axle of the cart.

OX YOKE

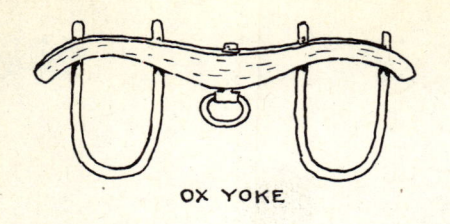

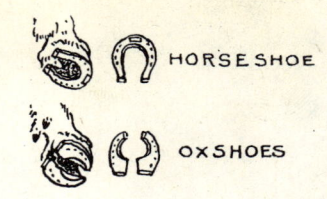

HORSESHOE

OX SHOES

A sharp call from Pa, "Stop it! Do you want those oxen to run away?" brought Tom to his senses. In another minute Pierre cracked the small ox whip above the yearlings' heads. "Giddap!" he called, and the boys and the calves walked quietly along the wagon path to the woods.

As they walked, the two boys began to get acquainted. Tom told Pierre all he knew about oxen, and that wasn't much. He knew that if you wanted them to go left, you said "Haw!" If you wanted them to go right, you said "Gee!" But it was Pierre who knew the important things because he had been helping Pa to "gentle" Red and Patch.

"You'll have to be quiet when these yearlings are around," said Pierre, shaking his head wisely as if he knew all there was to know about everything. "Get them excited, and they'll run away just as sure as a bear eats honey. Some days they will make you so cross that you'll want to yell at them. But yelling will only make matters worse. Just speak quietly and gentle them along. Carrots are good for that. Yearlings will do most anything for a carrot. And you never use the whip except to crack above their heads when you want them to gee and haw. These calves are going to be worth money someday if we break them in right, and that is what your pa is trusting us to do."

If Pa was trusting Tom to break the calves in right, Tom was going to begin that very minute. He walked backwards in front of Red and Patch and fed them carrots as they walked slowly along.

Now they had come to a lazy little creek which flowed westward to the river.

"Has this creek a name?" asked Tom, as the cart and the calves and the barefooted boys splashed through the water together.

"Indian Creek! That's what we call it," answered Pierre. He leaned over, picked up an Indian arrowhead which was stuck in the mud on the north bank, and handed the arrowhead to Tom.

Tom could hardly believe his eyes. Where there was one arrowhead, maybe there were two. He walked along with his head down and paid no more attention to Pierre and the cart.

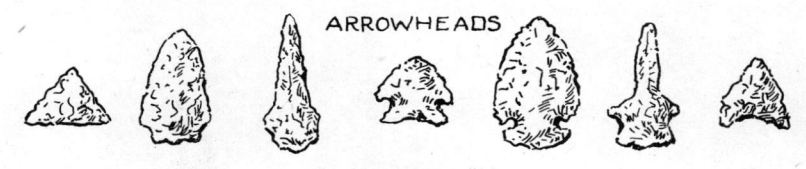

ARROWHEADS

"Get along there," shouted Pierre. "Better not let your pa find you lazying along. He'll fix you. Anyway, what's an old arrowhead? I can show you where you can get a pocketful."

"A pocketful! Where?" asked Tom, hurrying after him.

"In the cave," replied Pierre, as if he were not a bit interested.

"The cave! Where is it? Show me the place! Can we go today?" asked Tom.

"Today?" said Pierre, as if he thought Tom had lost his mind. "When the woodpiles behind your cabin and my cabin and Mr. White's and Mr. Carter's are each as big as a house, then maybe we'll get a day off to go to the cave, but not before."

"Woodpile? Behind my house? I thought we were going to cut logs for the mill," said Tom.

Now Pierre did think that Tom had lost his senses. He just stood and looked at Tom in disgust.

"Do you think that you can cut down a tree, a big tree like the ones in the Big Woods?" asked Pierre.

Tom did not answer. He just looked red-faced and ashamed. Now that he came to think of it, he knew that he had said something foolish.

"Why, sometimes it takes four men, my pa and your pa and Indian Jack and Charlie, to handle one of those big trees, the kind your pa wants for his mill. And men don't want boys around while they're doing it, either. All we are going to do is load the small logs onto this cart. Even that is hard enough. All we are going to do is to get people's woodpiles ready for winter."

Woodpiles! Tom was never so disappointed in all his life. He knew all about woodpiles. First you broke your back piling up wood so that it wouldn't fall down. Then, when you were all through, you started unpiling it again and dragging it into

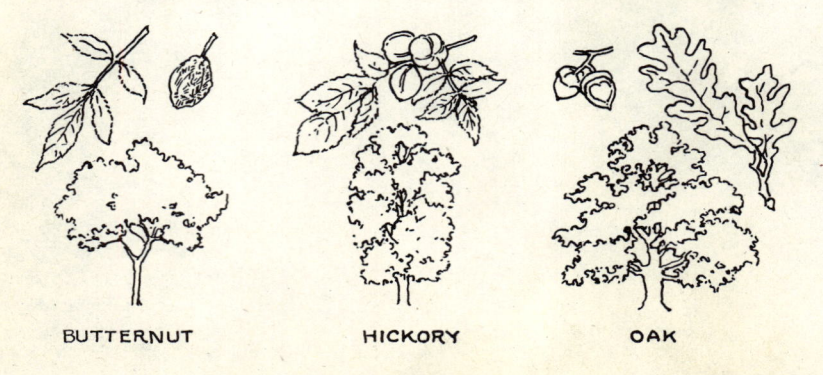

BUTTERNUT   HICKORY   OAK

the house. Yes, Tom knew all there was to know about woodpiles, and he hated them.

Tom wouldn't care now if they never reached the Big Woods, but they did. Again he thought of Lightning Joe. "Hundreds of trees reaching right down to the riverbank," is what Lightning Joe had said. And that was just the way the Big Woods looked. There were maple, walnut, and hickory nut trees without end. And the woods were "plum full of animals waiting for Jenny and him." The rabbits were so thick that he could step on them. Tom began to count them by the white spots under their tails as they raced across the road.

"Look, Tom! A fox!" yelled Pierre, as the end of a bushy tail disappeared into the underbrush.

The next minute Tom was sure he saw a bear.

"That's only your pa's pig which has been running wild in the woods all summer," laughed Pierre. "That wasn't a bear."

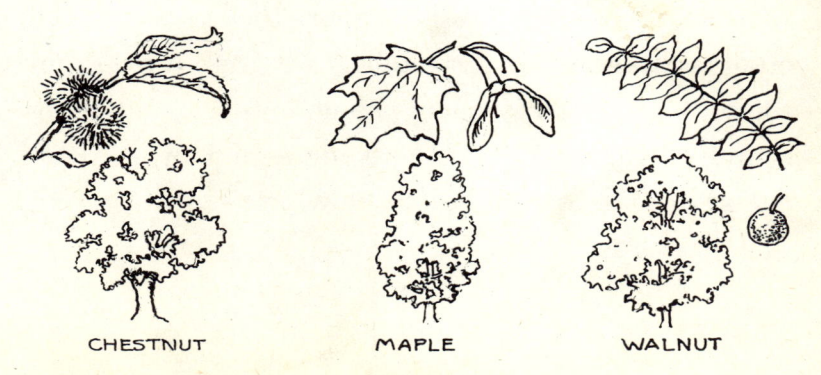

CHESTNUT   MAPLE   WALNUT

All Work and No Play

It was dark and still under the trees. The crooked wagon road stretched on and on. From some place far away came the chop, chop, chopping sound of an ax and the z-z-z-ing sound of a crosscut saw. The oxcart jolted slowly on to a clearing in the woods.

There was Frenchy busy at work with his ax, cutting a notch in the trunk of a tree at the edge of the clearing. He was cutting a big notch on one side of the trunk not far from the ground. He had already cut a small notch on the other side of the trunk. When Frenchy finished cutting through to the small notch, the tree would be sure to fall to the side where the big notch was, and that was out into the clearing.

AX CROSSCUT SAW MAUL

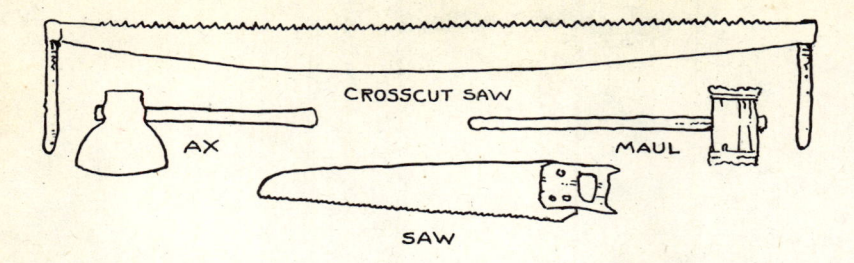

SAW

Indian Jack and Charlie were busy with axes, chopping the upper branches from a tree which had been cut down the day before.

"Morning, woodcutter!" called Indian Jack.

"There's a queer animal in the woods this morning," grinned Charlie.

"Things will begin moving now," chuckled Frenchy. "I wouldn't be surprised if this whole woods were cut down by night."

"Let them joke! I'll show them!" thought Tom.

Over at the edge of the clearing was a pile of small logs. The boys led the calves across the clearing and began to load the logs. Tom worked with a will. Pierre was quick, but Tom was quicker.

"What's the hurry?" grumbled Pierre. "It isn't good sense getting all tired out at the very beginning. We've got to haul wood all day."

Minutes went by. Tom, trying to lift a heavy log all by himself, stumbled over the root of a tree. He stubbed one toe badly and cut another.

"Pooh!" said Pierre when he saw the toes. "That's nothing." But Tom thought it was. You see, they were Tom's toes.

That stumble slowed Tom up a bit. Now he had to be careful where he stepped. Thinking about his sore toes made him a bit careless. One of the logs slipped and scraped a big piece of skin from his left arm.

When the oxcart was loaded, Tom looked proudly around. Now Frenchy would see what a fast worker he was! But Frenchy didn't find anything surprising in that load of logs. He didn't even pay any attention when the cart left the clearing.

It was a mile from the Big Woods to the Hastings cabin. Early in the morning it had not seemed long at all. Now Tom thought they would never get there. Of all the animals in all the world, yearling calves were the slowest.

"Giddap! Giddap!" called Tom every now and then, until Pierre turned on him angrily.

"You'll spoil these calves yet. You'd better not let your pa hear you. He'll fix you," said Pierre.

Tom was glad when they reached the creek. The cold water felt good on his sore toes.

When the boys drove up to the barn at last, Jim and Sally came hurrying out to help with the wood piling. Tom thought he had better show Ma what had happened to him. She wasn't a bit alarmed. She washed the cut places and tied a clean cloth around each toe. Then she hurried him right out of the cabin. "Run along, Tom! Don't leave Pierre with all the work."

By the time the boys had walked back and forth to the woods a time or two, Tom's back ached. His legs ached and his arms ached. He was sure it must be noon, even though the sun was not high in the sky. No boy could get as hungry as he, in just one morning. He couldn't hurry now. A boy can't hurry when he is starved, simply starved.

When dinnertime did come and Tom walked into the cabin, he was limping badly. Pa noticed the limp, but he didn't say anything. The minute Tom was so full he could hold no more, Pa spoiled it all by saying, "Move along, now, and be smart about it. There is a sight of hauling still to be done."

From the minute the boys reached the woods, Tom had a miserable time. If you have to haul logs, you may as well haul as many as you can at one time. In spite of everything Pierre could say, Tom insisted on piling more logs on the cart.

"All right! You'll see!" said Pierre in disgust when the cart would hold no more. He handed the whip to Tom.

"Giddap!" called Tom, as he cracked the whip.

The yearlings gave one pull. The cart didn't move. Then they stopped pulling. They couldn't pull, and they wouldn't. The boys had to unload the cart until it was only half-full. Even then it took a good many carrots to get the calves started.

Tom walked along by the cart, feeling cross and mean and miserable. Surely, with only half a load, those calves could walk faster. There was no sense in the way they were acting. Just as they came to the creek, Tom cracked the whip so close above their heads that the tip of the whip touched Red's back.

The next minute all Tom could see was flying feet, splashing water, and falling logs. All he could hear was Pierre's angry voice calling, "I'll tell your pa! I'll tell your pa!"

Tom stood still. He looked as if he were frozen to the spot. What had he done? He had hit one of the yearlings with a whip! How could he ever have done that? And now Pierre was going to tell Pa. Tom's heart sank. He knew what would happen then. The worst of it was that the mischief was done, and he couldn't do a thing about it.

When Tom looked up, there was Pierre away up the hillside on the other side of the creek. Tom hung his head and walked over to join him.

Pierre was talking softly to the calves, fixing the yoke in place again and rubbing their soft necks. He never even noticed Tom.

Tom dropped the whip on the ground and helped Pierre with the yoke. He smoothed the calves' shiny coats and whispered into each big ear, "I didn't mean it! I didn't mean it!"

At last Pierre called softly, "Steady, Red! Steady, Patch!" The boys led the calves back to the creek and began to reload the logs. Then Pierre spoke to Tom.

"You haven't any pluck. My pa says that when you grumble and won't stick to a thing because it's hard, you're plum no good. And that's what you are — plum no good. A lazy Tom!"

Tom hung his head and said nothing. But all the rest of the afternoon he worked, not as hard as Pierre, perhaps, but as hard as ever he could.

When the boys drove up to the barn with the last load for the day, there stood Pa.

"Now," thought Tom, "now!" His heart began to beat faster and faster.

"A good day's haul, boys," said Pa, with a pleasant smile in their direction. "You are good workers, the pair of you. I'm proud of you!"

Then Pierre helped Tom lift the yoke from the necks of Red and Patch and lead the yearlings into the barn. He even stayed long enough to help

Tom feed and water the calves and brush their red coats until they were smooth and shiny. And still he didn't say a word to Pa, not one word.

"Aren't you going to tell?" whispered Tom in the dark stillness of the barn.

"Of course not!" answered Pierre. "But you be careful how you handle these calves, or I'll tell. I wish they were my calves. And you're still plum no good."

Tom was "tired enough to drop in his tracks," as his grandpa used to say. But when Pierre finished speaking, Tom was so surprised and so happy that he went with Jack after the cows, he dragged bucket after bucket of water for the animals, he milked Brownie, and he whistled all the time. Even if he did limp, there wasn't a grumble out of him.

When supper was over and Tom was all full of Ma's good hasty pudding sweetened with maple sugar, the blacksmith came walking over to the Hastings cabin. Sam and Joe were with him. Joe was almost as big as his pa.

Then all together, Pa and the blacksmith, Joe and Sam, showed Tom how to shoot Jenny. They showed him how to hold the gun. They showed him how to close one eye, look down the barrel, and sight the mark. But when Tom shot at a rabbitskin fastened to the rail fence, he missed the rabbitskin, and the "kickback" from the gun almost threw him to the ground. Everyone had remembered everything else, but no one had remembered the "kickback." Pa reloaded the gun, and Tom tried again. This time Tom was ready for the "kickback," but again he missed the rabbitskin.

"Not ready for bear hunting, yet!" smiled Joe. "But never mind, Tom. You did well for the first time, and you'll do better tomorrow."

From that minute on, Tom liked Joe.

Then Pa and Tom went into the house, and together they made some bullets. First they heated bits of lead in an iron pan held over the red coals. Then they poured the melted lead into the holes in the bullet mold. They waited a minute and then opened the mold. Out rolled some bright new bullets.

"Be careful! They're hot!" called Pa. But Tom had already touched the bullets and burned his fingers. Even then he did not grumble. He blew on his fingers to cool them off and went right on making bullets.

Then at last Tom took his sore toes, his skinned arm, and his burned fingers up the ladder to bed. And do you know? He was so tired that he never waked up the next morning until Pa had called him three times and had started up the ladder to pull him out.

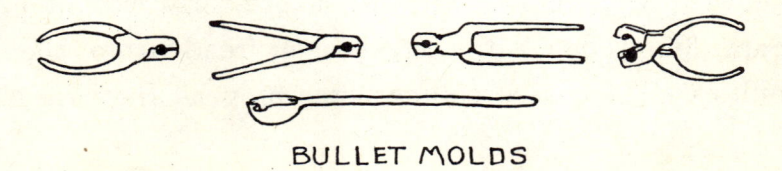

BULLET MOLDS

Cabins on the Hill

Days came and went. The ache and soreness in Tom's back and legs and arms grew less, but his hate for the long days of endless wood hauling grew more and more. By nine o'clock in the morning he was hungry; by eleven he was starved. By three in the afternoon he was certain he could never lift another log. Only the unexpected things that happened made the long days bearable.

No one complained if the boys stole a few minutes from work on the days when the stagecoach came to town.

"Hello, Tom! You're as brown as a berry and as fit as a fiddle!" Lightning Joe would say, as Tom climbed up onto the seat beside him. "That's what work does for a man. I'm glad you're not turning into a worthless, no-account good-for-nothing."

After that Tom couldn't complain. He just couldn't.

One morning the boys had just crossed the creek on their way to the barn when they saw Joe and Sam flying down the stagecoach road from the hilltop. They were calling something as they ran, but the boys were too far away to hear what Joe and Sam were calling.

In another minute Pa left his mill, Mr. White his blacksmith shop, Mr. Carter his general store, and Mr. Fields his inn. Joe and Sam pointed to the hilltop, and the men hurried after them up the hill.

This was too much for even Pierre. For once the yearlings would have to find their way to the barn as best they could. "Something's happening!" he said softly to Tom, so as not to frighten the calves. "Come on!" And he was off up the hill.

Something was happening. Coming right over the top of the hill in a cloud of dust were three covered wagons. Each wagon was drawn by four slow-moving oxen.

"I told you so! I told you so!" shouted Tom, as he caught up with Pa.

In another minute Tom was keeping step with a freckled-faced boy who was walking along by the oxen and driving the first wagon.

"This is Hastings Mills! This is where I told you to come! Are you going to stay? Are you?" asked Tom, and the words just tumbled out. "What's your name?"

"Silas Lane, after my pa," answered the boy. "But you can call me Si. Yes, I reckon we're going to stay. Anyway, we're going to look things over.

SPINNING WHEELS

FLAX WHEEL

WOOL WHEEL

SHUTTLE

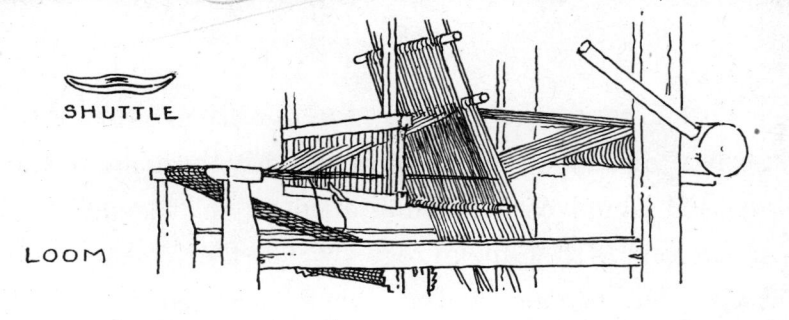

LOOM

Everywhere we stopped, folks would say, 'If you're wise, you won't stay here. You will go on to Hastings Mills. That's getting to be a lively town, and there is rich farm land in that valley.'"

Before long the parade of wagons and men drew up in front of the blacksmith shop, and all the rest of the people in Hastings Mills hurried out to welcome the strangers. What laughing and talking there was then! The more the people from the covered wagons talked, the wider grew the satisfied smile on Pa's face.

"It's a red-letter day for this town," chuckled the old harness maker, slapping Pa on the shoulder. "It's folks like these that make a town grow."

In the first covered wagon was the Lane family — Si and his ma and pa, his brother Bill, and his sister Mary. Mr. Lane was on his way west to find a good place to build a woolen mill. With him in the wagon was a carding machine, all ready to be put together, and a big loom.

When he saw Pa's mill on one riverbank, Mr. Gray's on the other, a dam already built, and the wooded island with nothing on it at all, the satisfied smile on Mr. Lane's face was wider even than Pa's. He needed water power, too, to work his machine.

"My mind is made up! I'm here to stay if you'll sell me the end of the island," he said to Pa. "What is this I hear about logs already cut for my cabin?"

There was another important man traveling with the Lanes. His name was Joseph Hunter, and his only reason for coming west was a desire to see what the country was like. Back East he had been a schoolteacher.

"And out West you'll be a schoolteacher, too," said Pa. "We need you sadly in Hastings Mills. We'll give you a school and a round dozen scholars before snow flies. As for boarding round, you can begin at my house. There is room for you in the attic with our Tom."

Tom was as tickled as a bear with a bee tree when he heard the word "school." At least, when you go to school, you don't have to haul wood. In all the excitement he was foolish enough to forget that even a school needed a woodpile.

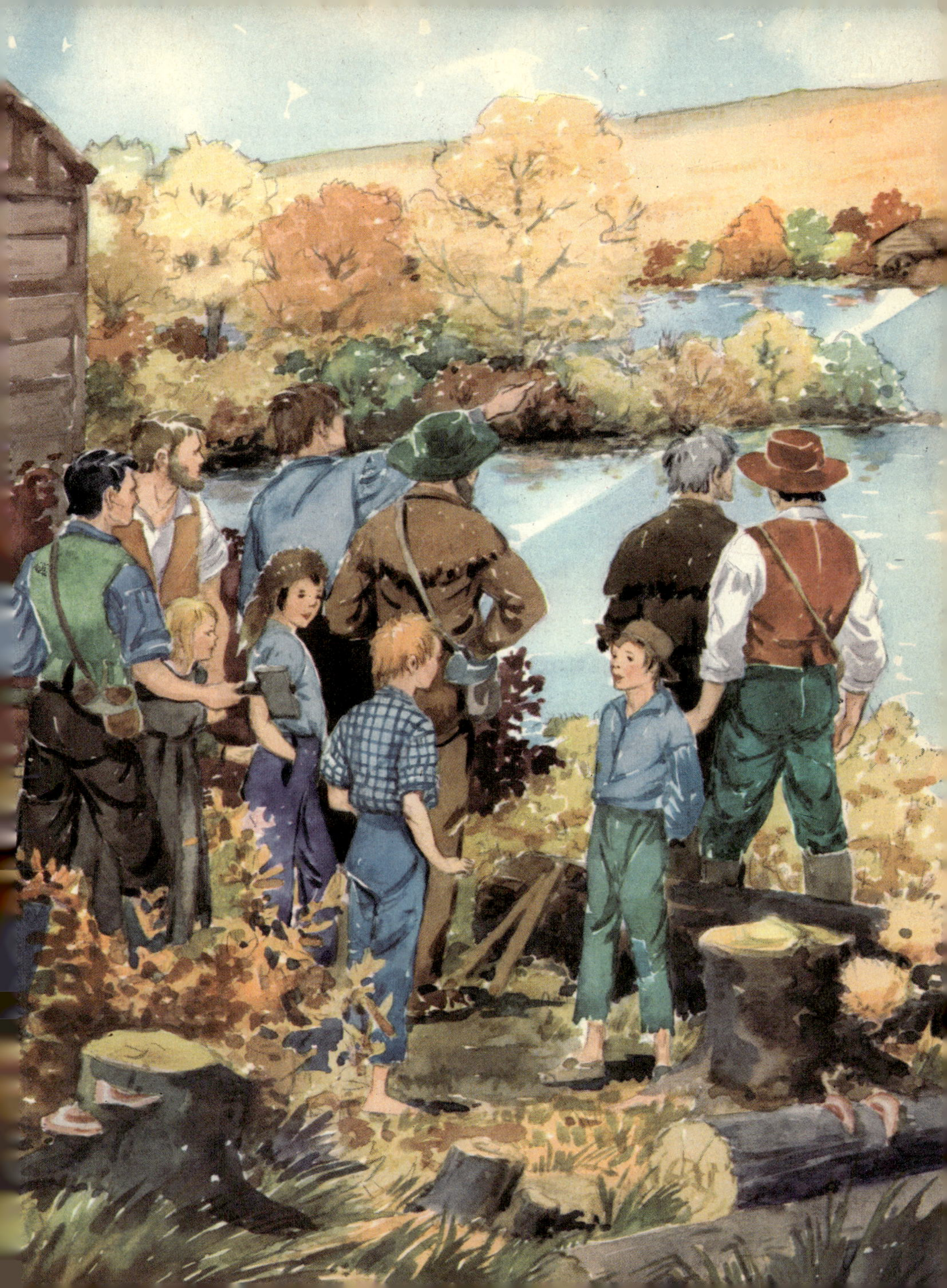

In the other two wagons were the Fuller and the Chase families. They were on the lookout for rich farm lands in the valley. So, while the women went home with Ma and Mrs. Fields and the children ran here and there all over town, Pa took the men down the river to stake their claims.

Mr. Fuller found a piece of land which just suited him. At each corner of the land he drove a wooden stake. This was a sign to anyone who might come wandering along looking for a place to settle that this land was already claimed. As soon as he could, Mr. Fuller would build a cabin on his claim and squat, or live, there. Then he would have squatter's rights to the land. That meant that he would have the first chance to buy that land from the government.

Before long Mr. Chase found a piece of land which suited him, and he staked his claim.

All this time Grandpa Fuller, who had come along, too, was talking to Pa. Pa was certainly surprised to hear that he was a preacher.

"That's the best news I've heard today," said Pa. "No one in Hastings Mills has been to church since the town was built. You can preach in my cabin next Sunday morning, and the whole town will be there. We'll even build you a church of your own on the hillside."

Grandpa Fuller was pleased but not quite satisfied. He had an idea all his own. He wanted to ride a circuit. He was still young enough to ride a horse. He would preach in Hastings Mills one Sunday. Then he would start south along the river on horseback and reach the settlement of Graytown in time for church the next Sunday. He would go on to Four Corners the next Sunday, and Ford's Mills the next. Then he could ford the river and head north again, stopping in every settlement on the way. In about six weeks he would be back in Hastings Mills once more.

"You'd better stay where you are," said Pa, "and I'll build you the church I promised. Circuit riding may be all right in the autumn but not when the snow hits these prairies. It's too hard work for an old man like you."

When Grandpa Fuller thought it over, he agreed.

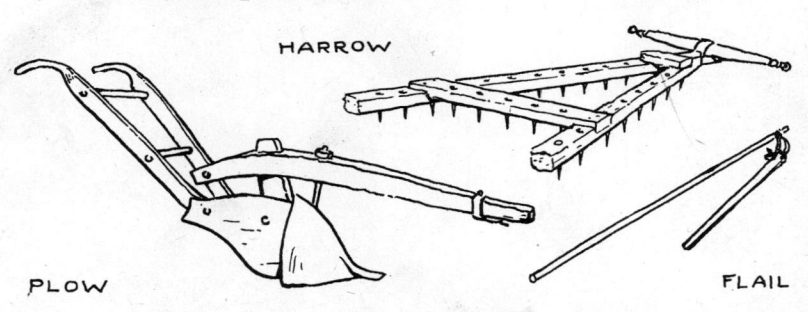

PLOW   HARROW   FLAIL

That night the Fuller and the Chase families made camp and slept on the ground or in covered wagons on their own land. The Lane family slept in the inn — that is, all but Si. He slept in the attic with Tom and the teacher. Mr. Hunter had Tom's bed, and the two boys slept on thick beds of prairie grass covered with blankets.

In the days that followed, Frenchy, Indian Jack, and Charlie stopped their work in the woods. Pa went to his mill only once in a while. The blacksmith shop, the general store, and the inn were left to care for themselves, and every man helped to notch logs and build cabins. The coverings and the great wooden bows were removed from the tops of the covered wagons. Then the wagons went up and down the river road carrying notched logs for the Chase and the Fuller cabins. Even Pierre and Tom escaped the everlasting wood hauling while they worked with Sam and Si hauling cobblestones for chimneys and fireplaces.

Pa was as good as his word. The building went on until every family had a comfortable cabin and until a church and a school stood side by side on the stage road leading up the hill.

Even then school did not begin. When you are a pioneer, there are more important things than school — food and warm clothes for the hard days ahead and woodpiles to keep out the freezing cold of a prairie winter. Time enough to talk of school when important work is over!

The day the Lane cabin was finished, all the men gathered about the stove in the general store. When there was something to talk over, that was the meeting place — the general store.

The building of the woolen mill was yet before them. But more important than that was the question of a bridge. Now, at this time of year, the water below the dam was low, and the building of a bridge was possible and not too dangerous. There would be no chance at all when the river was frozen over or when the breaking up of the ice and the spring rains turned the quiet stream into a rushing torrent.

No, the bridge must be built now, and everyone must do his part. Pa agreed to furnish the logs, since the Big Woods belonged to him. Mr.

Fields would donate a week's work, Mr. Carter an oxcart and a pair of oxen, and Mr. Gray ten bags of grist to pay for some man to take his place, since he would be too busy at the mill to work himself. Everyone else agreed to do his part, and the next morning the bridgebuilding began.

Everyone was so well pleased that the long-looked-for bridge was started at last, that even the boys had a half day off from wood hauling to stand on the bank and watch. They asked a hundred questions and were always in the way, but everyone was so much interested in the bridge that no one even took the time to get cross.

Long tree trunks were loaded from oxcarts onto flatboats. About eight feet from shore three upright tree trunks placed six feet apart were driven down into the mud of the river bed. Large stones were dropped between and around the trunks to hold the trunks in place. The tops of the trunks were notched, and a log placed crosswise through the notches joined the tree trunks together. This was one of the pilings for the bridge.

EARLY AMERICAN STOVES

Eight feet farther out in the river three more tree trunks formed the second piling, and so on until the island was reached. Then logs were laid lengthwise from the shore to the first piling and from one piling to the next and were nailed fast. Shorter logs, nailed crosswise, formed the flooring for the bridge.

Before the week was over, lumbering oxcarts were jolting over the corduroy bridge from the east bank to the island. The bridge from the island to the west bank was already begun. Only the woolen mill was yet to be built, and the work of building would be over.

The Screech Owl

Weeks came and went, and the maples on the hilltop were a blaze of color. Walnuts and hickory nuts lay thick on the ground under the trees in the Big Woods.

Flocks of wild geese passed overhead, and the wild ducks on their way south settled at night among the reeds in the river.

Turtles no longer sunned themselves on the rocks, and woodchucks no longer sat in the sun at the doors of their holes. Sally and Jim, wandering through the long prairie grass, found the empty nests of the meadow larks. Prairie chickens gathered about the barns and in the small corn patches near the cabins.

Indian Jack told of seeing bears, fat from their good summer's feeding, moving lazily through the woods as if they were already on the lookout for a place to begin their long winter's sleep. Wise old men like the harness maker pointed to the heavy coats of the animals and predicted a long, hard winter.

One sunny morning Sally and Jim took a big bag and followed the wagon road to the woods. "Don't go into the woods," Ma had told them. "There will be nuts aplenty at the wood's edge, and you can pick there in safety."

The children turned off from the wagon road and stopped under a big walnut tree. For days they had been waiting for this chance to go nutting. There must be bag after bag of nuts stored in the attic, bag after bag to be enjoyed in the long winter evenings. Gathering nuts was Sally's work and Jim's work, and the children were eager to begin.

Jim was trying to beat Sally, and the nuts were popping merrily into the bag. All at once the children heard a screech, a terrible screech. It came from a tree not far away. For a second they were so much frightened that they could not move. They could only stand with eyes and mouths open,

NUTS

staring at each other. One more second and they dropped the bag and started for home on the run.

Tom and Pierre, returning from the barn, met them on the way and laughed and laughed when they heard the wild tale.

"It was just an old screech owl waked up from his nap and trying his screech in the daytime," laughed Pierre. Tom made all kinds of fun of Jim and Sally for being afraid of a bird.

"But it wasn't a bird," insisted Sally, about to cry. "It was something terrible! You would have run, too, Tom Hastings!"

"Terrible! Just terrible!" teased Tom.

At last Jim and Sally agreed to go back for the bag if Tom and Pierre would stay right with them. When they came to the wood's edge, there was the bag just where they had left it. All was quiet except for the faraway sound of the woodcutters and the rustle of the fallen leaves beneath their feet. Again Tom began his teasing about being afraid of a bird.

131

"I tell you it wasn't a bird!" insisted Jim. "I guess we know!"

"Was it something like this?" smiled Pierre. He opened his mouth and gave the most terrible screech he could possibly give. Even Tom jumped when he heard it.

And then something happened which Pierre didn't expect. From a far-off tree came an answering screech, the same terrible screech which had frightened the children. Tom and Pierre were scared out of their senses. "Run!" they cried. They were off like a flash, leaving poor Jim and Sally to follow as best they might. Not one of the four stopped running until he reached the mill. Then, all together, they poured out the wild tale into Pa's astonished ears.

"Whatever it was, we must find out at once," said Pa with a worried look. He took his gun and went to find Frenchy.

Ma wouldn't think of letting the boys go on with the wood hauling. Red and Patch, frightened also, had come racing back to the barn. Ma was even too much alarmed to find some work for the boys to do. So they went fishing on the riverbank, with one eye on the woods and the other on the fish.

Sometime later a shot rang out.

"He got him! My pa got him!" shouted Tom. The boys dropped their fishlines and fish and made for the wagon road.

And Tom was right. Pa had shot a wildcat.

"Mark my words! It means a bad winter!" said the old harness maker. "When animals like this come down from the north, it means that a cold winter has set in early."

For days no one talked of anything else but the wildcat. For days every man carried a gun, and Indian Jack went back and forth with the boys on their trips to the clearing. But no more wildcats appeared in the Big Woods.

Ever after that, when visitors came to the Hastings cabin and asked about the wildcat skin hanging on the wall, Sally would give Tom a teasing look out of the corner of her eye.

"Oh, that!" she would say. "That's nothing! That's just the bird that scared Jimmie and me when we were nutting in the Big Woods."

PRAIRIE CHICKEN   WILDCAT   WOODCHUCK   OWL

Secrets Astir

There was a secret astir in the Hastings cabin. Ma knew all about the secret because she was the one who had thought of it in the very beginning. Pa had to be told because Ma counted on him to help her out. Then Tom had to know because, when Pa found that he couldn't help out after all, Tom had to take his place.

You couldn't have called it a family secret, that was certain. Jim didn't know a thing about it. It wasn't quite safe to trust Jim. Sometimes he didn't think before he talked, and he told more than he meant to tell. Sally hadn't an idea that there was a secret in the air because —. Well, you see, the secret had to do with Sally and with something that Ma thought Sally should have and that Pa wasn't sure about.

"Mark my words, you'll spoil that girl. You had better let her stick to her knitting and not put ideas like that into her head," said Pa. But the pleasant ring in his voice made Ma decide to go right ahead and have her own way.

The secret had flashed into Ma's head late one afternoon just about suppertime.

Sally was sitting on the log stool, busily at work turning the heel in the big woolen sock she was knitting for Pa.

Tom came into the house dead tired after a day of wood hauling. His face was red from the wind and from the cold water he had dashed upon it from the rain barrel at the back door. Tom threw himself on the floor before the fire. All he wanted to do was to lie there and smell the good supper smells and enjoy the good feeling he always had when the day's work was over.

"Four weeks from today I'll be ten years old," announced Sally. "I'll be as old as you are."

Why couldn't Sally have let him alone? Why did she have to begin right away with her teasing?

"As old as I am? How do you figure that out?" asked Tom, sitting up to stare at her. Sometimes Sally made him so mad!

"You won't be eleven for another whole week after that," teased Sally. "So I'll be ten, and you'll be ten, and I'll be as old as you are."

"Of all the silly things!" said Tom in disgust. "Just like a girl! You won't be as old as I am, and you know it! Silly!"

"I will!" insisted Sally.

"You won't!" insisted Tom.

They went right on saying, "I will!" "You won't!" and every time they said it, their voices grew louder and louder.

"Maybe we need a taste of something else around here besides supper," said Pa, as he came in at the cabin door. His eyes turned in the direction of the strap on the wall by the fireplace. Then Tom and Sally kept still. That is, they didn't really keep still. They went on whispering under their breath, "I will!" "You won't!" But they were very careful that Pa didn't hear.

Would you ever think that a quarrel like that could start a secret? Well, it did.

"Four weeks from today," thought Ma. "I declare, I had almost forgotten." All the time she was putting supper on the table, she was looking at Sally out of the corner of her eye.

Sally had big brown freckles on the end of her nose, and blue, blue eyes that twinkled and twinkled. She had two long braids of yellow hair that never stayed smooth the way they were supposed to stay. No one could say that Sally's hair was curly. No one could ever say that. But it was wavy enough to pull out of the braids and to make little rings around her face and to look as if it had never been combed. Along with her freckles and her twinkly eyes and her yellow hair, Sally had a mouth that turned up at the corners. Maybe that is what made her a "tease." When your mouth turns up at the corners, you can't always help what it makes you do. Not always!

If you had looked at the rest of Sally and not at her face and her two yellow braids, you never would have guessed that she could have started a quarrel. You certainly wouldn't. All the rest of Sally was just a plain dark dress of sheep's gray wool. The dress had a short, tight waist and a long skirt that reached down to her shoe tops. A black sheep and a white sheep had furnished the wool that went into its making, and that is why it wasn't black and it wasn't white, but just a sheep's gray. "Pepper-and-salt" is what you might have called it. No one could see anything pretty in that dress. No one could possibly stretch his imagination that far. But then, it wasn't supposed to be pretty.

"It's good and warm and comfortable," thought Ma, and just as she was thinking that, Sally's eyes twinkled up at her.

"Why didn't I think to dye it blue," thought Ma, "just the color of her eyes. It wouldn't have been very much trouble." The next minute she was mad at herself for having thought of anything so foolish.

"What's come over me?" said Ma to herself. "That dress is good enough as it is. It will last all this winter and all the next." Then, in spite of herself, she began to think, "Blue would look good on Sally, and she does need a — ."

And that's where the secret comes in.

That night after Sally was in bed, Ma took yards and yards of sheep's gray cloth from the big chest. There was enough to make warm clothes for the whole family, no matter how cold the winter. Ma had spun the yarn for that cloth and woven it on her own loom. The cloth was all wool and a yard wide; and Ma was proud of her spinning. But it had never entered her head until tonight how homely sheep's gray homespun could really be.

"I'll spin another fleece," said Ma to Pa, "and this time I'll dye it in the wool."

Then Ma happened to remember that there wasn't a fleece in the house, not one. "I've always thought we should have sheep of our own," she said, "and now I know it. Then we would have a fleece on hand when we needed it, if not in the house, at least on the sheep's back."

"Come now," said Pa. "You wouldn't shear a sheep coming on winter, would you? Of all the animals a pioneer needs, sheep are the hardest to raise. Wild animals have a way of killing them under our very noses. A man hadn't better raise sheep without time to keep his eye on them, and I'm too busy at the mill."

"If your heart is still set on a fleece," Pa said after a while, "I'll get on my horse and bring you a few in the morning. Silas Lake owes me many a fleece in trade for the lumber I sawed for him at the mill. The chest in his barn is filled with fleeces cut last spring."

But the next morning Mr. Lane needed Pa's help at the mill, and Pa could not get the fleece.

"Your ma will be right disappointed," said Pa to Tom, on one of Tom's return trips from the Big Woods. "If I thought you could keep your head about you, I'd let you go in my place."

Keep his head about him! Tom could do that! He had never been so sure of anything in all his life. Before long he made Pa believe so, too.

"All right," said Pa. "The east river road is the one to take. Get on Thunder's back and ride along until you come to the Horseshoe Ford. Mr. Lake's cabin is right across the river from the ford. 'Hello' to him from the east bank and ask if it is safe for a boy to cross. If it isn't, he'll do the fording.

SOURCES OF WOOL

GOAT ALPACA CAMEL SHEEP

And mind you, don't move a step until he answers. Get a half dozen fleeces and start home at once. Don't leave Pierre with the heavy end of the work."

What if Pierre was left with all the work? Tom didn't have time to bother about nonsense like that. He was going down the river on Thunder all by himself, and he was going to ford a river on horseback.

"Now, remember your promise," said Pa, as Tom climbed into the saddle. "Go no faster than a trot, and keep your head about you."

It was only two miles down the river to the fording place. Tom wished it were a hundred. What could be better than this? Riding out over the country on your own horse! Maybe he'd have an adventure. Maybe he'd meet a bear. Maybe he would.

But there were no bears and no adventures waiting around for Tom that morning. The road lay straight before him. There was little to see, only the prairie and a few rabbits running across the road. Before Tom knew it, he was at the fording place, and there was Mr. Lake standing on the other bank. Tom didn't even have to "hello." Mr. Lake did the "helloing."

"Come ahead," called Mr. Lake. "It's safe!"

The water wasn't a bit deep, and Thunder was sure-footed. In no time at all Tom and the horse were on the other bank.

Mr. Lake went to his chest in the barn and took out six fleeces and one more for good measure. There wasn't a black fleece among them. Then he fastened them to Thunder's saddle.

"Tell your ma that they are the best fleeces in the chest, and I'm glad to be sending them to the best spinner and weaver in Hastings Mills," called Mr. Lake, as Tom and Thunder went splashing through the river on their return trip.

Tom made up his mind not to forget to tell Ma what Mr. Lake had said. When Tom had done something well and someone told him about it, Grandpa used to say that Tom was as proud as a turkey cock. Maybe Ma would be that way, proud as a turkey cock.

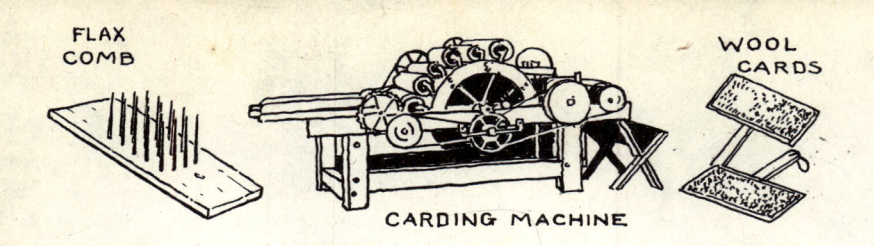

Indigo Blue

Tom hardly had time to stop Thunder at the door before Ma had her eye on the two best fleeces.

"I won't need two, but as long as I'm dyeing, I may as well dye," she said, as she put the other fleeces safely away in the chest in the barn.

All the rest of the morning Ma was busy washing the wool in warm soap and water. Then she spread it to dry in the sun on the crooked rail fence.

When Pa came in for supper, there were Ma's wool cards all ready and waiting. They looked like two wooden brushes with sharp wire teeth. Ma would use them to comb the wool until all the threads lay straight and even.

"Don't tell me you're going to stick to your old-fashioned ways," said Pa when he saw the cards. "There is a woolen mill in this town now, and a carding machine, too. Have you forgotten that?"

"I declare," said Ma, "I never gave it a thought. I've been carding by hand so long that I forgot there might be a better way."

The next day Ma took the washed wool and went across the corduroy bridge to the island. And there she had a long talk with Mr. Lane.

"We'll do the carding," he said, "and you can do the spinning and dyeing. It takes a woman to have an eye for color. Then suppose you let me do the weaving. What is a woolen mill for if it is not to weave cloth?"

Ma didn't care a bit about the carding, but she remembered what Mr. Lake had said. When you are the best spinner and weaver in town, you like to show what you can do. No, Ma didn't care a bit about the carding, but she wanted to make her own homespun.

"We won't get far with a woolen mill if all the women in this town feel that way," said Mr. Lane. "How are you going to keep the secret from Sally if she sees you weaving this cloth?"

Mr. Lane's words decided Ma. "You can do the weaving," she said. "I may as well change one time as another. There is no sense in sticking to old-fashioned ways."

So Mr. Lane carded the wool on his carding machine, and he took home to the Hastings cabin the soft rolls of carded wool.

Then all day long whenever she could take a minute from her other work, Ma was busy at her wool wheel in the warm chimney corner. Yes, the chimney corner was the only place for a wool wheel, for Ma must be warm and the wheel and the wool must be warm if Ma was to do good work.

Round and round went the big wool wheel, round and round until each soft roll of carded wool was spun into yarn. All the time Ma was spinning, there were her own happy thoughts and the pleasant sounds of the cabin to keep her company. There was the crackling sound of the fire and the soft falling of the logs in the fireplace. There was the loud ticking of the Christmas clock, the humming sound of the wheel, and Ma's low voice as she sang the spinning song,

"Round and round the wool wheel turns,
Bright and warm the red fire burns."

Beside the big wheel was Ma's reel. When the yarn was spun, the reel was there to measure the yarn into skeins. Round and round went the reel until there were twenty threads around the reel. Then Ma ran a thread around the twenty threads to hold them. The twenty threads were called a knot. Round and round went the reel again until there were six knots on the reel, and six knots made a skein.

WOOD ASHES

WATER

LYE MAKING

LYE

Ma's spinning kept her as busy as a bee, but she still had time to think of other things.

Outside the cabin door a big barrel filled with wood ashes was always standing. The barrel was raised from the ground because its edges were resting on two flat stones. There was a hole in the bottom of the barrel, and under the hole was one of Ma's big kettles. Every now and then Ma would pour some water into the top of the barrel. The water worked its way down through the ashes and out through the hole in the bottom. Then it wasn't water any longer. It was lye, and Ma used the lye to make soap. Now she was going to use some of it in her dye pot.

In front of the fireplace was a brown earthen jar with a round wooden cover. This was the dye pot. The dye pot, like the spinning wheel, must have its own place in the chimney corner where it would keep warm at all times.

Ma put the lye into the dye pot, and then from the chest she took something which had been carefully put away in a piece of white cloth. When Ma opened the cloth, there was a lump of dark blue something, and every time Ma touched the lump, some of it broke up into blue powder. The lump was indigo.

Ma's indigo came from a plant which didn't grow anywhere around Hastings Mills. It didn't grow in America except in a few places. Most of it grew in countries across the sea.

Just before the indigo plant was ready to blossom, it was cut down and put into great kettles of hot water. After a day or a day and a half, the water was poured off, and there at the bottom of the kettles was a blue substance. When this blue substance dried, it was broken up into lumps, just like the lump of indigo which Ma had.

Ships came and carried the indigo lumps to countries where people wanted the indigo to make blue dye. One of these ships had brought Ma's lump to America.

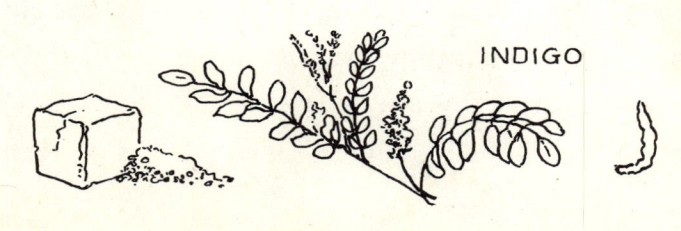

INDIGO

Indigo peddlers met the ships and started out on horseback or in their carts to peddle the indigo to housewives everywhere and to other indigo peddlers whom they met on the way. There was nothing like indigo to make beautiful blue dye. Ma was certainly glad that the indigo peddler had not missed Hastings Mills on his rounds the spring before.

Now Ma broke the lump of indigo up into powder and put the powder into little bags of white cloth. Then she dropped a few bags into the lye in the dye pot, and there they stayed for a day.

When the warm dye was ready, Ma dropped the skeins of soft yarn into it a few at a time. Two or three times a day she took the skeins out again, squeezed them dry, and hung them in the little room to air. The warm back of the fireplace was in the little room, and it was there that Ma hung the skeins.

Again and again and again the skeins were put into the dye pot. Again and again and again they were squeezed and hung up to air. Little by little the soft yarn was turning blue, a pretty light blue, but not as blue as Ma had expected.

"I won't give up until I have the right shade," she said, and into the dye pot went one, two, three more of the little white bags to make the blue dye stronger.

Down into the dye went the skeins again and again and again. At last Ma couldn't help being satisfied. The soft yarn had changed to a beautiful blue, not the same color as Sally's eyes, perhaps, but just as bright and just as beautiful. It had taken Ma several days to get that shade. Anyone else would have given up long before, but not Ma. You can't give up when you have an important secret.

As long as Ma was spinning, there was no danger of her secret being discovered. It seemed to Jim and Sally that Ma was always spinning when she was not cooking or washing or mending or knitting. Not once did they stop to wonder why Ma was spinning so steadily. They came and went, and paid no attention. But when the dyeing began,

DYE POTS AND KETTLE

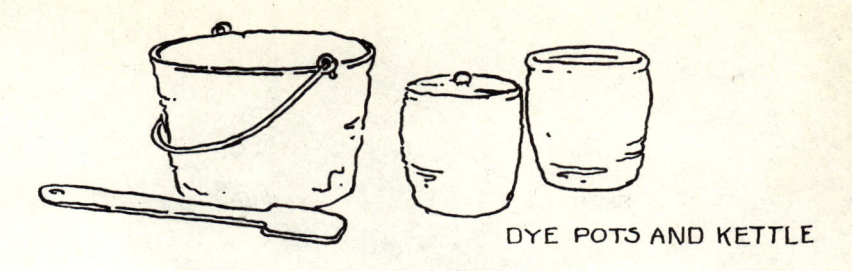

it was a good thing that the wildcat scare was over and that Jim and Sally were busy most of the day with their nut gathering.

Once Ma popped the cover back on the dye pot just the second that Sally entered the door. Sally walked right over to the dye pot and was about to lift the cover when Pa saved the day by saying, "Curiosity killed a cat, Sally. There is nothing in there for you."

Maybe Sally was too busy trying to figure out what Pa meant. Anyway, she let the dye pot alone, and after that she seemed to forget about it. Jim and Sally hardly ever went into the little room in the daytime, and Ma was careful to have no skeins hanging to air when Jim went to bed by candlelight or waked up the next morning. So far, Ma's secret was safe.

Then came the day when Ma wrapped all but a few skeins carefully in paper. Once more she walked across the corduroy bridge to the mill.

"Upon my word as a weaver," said Mr. Lane, "I've seen many a sight in my time, but I've never seen better spun yarn, and I've never seen a more beautiful blue. I'll do my best with the weaving, and I'll turn over to you the best piece of fullcloth ever seen in these parts."

Ma was as happy as a lark all the rest of the day. She was as pleasant as could be to everyone. You know how you act when you are pleased with yourself. Ma acted that way, too.

Mr. Lane didn't waste a minute in getting to work. He put everything else aside, and he stuck to his weaving until he had woven a long length of beautiful bright blue cloth. Never before had he been so careful.

Then what do you suppose Mr. Lane did? If you had been there, you wouldn't have believed that he could do such a thing. He put that beautiful cloth into hot, soapy water. Then, with some smooth pieces of wood which he called hammers, the cloth was beaten back and forth and up and down. The hammers made the cloth very soft, and the hot water made it shrink.

When the time came to take the cloth from the water, it would not be as long or as wide as when it went into the hot, soapy water. But that is just what Mr. Lane wanted. Shrinking brought the woolen threads closer together and made the cloth stronger and warmer.

The shrinking and hammering together were called fulling. So when the cloth finally came from the water, it was not just woolen cloth. It was fullcloth. And do you know? It was just as blue when it came out of the water as when it went in. It hadn't lost a bit of Ma's beautiful blue dye. Not one bit!

Next Mr. Lane fastened the cloth on a wooden frame to stretch it back into shape again. All along the edge of the frame were some iron hooks called tenterhooks. Mr. Lane didn't try to make the cloth as long or as wide as when it was first woven, but still the tenterhooks stretched it a little. Then Mr. Lane put the frame out in the sunshine and let the cloth dry.

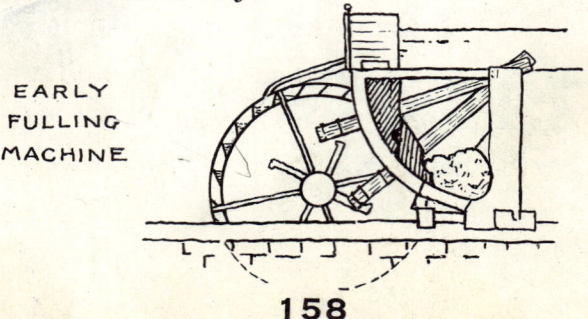

EARLY FULLING MACHINE

After that the strangest thing of all happened. Do you know what a teasel is? It is a plant which has a flower that looks for all the world like a sharp little wire brush. There were teasel plants growing in some of the gardens in Hastings Mills. And now Mr. Lane took some of the dried teasel blossoms, and he combed the finished cloth lightly and carefully. The more he combed, the softer and woolier the blue cloth became. Mr. Lane said that his combing was raising the nap.

Then came the evening when Mr. Lane took the beautiful piece of fullcloth home to the Hastings cabin. Of course, he waited until Sally was in bed. It was hard to tell who was the most delighted, Ma, Pa, or Mr. Lane. All Ma could think of was how lovely Sally would look in blue. All Mr. Lane could think of was how proud he was of the first piece of cloth that had come from his mill. And all Pa could think of was what a lucky day it had been for Hastings Mills when a weaver like Mr. Lane had come to town.

TEASEL

Fine Feathers

Ma could hardly wait to get Jim and Sally out of the house the next morning. Even if there hadn't been a nut left in the woods, she would still have told them to find some. Anything to get them out of the way so that she could take her big shears and begin at once to cut out a — !

Have you been thinking all this time that Sally was going to have a new dress? Well, she wasn't. It is your own fault if you thought so. I told you her dress would last all winter.

It was a cloak that Ma was making, a cloak that would reach right down to Sally's shoe tops. Fastened to the cloak would be a little blue hood that would fit closely about Sally's face and help to keep the rings of yellow hair in place.

For two days, whenever Ma could take a minute from her other work, she was busy with the cloak and hood. She cut and she sewed and she pressed wherever the cloak needed pressing. She used a tailor's goose for pressing. Do you know what that was? It was the big flatiron which the blacksmith had made for Ma.

All the time Ma was pressing, she was singing to herself, gay, lilting bits of songs which came and went. Ma couldn't help singing. The color and the feel of that fullcloth made her happy all over. Then, of course, there was the secret.

The cloak and hood weren't all there was to the secret. At night, when Sally was safe in bed, Ma would take out the skeins of blue wool that she hadn't taken to the mill and some skeins of creamy white wool which she hadn't dyed at all. Then she would begin her knitting. It didn't matter that there was only candlelight to knit by. Ma could knit just as well in the dark.

Ma knitted a pair of blue and white mittens for Sally. She fastened them to the ends of a blue and white knitted string. Then she made a muffler, a pretty blue and white muffler to tie around Sally's neck.

When Ma put the pair of blue mittens and the muffler on top of the cloak in the bottom drawer of the chest, you couldn't believe how beautiful they looked. Even Tom, who had no use for girls' things, thought they were lovely.

Days went by, and work went on as usual. At last the big day came. When Sally waked in the morning and saw the cloak and muffler and mittens, she couldn't say, "Thank you." Every bit of her wanted to say it, but the words wouldn't come out. She couldn't even say, "How pretty!" All she could do was look her happiness and say "Oh!"

I wish you could have seen Sally when she put on her cloak and muffler and mittens. I certainly wish you could have seen her. Do you know what that cloak did for Sally? It covered up every bit of that homely sheep's gray dress. It made her eyes bluer than ever, and it made her mouth turn up still more at the corners. It even made you forget her freckles. Sally looked beautiful, just beautiful.

Now, because the cloak and muffler and mittens did all this for Sally, Pa was a bit worried.

"Fine feathers don't always make a fine bird," he said, shaking his head at Ma. And now, if you don't know what that means, I am sure you can figure it out for yourself.

When breakfast was over, Sally whispered something in Ma's ear, and Ma smiled and said "Yes!" Then Sally put on her cloak and muffler and little blue mittens again, and she hurried from the cabin. She knew who wanted to see her. Yes, Sally knew.

In a minute or two she was standing in the door of the harness shop. The old harness maker jumped to his feet in astonishment when he saw that beautiful blue something in the door of his shop.

"Well, if it isn't my girl," said the harness maker, over and over. "If it isn't my girl!"

Sally knew he would say that. That's what he always called her, "My girl."

All the time that Mr. Harding was looking her over and telling her how lovely she looked, he was putting Sally's hand right down into the big leather pocket of his coat. And there she found a little brown bag, a little brown bag of peppermint hearts with writing on them. "Roses are red." "Forget-me-not." "Love me truly." That's what the hearts said.

"Now, where do you reckon they came from?" said the old harness maker. But how could Sally tell him? She had picked out a heart which said

"Sweets to the sweet," and she was trying not to bite it so that it would last as long as ever it could.

In a few minutes Sally went home, and all the rest of the day she helped Ma. All the time she was working, there was a big smile on her face. Maybe that was a good way to say, "Thank you."

This was one of Pa's forgetful days. He had to come home from the mill several times for things which he had forgotten. Every time he came, there was Sally working as hard as ever. Then, little by little, Pa changed his mind about something, and can you imagine what he said to Ma?

"I reckon fine feathers can't spoil a fine bird, and our Sally is a pretty fine bird." That's what Pa said.

If you are a boy and are reading this story, I hope you haven't been thinking, "Tom's birthday is only a week away, and he won't get a thing, not a thing." How could you believe that?

When Tom started down the ladder on his birthday morning, he climbed halfway and jumped the rest. You would have jumped, too. There at the foot of the ladder was a new sled, a shiny new sled of hickory wood which Pa had made at the mill. One look at that sled and Tom knew that it would go like the wind.

"Do what we will," said Pa, as he looked at Tom's happy face, "we can't keep the snow away forever. You'll need that sled before long."

You can never imagine what happened next. Sally brought Tom a coonskin cap with a long tail hanging down behind.

"I made it all by myself," she said, "because you are eleven years old. Frenchy gave me the skin. Now I'm not as old as you are." And then, because she couldn't help it, she added, "But yesterday I was. Don't forget that. Yesterday I was."

But do you know? Today Sally's teasing didn't make Tom a bit mad, not one bit.

Bringing Home the Deer

Now came a few days when the wind blew cold from the north and the sky was full of hurrying gray clouds. The weather-wise looked at the clouds and predicted snow, but no snow came. Yet the thoughts of everyone in Hastings Mills turned to the long, cold days ahead, and preparations for winter went quickly forward.

One morning Tom and Pierre, and Sam and Si, went with Joe to a spring on the riverbank in the Big Woods. Joe and Pierre carried saddlebags filled with salt.

"Who says there are no salt licks in these parts? If there aren't any, we'll make one," said Joe laughingly, as he helped the boys spread the salt lightly over the wet mud about the spring.

As they worked, Tom thought he saw a deer watching them from the shadows. The deer was so much the color of the underbrush and it raced away so lightly, that Tom could not be sure.

Late that afternoon, when the boys stopped with more salt, the mud about the spring was filled with the prints of deer hoofs. The deer had found the salt lick.

Early the next morning Pa, with Tom beside him, lay in waiting behind a tree near the spring. Pa had his gun loaded and ready, and of course Tom had Jenny. Before long a big deer stepped lightly over the fallen leaves on its way to the salt lick. Before Tom had time to raise Jenny to his shoulder, Pa's shot had brought down the deer.

While Tom ran to call Frenchy, Pa tied the deer's legs together, first the front legs and then the back. Then he ran a long pole under the tied legs. With one end of the pole on Frenchy's shoulder and the other on Pa's, the deer was carried home and hung in a tree near the cabin. That day the Hastings family had fresh venison for dinner.

That same afternoon Pa's sure shot brought down another deer. Frenchy helped Pa, and with their hunting knives they skinned the deer. Then, while Pa cut up the meat and sprinkled salt over the pieces, Frenchy stretched the hides. Later Frenchy would oil the stretched hides and make them into soft leather. It took a good trapper to know how to handle the skins. Someday Pa would have trousers made from the soft leather.

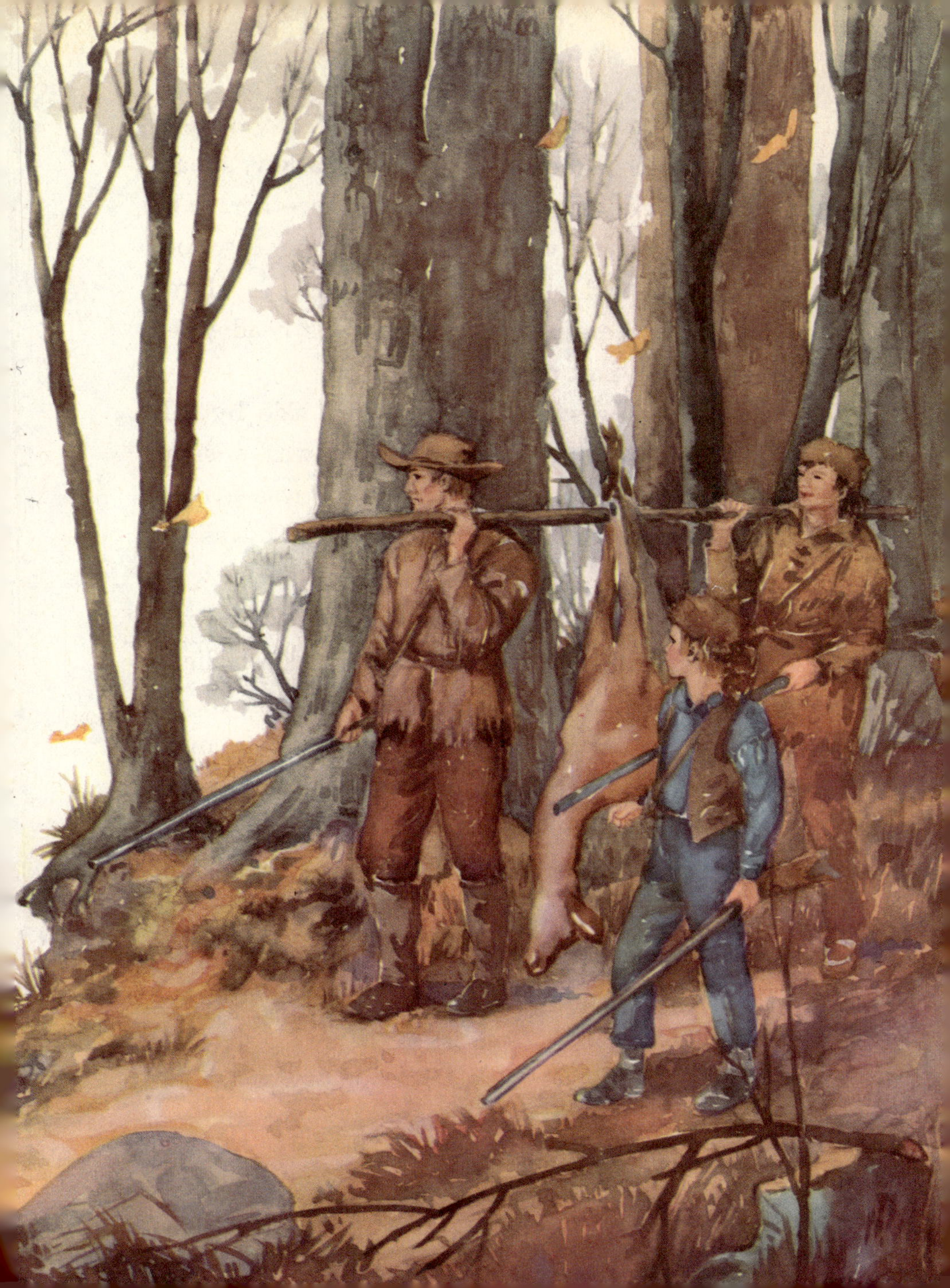

Out near the barn in one corner of the crooked rail fence was the smokehouse. It was a low, square house made of cobblestones plastered together. The smokehouse had no windows, only a low, log door which opened and shut on leather hinges. Even Jim had to be careful not to bump his head when he went in at that door.

The flat roof was made of logs laid side by side and plastered together. In the roof was a small chimney hole, and fitted into the hole was a piece of a hollow tree trunk. The hollow trunk was the chimney.

It was dark inside the smokehouse, with only the chimney hole and the door to furnish light. There was no floor, just the bare ground. In the center the ground had been hollowed out to make a place for a fire. Into the logs of the roof Pa had driven many nails and iron hooks.

One morning, after the deer meat had been salted for several days, Pa took each piece of meat and fastened it to one of the nails or hooks in the smokehouse roof. Sally and Jim squatted in the doorway to watch him.

"Now, if I only had some bits of dry wood and some sawdust," said Pa, when he caught sight of them, "I might start a fire. I don't suppose there is anyone around here who would bring me some."

Jim and Sally were off like a flash. While Jim brought the dry wood, and Sally an apronful of sawdust, Pa walked over to the woodpile.

"Good hickory wood! That's what I want to make sweet-tasting venison, or any other kind of smoked meat for that matter," thought Pa, as he chose a freshly cut hickory log. "Meat smoked with hickory will keep well in any weather."

Pa chopped the hickory log into small pieces. Then, with the bits of dry wood and sawdust, he made a fire in the hollowed-out place in the center of the smokehouse. When the fire was burning brightly, he put the pieces of hickory wood carefully on the fire. The hickory wood had come from a freshly cut log, and the wood was still green. It smoldered instead of burning brightly, and it filled the smokehouse with thick, gray smoke.

Pa came out and shut the door. Smoke came out from around the door, and smoke came out of the chimney. Sally stuck some old pieces of cloth into the cracks about the door, and Pa put a piece of bark over the chimney top. Still a little smoke came out, but most of it stayed in with the meat.

For the next few days Sally kept her watchful eye on the smokehouse. Whenever smoke stopped coming through the cracks, she opened the door and added fresh hickory wood to the fire. The good smell of meat mingled with the smell of the hickory smoke.

Then came the day when the hickory-smoked venison was done. Pa let the fire go out, and Ma hung each piece of meat on its own nail in the attic.

While all this was happening, other boys sprinkled salt near the spring in the Big Woods, other deer found their way to the salt lick, and other hunters from Hastings Mills brought home their winter's supply of venison.

In the days that followed, Pa and Tom were busy with other things. Outside the back door of the cabin they made a long trench as deep as Pa was tall. Things placed on the bottom of the trench would be below frost line and would not freeze when the trench was refilled with earth. Into the trench went potatoes and carrots and cabbages, enough to last all winter. Pumpkins in orange piles filled the corners of the attic, and onions with their tops braided together hung from the nails beside the smoked venison.

The work which Tom enjoyed most of all was the long days of fishing on the river. Catching fish for winter may be called work, but it really isn't. You come home at night with a string of fish too heavy to carry. You feast on good fresh fish, and those you cannot eat are salted away in barrels for winter. Yes, catching fish is one way of getting ready for winter. But wood hauling is another. Strange how things can be so different!

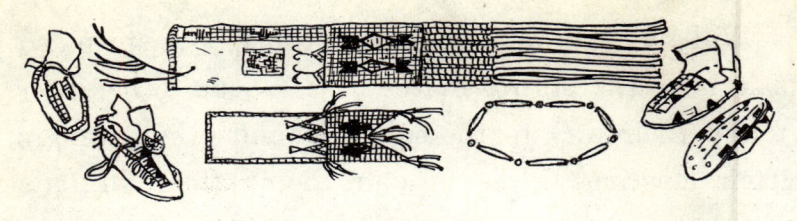

Waubonsie

Then suddenly the weather changed.

"Why think of winter?" laughed the sun. "There are golden days still before you."

Each day the sun shone, warm as in the summertime. The valley, the Big Woods, and the endless stretches of prairie were veiled in the hazy mists of Indian summer. Except for the bare trees and the brown grasses, one might have thought that summer had returned.

"Indian summer! The rest before the blizzard!" said Pa, as he stood in the doorway one evening at sunset. He shaded his eyes with his hand and looked to the westward.

"He'll be coming most any time now," said Pa to Ma, as she came to stand beside him in the doorway. "He'll never miss the Indian summer days in the valley of the Big Turtle."

All that evening and the next morning, the sharp eyes of Tom noticed that Pa was uneasy, as if he were expecting someone. But who that someone was, was Pa's secret, and Pa would not tell.

That noon Tom sat down to his dinner of prairie chicken and good-tasting succotash which Ma had made by boiling beans and corn together. His back was to the front door of the cabin, and all he was thinking about was filling the big hole inside of himself.

"How, Shmokoman!" grunted a voice behind him.

For a second Tom sat rooted to the spot. He could not move. But Pa, pushing back his log stool, jumped to his feet like a flash, a big smile of welcome on his face.

"Waubonsie!" he cried. "I knew this weather would bring you!"

Tom turned with a start, and there in the doorway was a big, powerful-looking Indian. By his side was an Indian boy. Their trousers, coats, and moccasins were of deerskin, and on the man's head was a beaver-skin cap. The boy was carrying the two biggest fish Tom had ever seen.

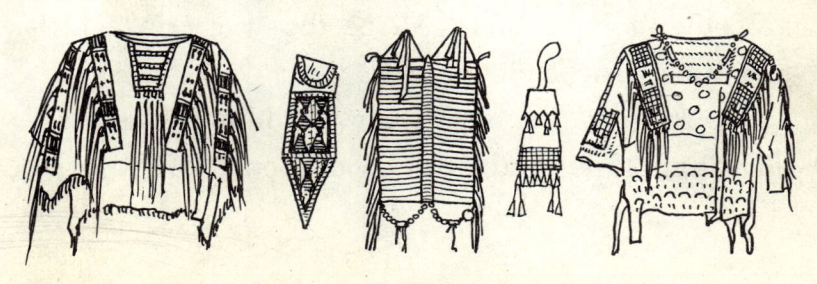

"Indian's summer!" grunted Waubonsie, pointing to the river valley outside the doorway. Then, as a slow smile spread over his face, he pointed first to Ma and then to the table before him.

"Succotash! Good Succotash! Fish! Boy! Waubonsie!" he grunted.

For once Tom was speechless. Even Jim and Sally, who had seen these Indians before, had not a word to say.

Waubonsie and the Indian boy crossed over to the fireplace, covered the fish with ashes, and placed them carefully among the red coals.

"Shmokoman?" said Waubonsie, pointing first to Tom and then to Pa. "You, Shmokoman?"

Pa nodded his head "Yes." "'Shmokoman' is the Indian word for 'white man,'" he explained to Tom. "Waubonsie wants to know if you belong to me."

"Shmokoman, good shot?" Waubonsie asked next, pointing to Tom and then to the place where Jenny lay on her wooden pegs above the door.

If anyone had asked Tom why he didn't answer, he couldn't have told. All he did was grin a little and hang his head.

"Fair," said Pa, answering for him. "Just fair! Give him time, and he'll be a good shot!"

"Boy, good shot!" grunted Waubonsie, pointing to the bow and the quiver full of arrows hanging over the Indian boy's shoulder.

177

Tom stood with his eyes glued to the redskinned faces as the Indians squatted before the fire. Before long they pulled the fish from the fire, shook off the ashes, and skinned the fish.

Then white man and Indian together sat down at the log table, and dinner began all over again. The prairie chicken was good, and the succotash was better. But never before had any one of the Hastings family tasted anything so good as the white meat of the fish which the Indians had cooked among the ashes of the fireplace.

By the time dinner was over, a dozen boys and girls had gathered at the Hastings cabin. And not one among them ever forgot what he saw that afternoon.

Waubonsie placed a white man's penny upright in a small crack in the top of the crooked rail fence. The Indian boy hit the penny with every arrow he shot from his bow. Again and again he shot, until not an arrow was left in his quiver.

Tom and Sam, overcome with astonishment, stood and stared at the Indian boy as if they were sure there was magic in his bow.

"It takes an Indian to do that, I tell you," insisted Sam, and Tom agreed.

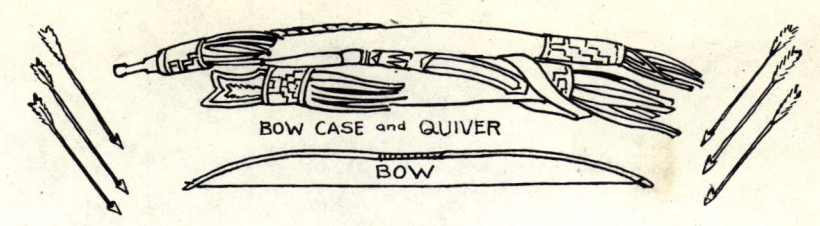

Fox Fire

Because Pa understood how a boy felt, and Frenchy did, and Sam's pa and Si's, there was no wood hauling that afternoon, and no brickmaking, and no work for Si at the mill. All afternoon the boys, with Jim and Sally following after, wandered here and there wherever the moccasined feet of the Indians led. The better acquainted they became, the easier it became to understand Waubonsie's signs and grunts.

They sat about the stove in the general store while Waubonsie traded fish for the white man's tobacco and told of his new home by the great river.

They crossed the corduroy bridge to the west bank and followed the Indian trail along the river to the place where the bark lodges of an Indian village had once stood. Waubonsie, pushing aside the fallen leaves and thick prairie grass, pointed to a circle of blackened earth where the feast fires of his people had once been lighted.

They crossed the river on an old flatboat which they found caught among the reeds along the shore. As they wandered back again along the east bank, Waubonsie taught the boys an Indian war cry, soft at first and slow, then louder and louder, faster and faster, until it ended in a mighty yell. There were no words to the war cry, just strange Indian sounds and grunts. Again and again the boys tried the war cry. A stranger walking that day in the Big Woods would surely have thought that he had come upon a party of Indian braves off on the warpath.

And then, just at sunset, they came to the cave. Frenchy, following his line of traps through the woods when his day's work was over, came upon them sitting in a circle outside the cave's mouth.

The cave was large, reaching well back from the riverbank with a well-marked Indian trail following the shore line in front of it. It was cold and dark and "scary" inside, but the kind of "scary" which makes you want to go farther and see more. An Indian war party could camp in that cave, and a man could hide safely in one of the long rooms opening from the large room.

KNIFE TOMAHAWK WAR CLUBS

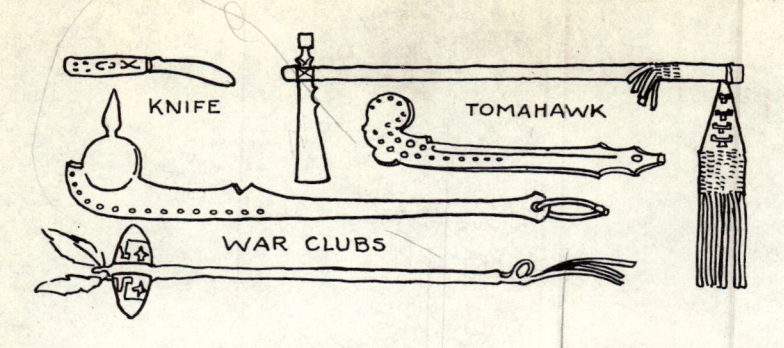

By the time Frenchy found them, Tom had already explored the cave to his heart's content. Now he sat turning over and over the handful of arrowheads he had found along the trail.

Frenchy squatted on the ground and joined the party. Waubonsie sat smoking his pipe and looking out across the river as if through the Indian summer haze he could see once more the bark lodges of his people. Slowly he turned his head toward the cave, laid aside his pipe, and grunted some Indian words which Frenchy understood.

"'Cave of the Evil Spirit' the Indians call it. That is what he is trying to tell you," said Frenchy.

As if satisfied that Frenchy could understand, Waubonsie began to talk.

"There are good Indians and bad Indians, as there are good white men and bad," interpreted Frenchy. "Once, in the lodges of the Indian village by the Big Turtle, there was a young brave who stole from other Indians and from the cabins of the white man. His stealing was drawing his people into war. If it did not stop, he would be banished from the village, warned the chief and the old men.

"One evening at sunset the young brave returned to his lodge with a cream-colored pony stolen from the trading post of the white man. That night he was stoned from camp, never to return.

"In the days that followed, strange things began to happen in the valley of the Big Turtle. Each night, when darkness came upon the valley, a man of fire appeared and disappeared, now to the north, now to the south, now to the west, but most often near the cave on the riverbank.

" 'The Evil Spirit is upon us,' said the Indians in alarm. 'The river will dry up, and our cornfields will not grow. The animals will leave the Big Woods, and the Indians will starve.'

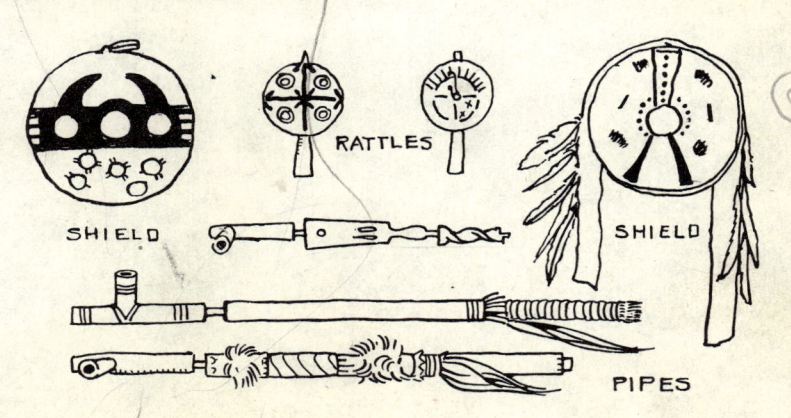

SHIELD   RATTLES   SHIELD

PIPES

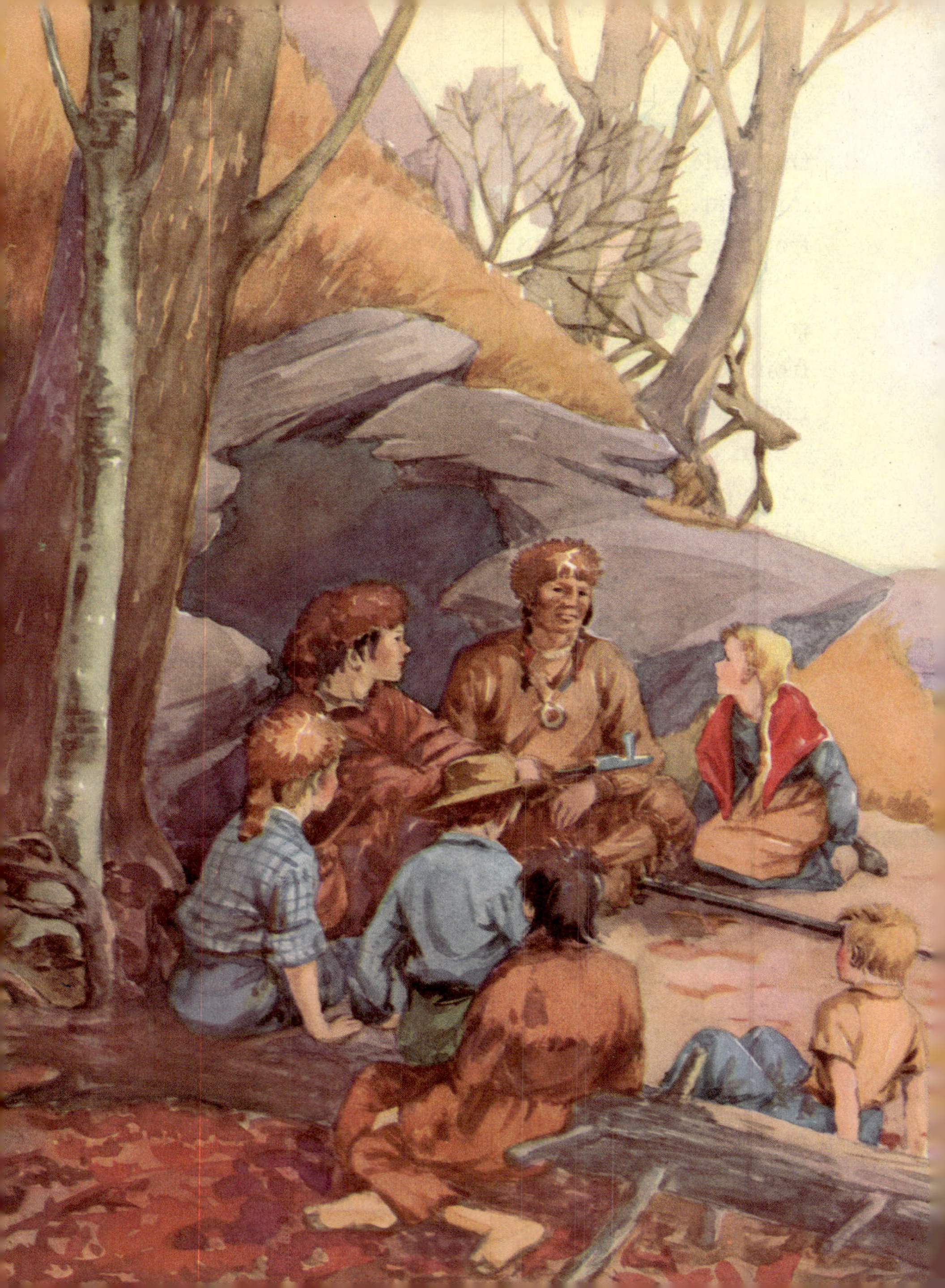

"Sickness broke out in the lodges of the red men. 'The Evil Spirit has begun his work,' said the frightened Indians. And still, at night, the man of fire appeared and disappeared, appeared and disappeared.

" 'His home is in the cave,' said the wise men. 'We must burn him out.'

"In the dark of night the Indians crossed the river. In the dark of night they piled brush and prairie grass and branches of fallen trees at the cave's mouth.

"As the fire lighted the night sky, the Indians watched as only Indians can watch, but nothing happened. More brush, more grass, more branches! Hotter and higher, hotter and higher rose the fire. No one, neither man nor spirit, could stand the heat within the cave.

"Then suddenly out from the door of the cave leaped the Evil Spirit, the man of fire. Over the fire at the cave's mouth with one mighty leap, and down into the river below! In the light of the fire the Indians could see that his face was the face of the banished brave. A few days later his body was washed up on the riverbank below the village."

"But a man of fire, Frenchy! How could he be that? Ask him! Ask Waubonsie!" begged Tom.

"In the trunks of decayed trees in the forest," Waubonsie went on, and Frenchy interpreted, "a substance was found which the Indians called fox fire. It was like phosphorus and would glow in the dark. It was by covering his body with this that the young brave changed himself into the Evil Spirit, the man of fire. By holding his blanket spread before him and pulling it quickly aside, he could appear and disappear.

"Many days later an Indian boy from the village came upon the young brave's supply of fox fire stored away in a corner of the cave."

Waubonsie's tale was over. At once and almost without a word, all the boys, with Sally among them, made their way into the cave. But look where they would, there was no fox fire shining in the darkness. The fox fire, like the Indian brave, had disappeared.

"'Cave of the Evil Spirit,'" said Frenchy, as they all walked back to Hastings Mills together. "But the white man has renamed it 'Devil's Cave.'"

That night Tom could not sleep for a long, long time. He lay on the attic floor near the ladder hole, staring down at two red-skinned faces asleep before the fire. Even when he crawled into bed, his dreams were of fox fire and evil spirits, of caves and cream-colored ponies and Indian braves.

For two days longer Waubonsie and the Indian boy wandered at will through the valley of the Big Turtle. Then, as silently as they had come, they disappeared.

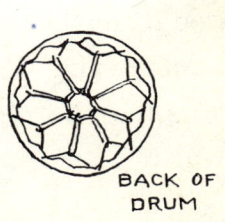

MEDICINE DRUM   WATER DRUM   BACK OF DRUM

Butchering Time

There was one Indian summer day which Tom never forgot. That was the day when Pa took the pig catcher down from the nail in the barn. Then Pa and Tom together started for the Big Woods. The pig had been running wild in the woods all summer, feeding on roots and berries. Now it was time to bring the pig home and fatten it.

The pig catcher was like a big pincers, with one handle longer than the other. A piece of rope joined the two handles. You held the pig catcher by the long handle until the pincers were around the pig's leg. Then you pulled on the rope, the pincers and the handles closed, and there was the pig, caught by the leg.

Has anyone ever told you that you can catch a bird if you sprinkle salt on its tail? Well, pig catching is like that. You can catch the pig if you can get the pincers around its leg.

All the way to the woods Tom begged Pa to let him have the first chance at the pig catcher. Tom would have that pig in a minute. He knew he would. But Pa would not listen. Pa was going to catch the pig in a hurry and be done with it.

The minute Pa caught sight of the pig, he started after it on the run. Pa may have been quick, but the pig was quicker. Around trees, across the clearing, into the underbrush, and out again went Pa and the pig.

Just as Pa almost had the pig, the pig turned around, doubled on its tracks, and ran between Pa's legs and upset him. I don't know how many more times Pa tried, but I do know that it was Tom who finally caught the pig. The best of it was that he caught it almost as soon as he got his hands on the pig catcher.

"I declare," said Pa with a hearty chuckle, "you are a better man than I am. It takes you to bring home the bacon."

Then Pa and Tom made a pen of logs beside the barn, and there they put the pig. They fed the pig until it could eat no more, and every day they watched it grow fatter.

Now Indian summer came to a close and was followed by the gray days of late November. Each day that passed grew shorter and colder. It was dark in the mornings long after Pa and Tom had finished their work in the barn. The frost lay thick on the long prairie grass, and there was a coating of ice on the rain barrel by the back door. Even

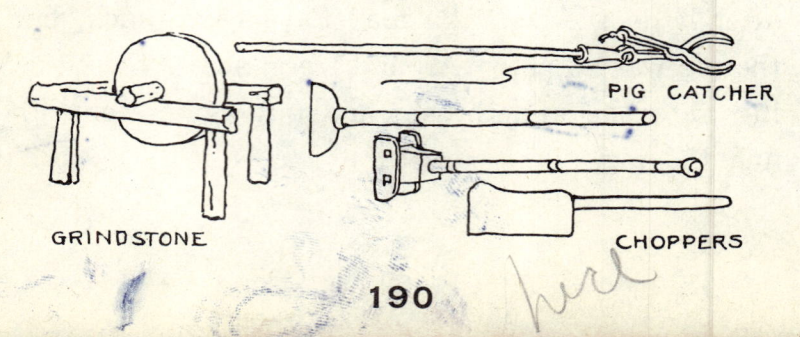

GRINDSTONE   PIG CATCHER   CHOPPERS

at noon there was a chill in the air which made Tom shiver inside his warm woolen coat.

"Wind's from the north! The cold has come to stay," said Pa one morning at breakfast. "Time to think about butchering!"

The next morning Frenchy and Indian Jack did not go to the woods as usual. They came to the Hastings cabin with their butcher knives already sharpened. They were going to help Pa kill the pig and a yearling bull.

Early that morning Pa had set Ma's great iron kettle upon some flat stones near the barn, and Tom had filled it with water. Then together they had built a big fire under it. Now the water had begun to boil, and Frenchy, Pa, and Indian Jack went to kill the pig and the yearling bull.

Sally, who was helping Ma, ran into the little room to hide her head deep down among the goose feathers in the big feather bed. She knew that the calf would bawl and that the pig would squeal, and she didn't want to hear them. She stayed there with her fingers in her ears until Ma called and told her not to be silly. The killing was all over. Anyway, it hadn't hurt the pig and the bull. It had happened too quickly.

As soon as the pig was killed, Frenchy and Indian Jack took hold of it by the legs and dropped it down into the boiling water. They lifted it up and dropped it again and again. Then they laid it on a board, and with their hunting knives they scraped off all the bristles.

When the yearling bull had been killed, Indian Jack hung the pig and the calf by their hind legs in a tree and cut them open. He took out the insides and put them into one of Ma's smaller kettles. Frenchy carried the kettle into the cabin.

Ma washed the hearts and livers and put them carefully aside. She saved all the bits of pork fat to make lard.

While Ma was busy in the house, Pa was skinning the calf. The skin came off in one piece. Pa would save the calfskin to make shoe leather.

As soon as the meat was cold, the men took it down from the tree and began the cutting. The calf was cut into quarters, and the quarters of beef were hung in the coldest corner of the attic where they would freeze and stay frozen until Ma wanted to use them.

All the pieces of fat pork were packed in salt in a big barrel. The hams and shoulders were put into another barrel filled with salt water called brine. After they had stayed in the brine long enough, they would be taken to the smokehouse and smoked like the venison, with good hickory smoke.

All morning long the men were busy with the meat. Tom and Jim helped whenever they could. It was a gay and busy time. Frenchy whistled and told jokes and sang French songs which Tom and Jim didn't understand but enjoyed anyway.

That noon there were spareribs for dinner, and Ma said that Frenchy and Indian Jack must stay for dinner. Everyone who sat down to the table declared that he had never eaten sweeter, juicier meat than the meat which had come from the flat ribs of what had once been the Hastings pig.

That day the men's work was over, but Ma's had just begun. All the next day she was boiling the pork fat in a big kettle over the fire. Ma said she was trying out the lard. Sally brought wood and kept a watchful eye on the kettle. The lard must boil, but it must not smoke.

When the lard was done, Ma poured it through a white cloth into a big earthen jar. Ma squeezed the cloth to be sure that all the lard went into the jar. Then she put the lard away to cool and harden. When Ma was through with the squeezing, there were some brown cracklings left inside the cloth. Jim liked good brown cracklings with salt on them, but Ma would give him only a few. Cracklings may taste good, but they are very rich, and it isn't safe to eat many.

The next day Ma made the headcheese. She boiled the pig's head and the calf's head until the meat fell from the bones. Then she put the meat into her wooden bowl, and she chopped it fine with her chopping knife. After that she seasoned it with salt and pepper and bits of dried leaves from certain plants in her garden. Ma called the plants herbs. Then she poured some of the water, in which the heads had been boiled, over the chopped meat and mixed it well. After that she set the chopped meat away in a pan to cool. When it was cool, it was like jelly and would cut with a knife. It was called headcheese.

KNIVES and CHOPPERS

SAUSAGE STUFFER

KNIVES and CHOPPERS

All the little pieces of meat that were left after the men had finished with the cutting were made into sausage. Ma chopped and Sally chopped until the meat was chopped as fine as fine could be. Then Ma seasoned it with salt and pepper and herbs, molded it into balls, and set the balls away in the attic to freeze. Ma set the sausage balls on one piece of cloth and covered them very carefully with another.

Now butchering time was over, but there was other work in preparation for winter still to be done. One of the most important things was the candle-making.

Pork fat makes lard, but beef fat makes tallow, and it is beef fat, or tallow, that you need for candles. Ma put all the beef fat into a kettle and melted it into tallow. Then she took out her candle molds.

If you had been there, you would have seen that a candle mold was just two rows of tin tubes fastened together. There were five tubes in a row in Ma's molds, and each tube was just the shape of a candle.

Ma had made the wicking for her candles many days before. You can never guess how she made it.

She made it from the soft silk of the milkweed. Jim had gathered the milkweed when he was wandering over the prairie. Ma took the soft silk, and she spun it on her spinning wheel into strong string to use for candlewicks.

Now Ma cut the wicking for each candle. The wick must be two times as long as the candle, and a little more. Ma doubled the wicking for one candle across a small stick. Then she rolled the two pieces of wicking between her hands until the two pieces were rolled into one. She wet her finger and rolled the tip end of the wicking into a sharp point.

When Ma had five wicks on the stick, she dropped the wicks down into the five tubes of the candle mold. She let the stick lie on top of the tubes. The pointed ends of the wicks came out through the little holes in the other ends of the tubes. Ma pulled the wicks tight and tied their pointed tips together to hold them in place.

When each tube in Ma's molds had its wicking, Ma poured hot tallow into the molds and filled each tube to the very top. A few minutes later Sally put the candle molds outdoors to cool.

When the tallow had hardened for a day or two, Ma dropped each mold into boiling water and took it quickly out again. Then she cut the tied tips of the wicks apart, lifted the sticks, and out came the candles, five candles on each stick.

Sally cut off the wicking until there was no wicking showing at the bottom and only a little showing at the top of the candle. After that she piled the candles away in the top drawer of the chest. Ma took her empty molds and began her candlemaking all over again. The pile of candles in the chest drawer grew slowly. Candlemaking was tiresome work, and it took a long time to make candles enough to last all winter.

Pigeon Pie

All through the long days of butchering and candlemaking, Ma's thoughts turned continually to Thanksgiving. The more she thought, the more she tried not to think; and the more she tried not to think, the more she thought. Ma's thoughts went around in circles.

The trouble was that she was bothered about something. She tried to think that the something didn't matter. She was going to laugh and forget about it. But she couldn't laugh, and she couldn't forget. She was too deeply disappointed.

Ma loved Thanksgiving. She enjoyed it more than any other day in the year except Christmas.

The thing that Ma liked best about Thanksgiving was the turkey. She didn't mind the hours of work it took to get the turkey ready for dinner. She didn't mind them a bit. She enjoyed picking the feathers. She enjoyed making the good dressing, even if cutting up the onions did bring the tears to her eyes. She was sure there wasn't a smell in the world as good as the smell of a turkey roasting in a Dutch oven among the red coals and hot ashes of a fireplace.

Then there was Pa's smile as he sat at the head of the table with the big bird before him. There was something different about that smile. It was jollier than on any other day in the year. Ma called it his Thanksgiving smile, and she said that he saved it just for Thanksgiving.

Ma knew exactly what Pa would say when the prayer was over and he looked out over the loaded table and the family faces.

"Which shall it be, dark meat or light? The wishbone is for Ma, and don't everyone ask for a drumstick."

That's what Pa would say, and Ma loved to hear him say it. Yes, Ma had her own good reasons for liking Thanksgiving.

But this year there would be no turkey — just ten or a dozen wild pigeons to make a pigeon pie. No wonder Ma was disappointed!

For some reason the wild turkeys had disappeared from the Big Woods. In spite of what Lightning Joe had said, Tom had not seen one in all the time he had been in Hastings Mills.

"They are scary birds," said the old harness maker with a wise nod of the head. "Ask Frenchy or any other trapper, and he will tell you that when white men settle in a place, turkeys are among the first of the wild things to disappear."

"The old harness maker is right," said Frenchy. And then, because he knew how disappointed Ma would be, he searched the Big Woods day after day. Not one turkey could he find.

But Frenchy was not one to give up easily. One morning, just before daybreak, Frenchy and Pierre, with their guns loaded, appeared suddenly in the doorway of the Hastings cabin.

Each of them held a lighted pine knot in his hand, and another pine knot ready to be lighted was sticking from the pocket of Pierre's deerskin jacket.

"If there is one turkey roosting in one tree in the Big Woods, I'm going to find him," declared Frenchy. "Two boys are better than one, and the boy who expects to eat the turkey should be the one to catch him. Come on, Tom!"

Ma and Pa had not been out of bed for many minutes, and Pa was just thinking about calling Tom. Now there was no need for calling. Tom was down the ladder and into his warm coat and coonskin cap without a thought for breakfast. Over his left shoulder and under his right arm went the leather strap to which were fastened the powder horn and bullet pouch that the harness maker had made for him. Pa took the pine knot from Pierre's pocket, lighted it at the fireplace, and handed it to Tom. Down came Jenny from her pegs on the wall, and Tom was ready.

All this time Ma was insisting that Frenchy should come in and have some breakfast and forget about the turkey. She was all through wanting one. Ma was sure she meant every word she was saying. But Frenchy knew that deep down in her heart she didn't mean a word of it. Thanksgiving without turkey would be too deeply disappointing.

Outside the door Limpy, Frenchy's dog, was barking and yelping. A long time before this, Limpy had been in a big battle with a wolf. When the battle was over, the wolf was dead, but Limpy's left front foot was never quite straight again. When you are a winner in a wolf fight, it makes no difference how you look. You are a hero. That's what the boys thought Limpy was — a hero.

There was a cold, biting wind blowing as the three turkey hunters made for the wagon road to the woods, but no one noticed the wind blowing.

"We won't need these pine knots long. We are later than I thought," said Frenchy, as the first streaks of sunrise appeared over the prairies to the eastward.

WILD TURKEYS

HEN   CHICK   COCK

When the hunters crossed the creek, they dropped the pine knots into the water and hurried on. All the time Frenchy was giving directions about what to do when they reached the woods.

"We'll spread out," said Frenchy, "and if either of you comes upon a turkey roosting in a tree, don't shoot. Call me! The bird will stay where you found it. That's the trouble with turkeys. They are as stubborn birds as ever I've seen. You can't hit them on the fly because they won't fly when you want them to fly. It's no easy matter even for a sure shot to hit them when they are roosting among the branches. We don't want to go home without at least one bird. So don't forget! Leave the first bird for the best hunter."

Frenchy need not have said all that. He just wasted his time giving those directions. Limpy did his best and smelled the whole woods over. Tom and Pierre wandered around looking up into the treetops until their necks ached. Look where he would, not even Frenchy could find a ball of black feathers which looked like a turkey in any tree in the Big Woods.

"I don't believe there ever was a turkey in those woods," said Tom, as, cold and tired and miserable, he led the way home.

So the turkey hunt ended, and it still looked as if there would be pigeon pie for Thanksgiving.

"Yankee-Doodle"

I told you that Frenchy wouldn't give up. I told you he wouldn't.

Early one morning a few days later, Tom was busily at work, feeding Red and Patch. Pa stopped at the log stall for a minute to talk to him.

"Did I hear you say that you would like a day's trapping with Frenchy in the woods? Am I right about that?" asked Pa.

A DAY'S trapping! A whole DAY off from wood hauling! Surely you have no doubt about Tom's answer. He dropped the grain on the calves' heads, he was so astonished.

"It isn't exactly trapping," Pa went on, "and yet again it might be. Thanksgiving is only three days away, but Frenchy is still determined to get Ma that turkey. He is going a dozen miles or more out over the prairie to a wild, unsettled piece of woodland that he knows about. It will be a long tramp and a hard one, and it can't be done in a day. It means camping out for the night. Frenchy thinks that you should go with him."

Should go with him! There could be no question about that! Of course Tom was going!

MOLE TRAP   SMALL ANIMAL TRAPS   OTTER TRAP

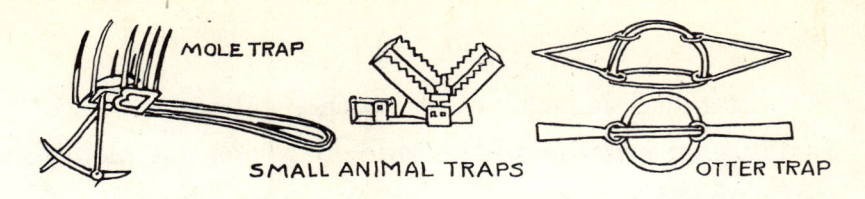

When Tom heard that Frenchy was starting this very afternoon and that this very night he, Tom Hastings, would be sleeping out under the stars, there wasn't a bit of work left in him. Pa had to bring him to his senses with a good hard shake.

"Settle down here," said Pa, and Tom settled.

It is a wonder that Tom didn't say something about turkeys to Ma that morning. It certainly is a wonder. Pa hadn't told him that getting the turkey for Ma was to be a secret. Thank goodness, Tom had sense enough to figure that out for himself. All he talked about was trapping.

When dinnertime came, wood hauling for that day was over. Before long Frenchy came whistling up from his cabin on the riverbank, leading his pack pony. The pony was loaded with blankets and a few small traps. With Ma around, Frenchy had to pretend that the traps were very important. Sam, Pierre, and Si were right by Frenchy's side, and Limpy was running on ahead. They were going, too. Each of the boys, like Frenchy, had his gun and powder horn and bullet pouch.

Ma added some blankets to those already on the pony, and into one of the saddlebags she put plenty of smoked venison and "rye-an'-Injun" bread.

"Don't come home without trapping a bear or two," laughed Ma, as if she didn't know that you couldn't catch bears in such small traps. Maybe Ma had her own ideas about that trapping party. Ma was a very wise woman.

Now the hunters turned their steps toward the corduroy bridge and the prairies to the westward. Before long Hastings Mills was left behind. The hunters started across the pathless prairies, making their own paths through the dead, brown grasses which at times were as high as Tom's head.

Once they stopped to rest on a rolling upland. The prairies seemed to stretch on forever on all sides. As Tom looked up into the great gray sky overhead, he understood for the first time how big a place the world really is.

It was hard work making one's way through the tangled grasses. The boys had to keep their eyes on the ground for fear of falling. The guns grew heavier with every step the boys took. Only Limpy, running here and there scaring up rabbits, seemed able to forget where he was going.

The boys might easily have become tired and cross as time went on. But Frenchy was so lively and so merry that the miles slipped away, and the boys had no idea how far they were walking.

"Frenchy is a singer if there ever was one," Pa used to say, and today Frenchy couldn't get enough of singing. When he wasn't singing, he was whistling. Each tune was gayer and more rollicking than the one before, and Frenchy sang each tune with such a merry lilt that the boys couldn't help joining in.

"Yankee-Doodle," sang Frenchy, and the boys took up the song at the tops of their voices.

"Yankee-Doodle keep it up,
Yankee-Doodle dandy,
Mind the music and the step,
And with the girls be handy."

On went the tune, over and over and over again. When at last the boys had to stop to get their breath, Frenchy began another.

"It's every Sunday morning,
When I am by your side,
We'll jump into the wagon,
And all take a ride.

"Wait for the wagon,
Wait for the wagon,
Wait for the wagon,
And we'll all take a ride."

Frenchy couldn't keep his feet still when he sang that tune. He started dancing over the tangled grasses, and he almost fell headlong over the poor old pack pony.

Then, when Frenchy himself was all tired out, he began a sad song.

"The old oaken bucket,
The ironbound bucket,
The moss-covered bucket,
That hung in the well."

The boys didn't like that. They couldn't see any sense in that song. So back they went to "Yankee-Doodle." No matter what else they sang, they always ended with "Yankee-Doodle."

Toward the end of the afternoon, Frenchy suggested that they try their luck at rabbit shooting. Rabbit stew would be better than smoked venison for supper. Si got a rabbit, and Sam did, and so, of course, did Frenchy.

"No more shooting," said Frenchy. "We have rabbits enough, and we'll save our shots for the turkeys."

JACK RABBIT

COTTONTAIL RABBIT

MARSH RABBIT

SNOWSHOE RABBIT

Just about sunset they came to a creek. On the west bank was the woodland where Frenchy hoped to find the turkeys. Frenchy and Limpy went at once on an exploring trip into the woods. The boys were left behind with directions to stay where they were until Frenchy's return.

Frenchy had no sooner disappeared from sight than the boys could hear Limpy's excited bark followed by another sound which they were sure was the gobble of a wild turkey. Tom was all for dashing into the woods to see, but Pierre soon brought him to his senses.

"You mind my pa," said Pierre, "or he'll fix you. He told you to stay here."

In another few minutes Frenchy was back. The wide smile on his face was sign enough that he had found what he was looking for.

"I wouldn't say the woods were full of them, but they are there aplenty," announced Frenchy. "We'll get them in the morning."

Even the boys could see the sense of not trying to shoot turkeys when it was growing dark. Anyway, all their thoughts were centered on building a campfire. They had been starved for hours, and they were so tired that they couldn't put one foot in front of the other.

TINDERBOX closed

WOOD

FLINT

STEEL

BURNED CLOTH

TINDERBOX open

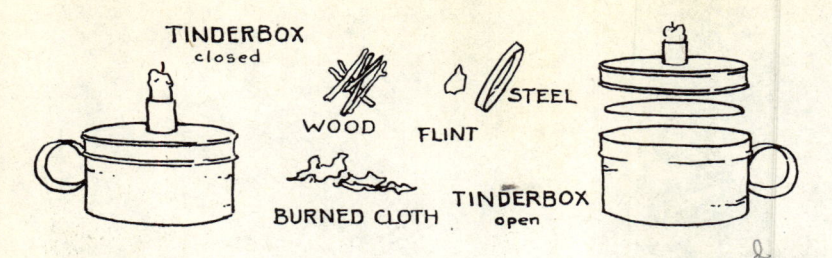

In another minute Frenchy had his tinderbox out from his pocket. From one of the saddlebags he took some bits of dry pine wood and put them in a little pile on the ground. Inside the tinderbox was a piece of very hard stone called flint. The flint was round and flat and had a sharp edge. Inside the tinderbox, also, was a piece of steel and some bits of half-burned cloth and string.

Frenchy held the steel in his left hand. Then, with his right hand, he hit the flint quickly against the steel until a spark flew out. He hit the flint against the steel again and again until one of the sparks fell among the bits of half-burned cloth and set it afire. Pierre dropped one of the pieces of pine wood on the burning cloth in the tinderbox. When one end of the wood was afire, he took it carefully by the other end and put it among the other pieces of wood on the ground.

All this time the other boys had been gathering dead branches from under the trees near the wood's

214

edge. The branches were added a few at a time to the bits of burning pine wood. In a few minutes the campfire was burning brightly.

Have you ever slept all night out under the stars, rolled up in a blanket with not even a tent over your head? Have you ever shot rabbits and cooked your own rabbit stew in a funny three-legged iron pot which sat right over the red coals? Have you any idea how good rabbit stew and "rye-an'-Injun" bread can taste when you're starved? Have you ever waked in the night to hear a wolf howl and a dog growl? Have you ever turned over with one eye open, and waited for someone who was not as sleepy as yourself to throw more wood on the fire to keep the wolf away?

If none of these things has happened to you, you don't know what an exciting adventure really is. But even an exciting adventure like this will seem nothing at all when I tell you what happened to Tom the next morning.

Bright and early the boys and Frenchy were in the woods.

"Be quiet, Limpy," said Frenchy in a low voice, and Limpy was quiet. There wasn't a bark or a yelp out of him.

Now, as the boys looked up into the trees, they could see big balls of black feathers with here and there a touch of red and white showing among the black.

Most of the trees had no turkeys, but a few had as many as two or three. Some of the turkeys were roosting low in the trees, but most of them had chosen their roosting places in the higher branches.

Again it was agreed that Frenchy was to have the first shot. It was hard for the boys to agree to that. They were sure that Frenchy's shot would send the turkeys flying. They would never be able to hit one on the fly. They were not good enough shots for that. But Frenchy told them that they didn't know turkeys. Anyway, Ma's turkey must be ready for the saddlebag before there was another shot fired in those woods.

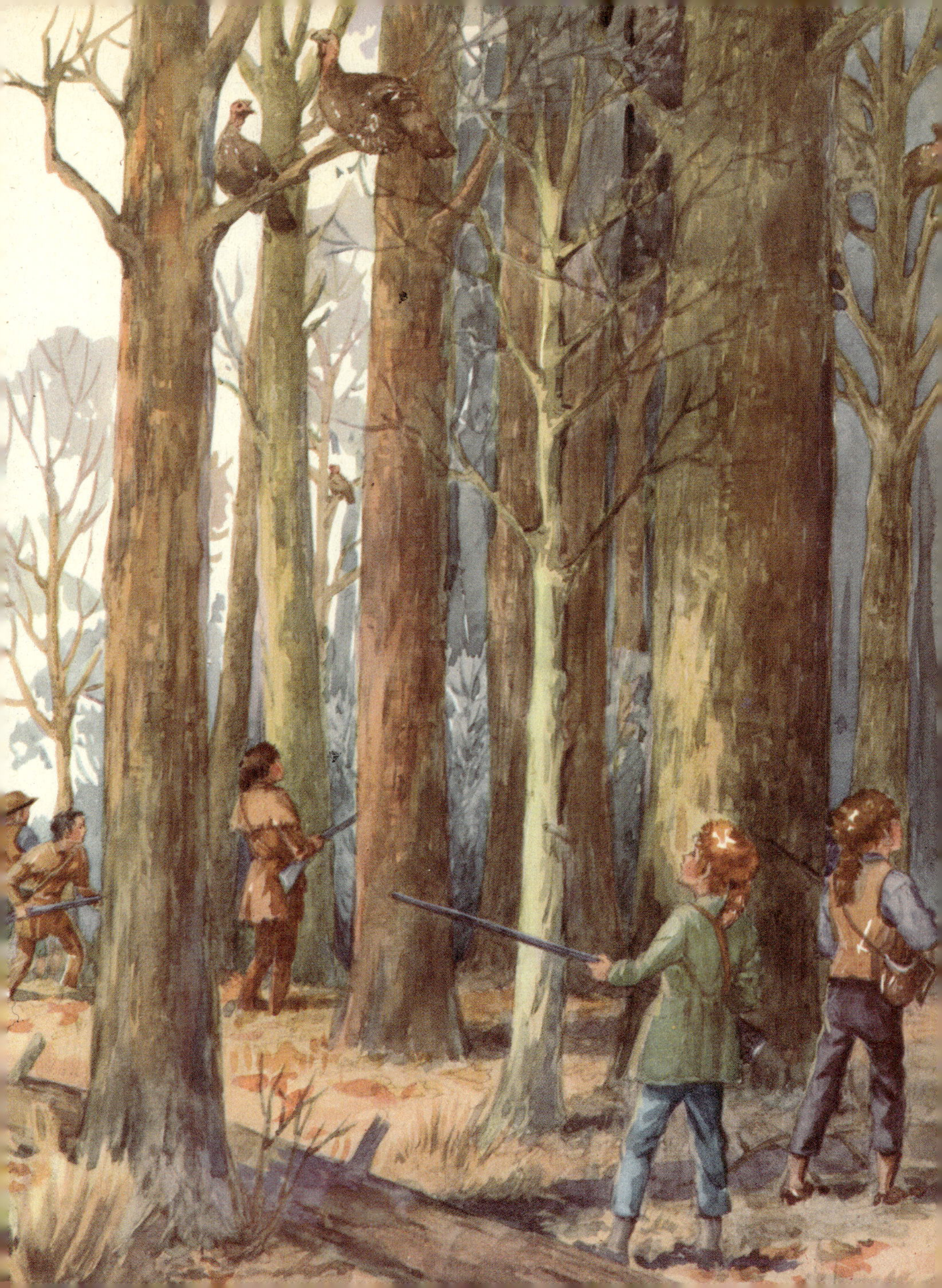

Frenchy walked quietly ahead, his sharp eyes choosing the best turkey in the woods. All at once a shot rang out, and a big turkey gobbler came tumbling down from a treetop. No pigeon pie for Thanksgiving now!

The boys scarcely looked at the big turkey. They were too busy choosing their own tree. If they had thought that the turkeys would fly, they saw now that they were mistaken. The turkeys seemed to know that with hunters in the woods they were safer in the trees than on the wing.

Sam and Si were each so eager to be the first to bring down a bird that they were in too much of a hurry. They hit the branches but not the turkeys. Pierre, more careful than they, missed also.

Tom for once was using his head. He had found a tree standing off by itself near the edge of the woods. There were three turkeys roosting in that tree. Limpy, standing close by Tom's side, was watching every move Tom made. Slowly Tom raised Jenny to his shoulder. He looked along the gun barrel to sight his mark. The big turkey on the high branch! Oh, if only he could get that bird! If only he could!

RACCOON   RACCOON TRACKS   FOX

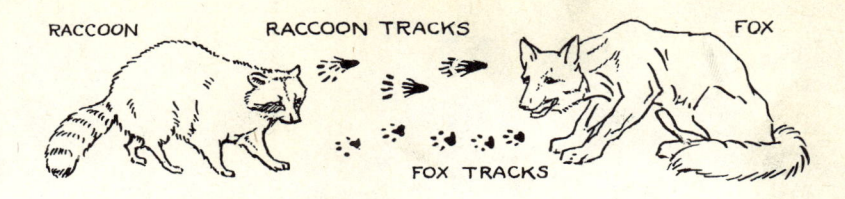

FOX TRACKS

Just as Tom was about to shoot, something big ran from the underbrush not far away and disappeared in the long prairie grass. Maybe it was a fox. Maybe it was a coon on his way to the creek for his breakfast. Tom, with his head in the air sighting the mark, could never be sure. Whatever it was, the sudden noise in the underbrush scared Limpy, who yelped loudly.

Then the unexpected happened — five or six unexpected things, and all at once. The turkeys flew — not into the woods, but out over the prairie. Tom gave a jump of surprise, turned his head to see them go, and fired Jenny. And then! Down into the prairie grass fell not one turkey, but two. Two turkeys killed with one shot! How did it happen? No one ever knew, least of all Tom.

Tom was the hero of the day. It made no difference that Frenchy got two more turkeys before he stopped shooting and that Pierre got one. Nothing mattered except that Tom had brought down two birds with one shot.

All the way home Tom was as proud as a turkey cock. He held his head as high in the air as when he was sighting the turkey. It is a wonder he didn't fall on his nose in the tangled grasses.

Tom's turkeys had a place of their own, tied by their feet to one of the saddlebags. Tom sang "Yankee-Doodle" and "Wait for the Wagon" with a will, but he sang them walking close to the pony's side with his eye on the turkeys. Just before the trapping party reached the corduroy bridge, Frenchy had an idea, a grand one.

"Hop up here, Tom," said Frenchy, with a big grin. In another minute Tom was on top of the blankets, and the poor pack pony was carrying Tom, too.

"Come on, boys," called Frenchy, and he began to sing "Yankee-Doodle" at the top of his voice.

Only this time the song wasn't "Yankee-Doodle" because the words were different.

>"Tom, the hunter, came to town,
>   Riding on a pony,
>   He had two turkeys at his side,
>   Killed with one shot only.
>
>"Tom, the hunter, had a gun,
>   Jenny was a dandy,
>   He kept her always by his side,
>   Where she'd be very handy."

That's what Frenchy sang, and the boys caught on to the words in a hurry. Oh, how they did sing! All the boys and girls in Hastings Mills, and the grownups, too, came running out to see. You never can imagine the excitement there was by the time Tom reached home. When Ma walked out of the door, it seemed to her that everyone in Hastings Mills was singing that song.

It took a long time before the excitement was over. But at last Si went home with one of Frenchy's turkeys for his ma, and Sam went home with another. Of course, Pierre's turkey was for his own ma. And what do you think Frenchy did with the last turkey? He gave it to the old harness maker.

And was Mr. Harding pleased! He showed that turkey to everybody in town.

Maybe you think that two turkeys were one too many for any family and that Ma gave one of Tom's turkeys away. Well, she didn't.

"I wouldn't think of such a thing," said Ma. "We'll roast the two turkeys, and we'll invite everyone in for a cold turkey supper."

That night Ma picked the turkeys and made the dressing. Things were just the way they had always been on other Thanksgivings except that Ma picked twice as many feathers and made twice as much dressing.

It was a good thing that Ma had two Dutch ovens, because the next morning there were two big turkeys to roast among the red coals and hot ashes of the fireplace. If one roasting turkey smells good, two roasting turkeys smell better. You just can't imagine the wonderful smell that filled the Hastings cabin that morning.

Pa sat down at the head of the table with the two big birds in front of him, and, of course, Pa's holiday smile was twice as jolly as ever before. Do you know what Pa said when the prayer was over and he looked out over the loaded table?

"Which shall it be, dark meat or white? The wishbones are for Ma, but there is a drumstick apiece for the rest of us." That's what Pa said.

It seemed as if everyone in Hastings Mills dropped in at the Hastings cabin that afternoon. Of course, the blacksmith brought his fiddle. The minute he arrived, he sat in Pa's big chair and tipped it back against the wall so that he could keep time better with his foot. Then the fun began.

"Give us a jig, fiddler!" called a laughing voice. "A jig, fiddler, a jig!"

Then, from the strings of the fiddle, came the rollicking lilt of "Turkey in the Straw."

"Turkey in the straw,
Turkey in the straw,
The funniest thing I ever saw,
Is to play the same old tune
And call it 'Turkey in the Straw.'"

You never would have thought that a fiddle bow could move so fast. No sooner had the tune started than Frenchy was right out in the middle of the floor, jigging as fast as a man can jig.

Round and round went the music, faster, faster, faster. Louder and louder grew the clapping and the tapping of the watching crowd. But you should have heard the laughing when Pa gave Ma a push and she was right out on the floor jigging, too.

Round and round went the music until Frenchy had to give up. He didn't have a breath left. But Ma went right on jigging. You couldn't beat Ma when it came to jigging.

But even a jig can't go on forever. Finally Ma had to stop. She dropped down on a chair in the corner, and Mr. Lane fanned her with his hat to help her get her breath back.

"Virginia reel!" called the fiddler. "Get your partners." At once the tune changed, and from the strings of the little brown fiddle came the rollicking lilt of "The Irish Washerwoman."

Pa, and the schoolmaster, and the old harness maker, and some more men lined up in one row. Grandma Carter, and Frenchy's wife, and some of the other women lined up in another. Everyone else crowded back against the wall ready to keep time with his hands and feet to help the dance along.

"Bow to your partner," called the big voice of the fiddler, and the dance began. But the cabin was too small and too crowded for the Virginia reel. When the fiddler called, "Mark time, march!" Pa opened the front door wide as he passed by. The dancers danced out into the yard, and there the dance ended.

When the merrymaking was over, there was cold turkey for supper, "rye-an'-Injun" bread, and hasty pudding with good maple sugar. You never would believe how fast that turkey disappeared. Before long there was nothing left but the bones, and Ma had to piece out the supper with sausage and ham and headcheese.

Right in the middle of the supper Pa called for the wishbones. Of course, they belonged to Ma, but it wasn't fair for her to do all the wishing. That's what Pa said. So Ma and Pa wished on one, and Frenchy and Tom wished on the other. Ma wished that there would always be turkey for Thanksgiving, and Pa, with a big grin on his face, wished for a pigeon pie. Would you ever believe that Pa could have done that? Tom wished that he would have just as good luck the next time he went turkey hunting, and Frenchy wished that he could beat Ma at jigging.

And then, when there was no good reason for staying any longer, the merrymakers went marching home, singing "Yankee-Doodle" with the new words. I don't know who was the tiredest person in Hastings Mills that night, but I do know who was the happiest. Maybe you do, too. It was Ma.

"Whipping the Cat"

Ma was cross, and every day she was growing crosser. Only last spring the traveling shoemaker on his rounds had promised, "I'll be in Hastings Mills before the snow flies. You can count on that." Still the days came and went, and he did not come.

Now Sally's shoes were so small that they pinched her toes, and she could not walk in them. Jim needed new moccasins, and Pa had not had new boots for years. As for Ma, she wished her everyday skirts were long enough to hide her own old shoes. Only Tom, who had brought new shoes from the East, was ready for winter.

Every now and then Ma would go to the barn and look up at the tanned cowhides hanging on the wall. Last year's hides ready and waiting! It had taken Frenchy a year to tan those hides. Must the Hastings family wear "store-bought" shoes with good hides hanging in their own barn?

"Why worry?" said Pa. "I reckon a day or two will bring him. Shoemaker Dan is a man of his word, but it is no easy matter for a man as old as he to be 'whipping the cat.'"

"Whipping the cat!" Of course you want to know what Pa meant by that. When a shoemaker traveled from place to place and had no shop of his own, people said he was "whipping the cat."

Just as Ma had given up all hope, the shoemaker came. Jim, on his way to the spring on the riverbank, was the first to discover him.

PEG CUTTER
COBBLER'S TOOLS

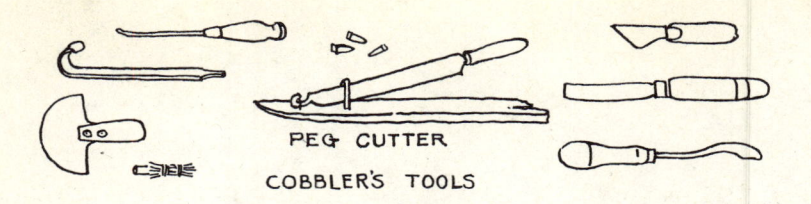

Shoemaker Dan was coming up the east river road with his wheelbarrow, merrily whistling a tune called "Old Dan Tucker." His spectacles sat on the end of his nose, and tied tightly about his waist was his shoemaker's leather apron. In the wheelbarrow were his shoemaker's bench and his box of tools, and sitting on top of everything else was his old felt hat. He never wore a hat if he could find a way out of it.

Shoemaker Dan had a shiny, bald head with hair around the edges. So, when he smiled, the smile didn't stop with his face. It wrinkled away up to the top of his funny bald head. He had sat for so many years on his low shoemaker's bench, driving home pegs with the tap, tap of his hammer, that he was very round-shouldered. You couldn't say that he had a hump on his back, but he did,

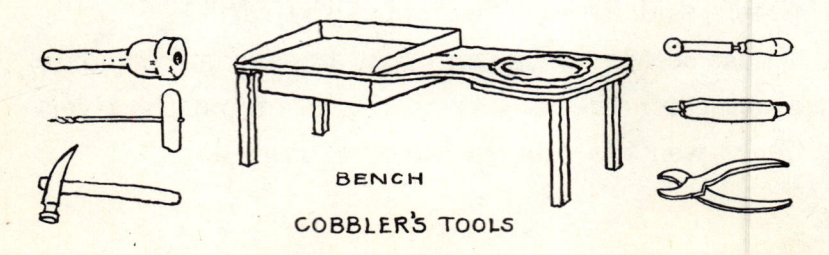

BENCH
COBBLER'S TOOLS

almost. The thing that Jim couldn't keep his eyes from was the shoemaker's funny bent thumbs.

"That's what pushing and pulling thread through thick leather does for a man," said Shoemaker Dan when he saw what Jim was looking at. "That comes from pushing and pulling."

Jim hurried to fill his buckets at the spring and walked along by the side of the wheelbarrow, his eyes big with interest at what he saw there.

"Change of work is rest," chuckled Shoemaker Dan. "Suppose we try it."

The next minute Jim was wheeling the wheelbarrow, and Shoemaker Dan was carrying the water buckets. You can imagine how Jim liked that. His face was just one big smile.

You never could believe how pleased everyone in Hastings Mills was to see the shoemaker. He knew stories and jokes without end, and he enjoyed telling every one of them.

"I declare! The newspaper has come to town," chuckled the old harness maker when he saw him. "There is nothing that has happened in these parts that we won't hear about now. Shoemaker Dan isn't one to sit in chimney corners with his ears closed."

And the old harness maker was right. Shoemaker Dan knew what Mr. Miller of Graytown used for the ache in his bones. He knew the hour and the minute when Mr. North's calf was stolen. He knew how many people were hurt when a robber tried to hold up the stagecoach, and the horses ran away. Shoemaker Dan knew everything. Pa said he even knew how to handle Ma.

"Hum-m-m!" said the shoemaker with a satisfied sigh, as he entered the cabin door. "It's good for an old man to be here. There isn't a house in the land where I'd rather spend the night. Tell me, is Shoemaker Dan a man of his word or isn't he? Didn't I tell you that I'd see you again before the snow began to fly?"

What could Ma say then? What could she say? Just seeing the shoemaker took a load of worry from her mind, and she had to smile in spite of herself. "You have missed the snow by a minute or two, but a miss is as good as a mile." That's what Ma said.

Shoemaker Dan set up his bench close to the window where the light would be good. Then Pa brought in the tanned hides from the barn, and the two men talked them over. Every minute that

Jim could steal from work, he was leaning over Shoemaker Dan's shoulder, watching everything.

"And now, where do I begin?" asked Shoemaker Dan when the talking was over.

"Suppose you begin with Jim," said Pa. "I wouldn't be a bit surprised if he'd like a pair of boots. I wouldn't be a bit surprised."

Jim's mouth opened, and his eyes almost popped out of his head. Boots! All he had hoped for was a new pair of moccasins. But oh, how he wanted boots! Pa must have made a mistake. He couldn't have meant what he said. He just couldn't! The next minute Jim was sure of it.

"Why, Thomas Hastings!" said Ma. "How you talk! You'll spoil that boy. His feet haven't stopped growing. What does he want with boots?"

Jim's face fell, but before he had time for more than a second's disappointment, Shoemaker Dan broke in.

"Well, I declare! What kind of shoemaker do you think I am? Can't I make boots big enough to allow for growing? Can't I, now?"

Ma shook her head as much as to say, "I give in!" As for Jim, he was just one big grin. When a boy gets his first pair of boots, he's growing up. He really is.

"There is one thing certain," announced the shoemaker. "I can't make boots for a boy if the boy is not right by my side while I'm doing it."

Then Ma looked at Pa, and Pa looked at Ma, and Shoemaker Dan looked at both of them. After that Ma didn't say a thing to Jim about bringing in the wood and the water. She just did it herself.

All Jim wanted to do was to hurry the shoemaking along. But Shoemaker Dan was in no hurry.

"The world wasn't made in a day, my lad," he said, as he looked his workbench over. "Upon my word, I need some shoe pegs. No sense in beginning without my shoe pegs!"

Then Pa and Jim and the shoemaker walked down to the mill together. Shoemaker Dan chose a piece of good hard maple wood. It had been standing in the mill for a long time and was very dry. Pa said it was well-seasoned.

Shoemaker Dan took Pa's saw and sawed off a piece of the maple wood one-half inch thick. He measured to be sure that it was just half an inch. Then back to his bench he went. With his sharp knife he marked the maple wood off into little squares, and he cut out the pegs. Each square made a peg. Each peg was half an inch long and was pointed at the end.

"Now, my man," said Shoemaker Dan when the last peg was finished, "I'm ready."

Jim took off his worn-out moccasins and his socks and stood on a thin piece of board. The shoemaker drew around each foot with his big pencil to make a pattern.

Then, from the thick part of the cowhide, Shoemaker Dan cut a pair of soles. From the thinner cowhide, he cut two inner soles. The soles were just the shape of the pattern of Jim's feet, which the shoemaker had drawn upon the wood, only bigger. You remember he had to allow for growing.

From the softest leather Shoemaker Dan cut the uppers. It took two pieces of leather to make the uppers for one boot. The two pieces had to be sewed together, just as the pieces of leather in the uppers of your shoes are sewed together.

Next Shoemaker Dan prepared his thread. From the long drawer under the bench he took some strong thread and his lump of beeswax. He rubbed the thread up his leg and broke it into pieces six feet long. Then, in his left hand, he held the beeswax. With his right hand he pulled one of the threads across the dark brown beeswax and rolled the thread down the front of his leather apron. Again and again he waxed the threads. When he was through, each thread was dark and stiff and shiny with wax.

SHOE — LAST, SIDE, SOLE

BOOT — LAST, SOLE

Then, out from one corner of the drawer, Shoemaker Dan took his pig bristles. Are you wondering what he could possibly want with pig bristles? Pig bristles were the shoemaker's needles, only they were much better than real needles because they never came unthreaded. Shoemaker Dan laid a pig's bristle along each end of the waxed thread. Once again he pulled the thread across the beeswax and rolled it down the front of his leather apron. He waxed and rolled until a pig's bristle was waxed tight to each end of the thread.

Now Shoemaker Dan was ready for his sewing. He fitted the two pieces of leather for the uppers of one shoe carefully together. He fastened them tightly in his vise, with the edges which he was to sew sticking up from the vise. Then, with one of his sharp tools, he made holes along the edges. In and out of the holes from side to side went the pig bristles and the waxed thread. Stitch by stitch he sewed the seams. Up went his hands, and he pulled the waxed thread so tight that it sank deep into the leather.

"That's the way to sew a seam that will hold water," said Shoemaker Dan proudly.

"Hold water? What do you mean?" asked Jim.

"We have queer ways of saying things," chuckled Shoemaker Dan. "When we sew a seam that will keep out water, we say that we are sewing a seam that will hold water. 'Hold it out' is what we mean, I reckon."

Jim couldn't see any sense in that.

Now the sewing of the uppers for the two shoes was finished, and Shoemaker Dan turned to his bench to choose his last. Do you know what a shoemaker's last is? It is a piece of wood cut and smoothed and shaped to look like a foot. Shoemaker Dan had big lasts for men's feet, smaller lasts for women's feet, and small lasts for the feet of boys and girls. He chose a pair of lasts the size of Jim's feet, only a little bigger. Don't forget. He had to remember the growing.

That night Shoemaker Dan put the soles for Jim's boots in water to soften the leather and make it easier to work with. Bright and early the next morning he was back at his bench.

Shoemaker Dan turned the last for one boot upside down and laid the inner sole upon it. Then very carefully he drew the uppers down over it and bent the edges which were to hold the uppers to the sole, back over the inner sole. He laid the heavy sole on top and put the upside down boot carefully across his knees.

Then he reached for his paste horn. This was just a hollowed-out cow horn filled with glue. He glued the two soles firmly together.

Next Shoemaker Dan tightened the leather strap of his shoemaker's jack. The jack was made from a narrow board and a long leather strap. The shoemaker held the board fast to the floor by keeping his feet firmly upon it. The leather strap reached under the center of the board and up over the boot held between the shoemaker's knees. By tightening the strap, the shoemaker held the boot firmly in place.

Now, with his sharp tool, Shoemaker Dan made holes around the edges of the sole. Into each hole went a shoe peg, and then, with two taps of his hammer for each peg, he pegged on the sole.

From the thickest part of the cowhide he cut a heel, and from the drawer of his bench he took some longer heel pegs. He made holes around the edges of the heel, and into each hole went a heel peg. Then he pegged the heel fast to the boot. When the sole was dry, the boot would be done.

It took three days for Shoemaker Dan to finish the boots, but they were grand boots. When Jim put on two pairs of heavy woolen socks and a thin pair, the boots weren't a bit too big. They didn't rub his toes or his heels. They fitted perfectly, and they made a grand clop, clop, clopping sound on the cabin floor.

It would take three days for Ma's shoes, three days for Sally's, and three days more for Pa's boots. Then Shoemaker Dan expected to go on to Sam's house and to Si's and to every house in Hastings Mills where shoes were needed. But something happened to change all that.

"I declare," said Ma to Pa one morning shortly before the shoes for the Hastings family were finished. "I hate to see him leave our cabin, to say nothing of the day when he will leave Hastings Mills to be gone for months. Everyone will miss his jokes and stories. He is the best shoemaker and the jolliest I have ever seen. I wish he would stay in these parts forever."

Ma's words gave Pa an idea.

"Have you ever thought of settling down?" Pa asked on the last day of the shoemaker's stay. "Hastings Mills is growing and needs a shoemaker.

If there are no shoes to be made, there are shoes to be mended. I reckon the harness maker will give you a corner of his shop for the winter. When spring comes round, we'll build you a shop of your own."

"A shop of my own!" said Shoemaker Dan. "Come now, that's good of you. Hastings Mills is a friendly place. I haven't run across another like it in all my travels. A shop of my own! I'll think it over."

The more Shoemaker Dan thought, the more he liked the idea. Late that afternoon the old harness maker looked up. There in the door of his shop was the shoemaker with his wheelbarrow before him and a smile on his face that wrinkled away up to the top of his funny bald head.

"Come in," said the old harness maker with a welcome ring in his voice. "There's a warm spot in the chimney corner waiting for you. Tomorrow we'll cut another window to give you light."

"Hum-m-m!" said the shoemaker with a satisfied sigh, as he set up his bench. "It's good to be here. Traveling the roads may be all right for young lads, but it's good to know that Shoemaker Dan will no longer be 'whipping the cat.'"

The Wolf Hunt

Every cabin in Hastings Mills was filled almost to overflowing with good food stored away for winter. The wood piles behind the cabins were as tall as the cabins themselves. Shoemaker Dan, in the warm corner of the harness shop, was making shoes for those who needed them. Busy mothers, spinning and weaving, had warm clothes ready for everyone. Now the wind could blow, and the snow could cover the prairies. Hastings Mills was ready for the long winter.

Work went on as usual, but more often than had been the custom, the men gathered about the stove in the general store. And always, when they gathered, the talk was of the wolves.

In spite of all the men could do, the number of wolves seemed to be growing. Frenchy set more traps and more traps. The minute it grew dark, the men lay in wait with their guns. The piles of wolfskins outside cabin doors grew larger and larger. But for every wolf killed, two came to take its place.

Now that winter was coming and food was scarce, the wolves were lean and hungry, and they grew bolder as they grew hungrier. At night they howled under the windows of the cabins, and watchdogs barked and growled at all hours.

The farmers up and down the river were having no end of trouble. Wolves were killing their sheep and chickens, and the pigs which had not yet been butchered. Even the cattle were not safe.

Mothers worried when their children were out of sight for a minute, even though the wolves did most of their killing at night.

Early one evening Mr. Fuller was returning on horseback from the home of a sick neighbor. A pack of wolves appeared suddenly from somewhere and followed him for half a mile, biting and snapping at his horse's heels.

One day Jim Hastings, on his way from the spring on the riverbank, heard a noise behind him and turned to find a wolf following him in daylight. Then everyone in Hastings Mills knew that the time for action had arrived. There was not a minute to be lost.

Sam and Si, and Tom and Pierre took every minute they could steal from work to stick their noses in at the general store, where plans for the big wolf hunt were under way.

When the boys heard that every man and boy who could carry a gun was to take part in the hunt, they almost shouted for joy. Si Lane said that it was the best news he had heard since the day he came to Hastings Mills.

All the rest of the day, while Sam was busy at work and Si was helping him, these two practiced the Indian war cry over and over. They were going to be ready to scare the wolves as well as to kill them. But Tom and Pierre couldn't practice a bit. They had to think of Red and Patch.

Early the next morning Pa, and Mr. Lane, and the old harness maker got on their horses and rode out over the country to ask every man for miles around to join the big wolf hunt. The meeting place was to be Turtle Rock Inn, and the time, late the next afternoon.

Plans for the big hunt had been carefully made. When everyone had arrived, each one was told where to go and what to do. Finally each man was in his place, waiting in a big circle. Each boy, with his gun loaded and ready, stood next to his pa. It was several miles across that big circle, and somewhere inside, though not in sight, were the wolves.

At the start, the men stood far apart from one another. All at once, from three different places, shots rang out. They were a signal for the hunt to begin. Each hunter began to move forward toward the center of the circle. As the hunters moved forward, they were drawing slowly together, and the circle was getting smaller and smaller.

As soon as the wolves saw or heard the men coming, they ran toward the center of the circle. There was nowhere else for them to go. While the hunters were still far apart, wise old wolves would sometimes try to run between the men and get away. But the Indian war cry saved the day. First the boys gave the cry. Then the men took it up, soft at first, then louder and louder, ending in a mighty yell. The frightened wolves, snarling angrily, turned about and dashed back the way they had come.

By now the hunters had closed up until they were very close together, and their circle had become so small that they could see the frightened animals crowded in the center.

"Pa! Pa! There's a deer!" yelled Tom, as he came near enough to be able to tell one animal from another. "I thought this was a wolf hunt."

"It is," answered Pa. "That deer is in for trouble. Since he has been caught with the wolves, he'll be killed with the wolves."

The circle grew smaller and smaller.

"Look out!" yelled Pa a few minutes later, as he stepped up close to Tom to protect him. "Shoot, Tom, and don't waste your powder."

Several big wolves, wild with fright, were running right toward Tom and Pa, trying to break through. At other points in the circle, other wolves were trying to break through, also.

Shots rang out here, there, and everywhere, and Tom's shot was among them. "I hit one! I hit one!" he cried at the top of his voice. And sure enough, Jenny had killed a big wolf. But when Tom had shot once, he was too much excited to reload Jenny. After that he just helped out by yelling. But oh, how he did yell!

When the hunt was over, sixteen wolves lay dead on the prairie. The dead deer was among them. There was a tired but satisfied look on the face of every man as he counted the dead wolves.

"No barking dogs nor howling wolves to keep us awake tonight!" said Pa. "We can sleep in peace."

Tom and Pierre, and Sam and Si — each boy had brought down his wolf, and each boy's pa was as proud as proud could be. Si could trade his skin for a knife if that was what he wanted. Sam and Pierre could figure how many caps they could get from a wolfskin. Tom knew what he was going to do with his wolfskin, and no one had to tell him.

"Lightning Joe! Lightning Joe!" called Tom the next day when the stage stopped on its return trip from the west. "Here's a wolfskin for my Uncle Will. You'll give it to him, won't you? Tell him we shot the wolf, Jenny and I. I promised him a bearskin, but a wolfskin is just as good. Don't you think so?"

"Bearskin!" said Lightning Joe in disgust. "Who wants a bearskin? Your Uncle Will wouldn't trade this skin for all the bearskins in the land. But come now, wouldn't this wolf be surprised if he were alive and knew where he was going?"

No doubt the wolf would have been surprised. But anyway, when the bugle called, "All aboard! Stage going!" Tom's wolfskin started on its long journey to the East.

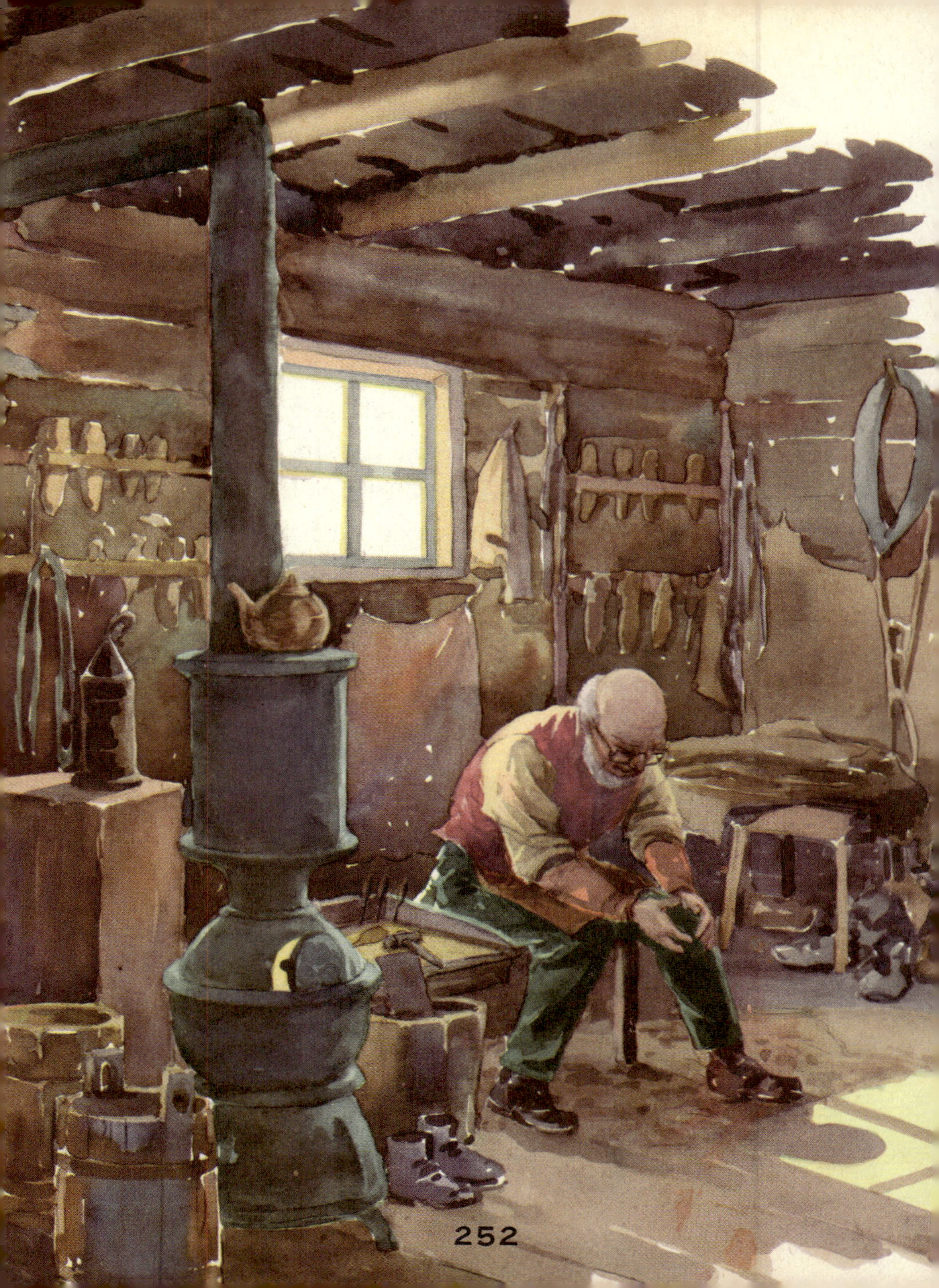

Snowbound

School Days

The morning that followed the wolf hunt was warm and sunny. Shoemaker Dan sat in a patch of sunshine near the new window of the harness shop, rubbing his knees and wrinkling his forehead.

"I'm as stiff as a log," he grumbled. "There is a change in the weather coming. I can tell by the ache in my bones."

"Wind's from the south, and that spells trouble," nodded the old harness maker wisely. "I don't trust a south wind at this time of year. There is snow on the way, or maybe a blizzard."

SNOWFLAKES

Time went by, and low down in the sky to the north and west clouds began to gather, slate-gray clouds with cold, silvery edges.

By early afternoon the cold, silvery edges had covered the sun, which shone through the clouds with a queer gray light. People went about their work with one eye on the sky. There was an uneasy, restless feeling in the air, as if at any minute the storm might break.

The wind died away. In the stillness that followed, boys like Tom hastened to bring home the cattle, and boys like Jim hurried into the cabins with wood and water.

By the middle of the afternoon the sun had disappeared. A strange gray darkness covered the prairies, a strange gray darkness which seemed to predict that anything might happen.

Suddenly the wind rushed cold from the north, and, carried along on the whistling wind, came the snow. At first the great flakes melted as they reached the ground, but as the wind grew sharper and colder, the snow no longer melted.

All through the night the snow fell. In the morning there was no stage road leading to the hill. No stretches of dead, brown prairie grasses! Over everything was the great whiteness of the snow, broken here and there by the gray logs of a cabin and the smoke of a friendly chimney. Winter had come at last to Hastings Mills.

Every boy and girl hailed with delight the coming of the snow. On the morning after the storm the work in the barns was no sooner over than the boys were following the ox teams and breaking the roads. Tom and Pierre, driving Red and Patch, did their part and cleared the roads from cabin to cabin.

Every now and then shouts of laughter rang out as the oxen were left to follow their noses, and the boys, and even a pa or two, tried their hands at a snowball fight.

As the sun rose higher in the southern sky, the snow sparkled in the sunlight, and for every cabin and tree and fence post there was a long, blue-black shadow. The roofs of the cabins were rounded with the snow. The branches of the trees snapped in the cold, frosty air, and the bells of the ox teams jingled merrily.

When the oxen had cleared the stage road to the hill, every sled in Hastings Mills appeared as if by magic. The longer the coasting continued, the smoother the snow became, until Tom, whose sled was swifter than any other, went whizzing from the hilltop to the riverbank in one grand slide.

There wasn't too much said about work in Hastings Mills that day. Certain things had to be done. Milking the cows was one thing. Bringing in wood and water was another. But aside from such things as these, work and the first snowstorm of the year didn't belong together. Every ma and pa understood that.

While the day passed merrily for the boys and girls, the thoughts of the grownups were on other things. No use to bother any longer about preparations for winter! Winter was here. What was not done must remain undone. In the meantime, there were boys and girls who needed reading, writing, and arithmetic. No doubt about it! School must begin.

Mr. Joseph Hunter, the schoolmaster, agreed most heartily. He had been wishing for this day for a long, long time.

SKATES

When you are boarding around, doing a little of this kind of work and a little of that, you grow sick and tired of being a Jack-of-all-trades. No wonder Mr. Hunter wanted school to begin.

On this particular morning, Mr. Hunter had promised Mr. Lake to help break the river road. So Pa and Mr. Carter agreed to do what had to be done to get the schoolhouse ready.

Waiting in one corner of the general store was a round iron stove which had come by pack train all the way from the East. The stove was to be Mr. Carter's donation to the new school. This very afternoon Pa and Mr. Carter carried the stove up the hill to the schoolhouse and set it up in the middle of the room.

For a time the boys coasted right by the schoolhouse door and paid little attention to anything that was going on there.

At last, overcome with curiosity, a few boys, with Tom among them, stuck their heads in at the door. The next minute they wished they hadn't.

"Just in time," said Pa with a big grin. "How thoughtful of you to come when we needed you."

Pa wouldn't let a single boy go back to his coasting until a goodly part of the woodpile outside the back door was piled in a corner of the room. Every log had to be placed just so to suit Pa. Of all things to have happen!

"You'd think your pa was the schoolmaster," Sam grumbled crossly to Tom.

As if that were not enough, Tom had to go all the way home and bring back some red coals from the fireplace in one of Ma's covered kettles. Tom couldn't see the sense in building a fire in a schoolhouse when there wasn't any school. But Pa insisted that they had to take the chill off the place. They couldn't wait until school started to do that.

During the past few weeks, whenever Pa could take time from his other work, he had been making the desks and benches and had been storing them in the mill. Each bench was made of a long board cut lengthwise from the trunk of a tree. The ends of the long board were nailed to shorter pieces of board. The desks were just like the benches, except that they were a little higher. Each bench was the same size as every other bench. The desks were the same way.

When Frenchy was through unloading his next load of logs at the mill, Pa told him to stop for the day and help to carry the desks and benches to the schoolhouse.

Bright and Flash were not pulling an oxcart now. They were pulling a big bobsled. By the time the desks and benches were on the bobsled, there was more than desks and benches for the oxen to pull. Every boy and girl who could find a place was on the bobsled, too. Things were certainly becoming interesting. Getting the schoolhouse ready was more exciting than coasting. Who ever would have thought it?

Up the long hill went the two big oxen, and the merry shouts of the boys and girls brought the grownups to the cabin doors to see what in the world could be going on.

Tom and Sam didn't mind the unloading a bit, not one bit. Before long the desks for the girls were on one side of the room, the ones for the boys on the other. Up in front was the master's desk.

Right in the middle of everything was the big round stove, glowing red with the newly built fire.

Just as the last bench was in place, in walked Ma and Grandma Fields. Ma had a wooden bucket in her hand and the half of a big yellow gourd for a dipper. The water bucket and the dipper were soon in place on a small bench by the back door.

Grandma Fields was carrying a big, round, wooden clock. It was an interesting old clock which had come overland with Grandma all the way from New England. There were pictures of the sun and the moon on its face, and it told the passing of each hour by the ringing of a bell. That is why it was called a bell-clock.

Pa couldn't believe that Grandma Fields really meant to donate that clock to the school, but she insisted that she did. Pa and Frenchy hung the clock high on the back wall where only the master could keep his eye on it.

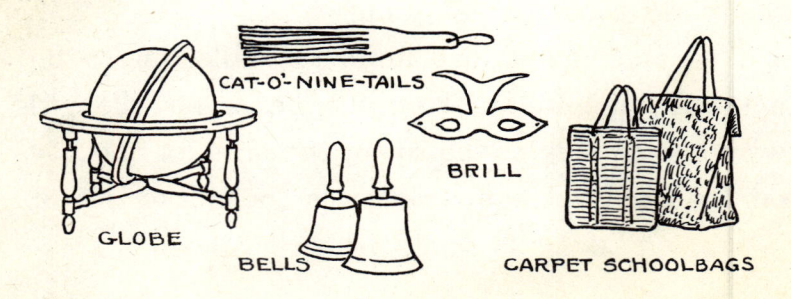

GLOBE

CAT-O'-NINE-TAILS

BRILL

BELLS

CARPET SCHOOLBAGS

Then Ma suggested that they all keep still for a minute and listen. It was surprising how cheerful and pleasant the ticking of the old clock sounded. It was good to see the smile on Grandma's face. She was so well pleased.

Just when everyone was listening, in walked the schoolmaster and Shoemaker Dan. They couldn't believe that all this work had been done in one afternoon. They simply couldn't.

"Upon my word, there is only one thing missing," declared the schoolmaster. But before he could say another word, Shoemaker Dan broke in.

"If it isn't a hickory stick you're thinking about, maybe I have it," said Shoemaker Dan.

Then, from the big leather pocket of his coat, he took a school bell.

"The blacksmith sent this," he said. "This bell has been sitting on a shelf in the smithy ever since the smithy was built. The blacksmith is very glad to find a use for it."

SLATES

HOURGLASS

PRIMER

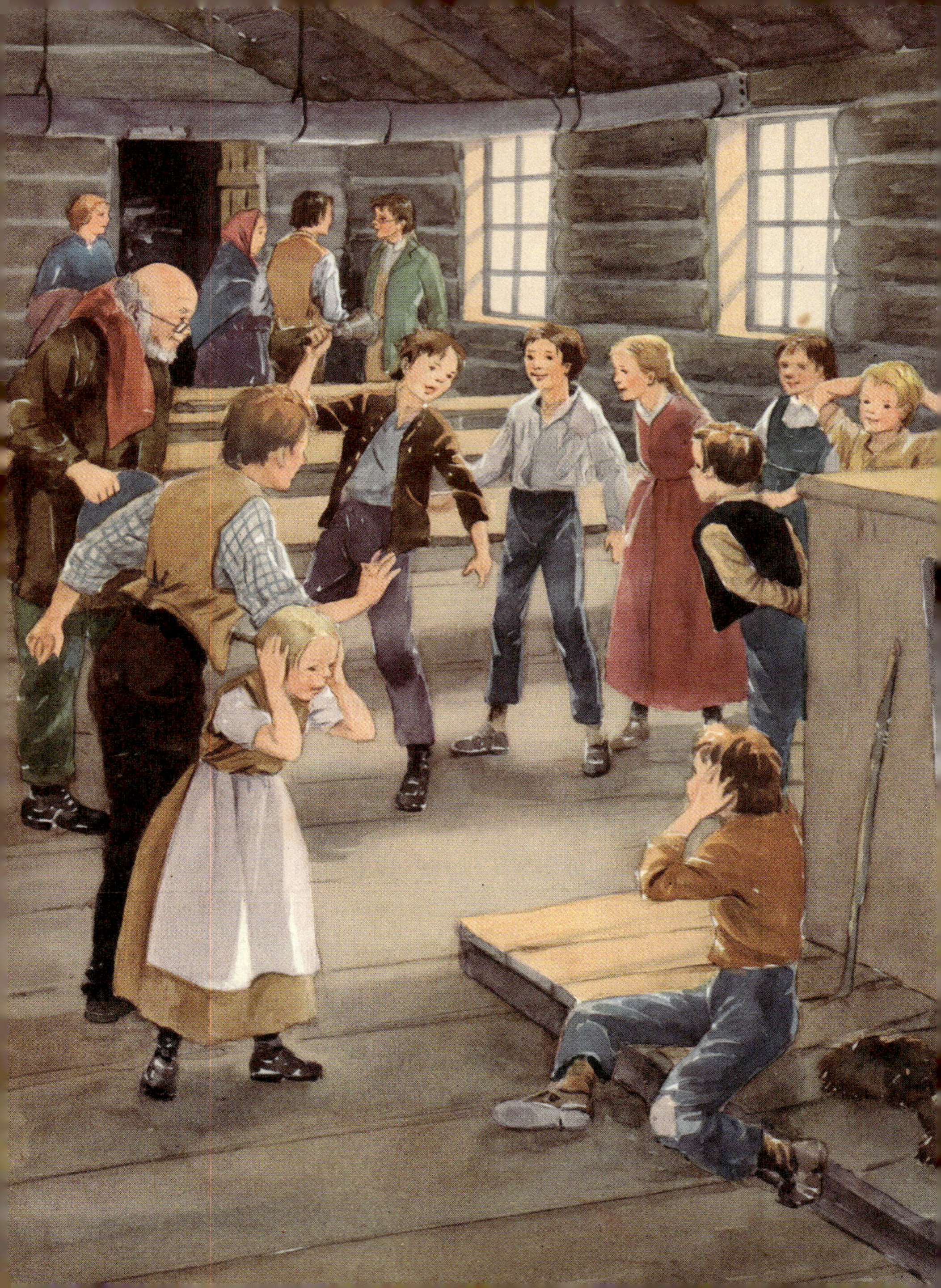

Of course, the boys had to try the bell. While the bell was ringing its loudest, Mr. Hunter turned to Pa.

"Is there a reason in the world why school should not start tomorrow?" he asked.

"Not a reason in the world," answered Pa.

Do you know what all the boys and girls who were old enough to go to school did before bedtime that night? They took out their slates and slate pencils and a book, if they happened to have one. Each slate pencil was tied to the wooden frame of the slate with a piece of red yarn.

Sam had a spelling book with a blue cover. His pa called it the "Blue-back Speller." The blacksmith had used it when he went to school, and he still thought that it was the best speller in the land. Sam's pa had been a famous speller in his day. He wanted Sam to be one, too. A boy ought to be, when he had a "Blue-back Speller."

Si Lane had a book called "The American Reader and Speaker." Tom had a very hard arithmetic called "The Scholar's Arithmetic." If you could have seen those books, you would certainly have been glad that Si was good at reading and that Tom was good at figures.

NUMBER BOARD COUNTING STICKS PENCIL CASES PENS and INKWELLS

Tom and Sally together were to use a book called "Easy Lessons in Reading," and Jim had a "Primer, The First Book for Children," with the A B C's in it.

It really looked as though every scholar in the school would have a different book. Some books would be too easy, but most of them would be too hard. That was all right. All a boy's father expected a boy to do was to take the book he had and learn out of it. With the girls it was the same way.

Long before time for the bell to ring the next morning, all the scholars were at the schoolhouse door. A few of the bolder ones were peeking in at the window. The red fire was shining through the holes in the door of the stove. There was the master sitting at his desk, reading a book as if he were really enjoying it. He must be a very smart man, the master.

Reading, Writing, and Arithmetic

The big boys couldn't wait around for a bell to ring. They had to have something to do. Of course, they had their sleds with them, ready for recess. So they made their little brothers carry their books while they themselves went coasting.

The girls stood in a group by the door and acted like little ladies. Before long Sally grew tired of that. Mary Lane did, too. What do you suppose those two did? They slipped away and went whizzing downhill on Sam's sled, books and all.

They took only one ride — just one. But what do you suppose happened? All the other girls turned up their noses and called Mary and Sally tomboys. The boys called them tomboys, too. Even Tom and Si did, their own brothers! Sally was so MAD! The madder she got, the more the boys ran after her and called her tomboy.

It was a good thing that the bell rang when it did. Everyone had to go into the school and behave.

The big boys and girls sat on benches at the back of the room. The next biggest scholars sat in the middle. The boys and girls in the primer class had the front benches.

This was Jim's first day at school. He wondered what it was going to be like. John Gray and Jim were the only boys in the primer class. So they had one front bench all to themselves.

Across from Jim and John sat Betsy Fuller, crying softly. Betsy was only five years old, and she wanted her mother.

First the master read a prayer. Then everyone sang "America." After that Mr. Hunter called one of the big boys up to the master's desk to stand with his toes on a crack in the floor and read.

Jim was supposed to study. That's what Mr. Hunter said. So Jim opened his book and studied. But his feet didn't touch the floor, and before long his feet grew tired of swinging. Jim thought that he would sit on one. So he did.

Suddenly Jim felt uneasy. He peeked up over the top of his book, and there was the master with his eye on him — on him, Jim Hastings. Down came Jim's foot in a hurry.

Jim went on studying for a while. Then his right foot went to sleep. When your foot goes to sleep, you have to rub it to wake it up. Jim rubbed and peeked over the top of his book at the same time. There was the master's eye on him again.

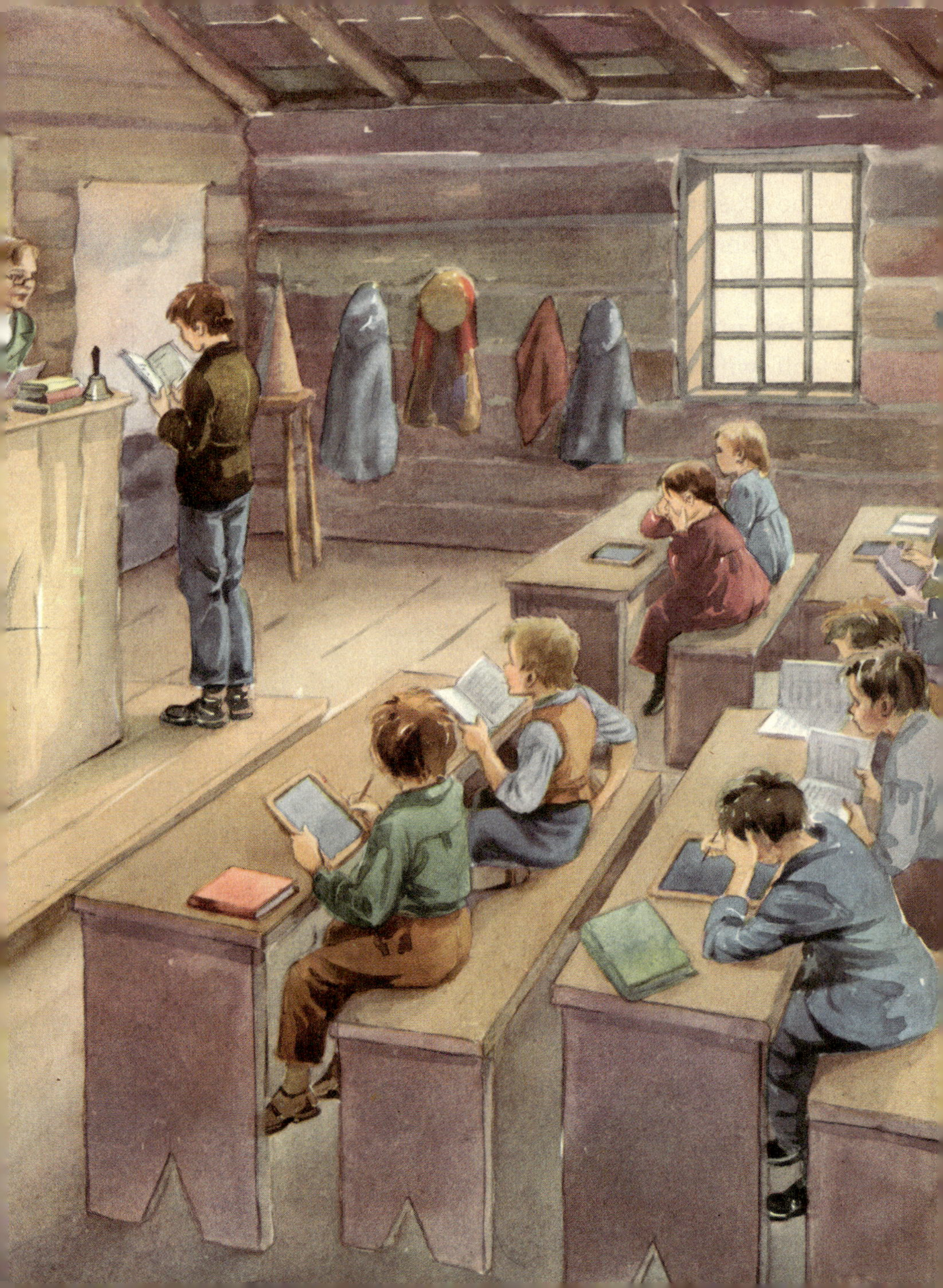

Jim stopped rubbing. My, but you had to be good in school! Jim guessed he didn't like school. No, he was sure he didn't.

Then Mr. Hunter called Jim's name, and Jim went up to the master's desk to stand with his toes on a crack and read. Mr. Hunter started him off with the A B C's. Jim knew those. Ma had taught him his A B C's. Jim knew more than his A B C's. He read away over to page 11 where it said,

He	is	up	He is up
So	am	I	So am I
As	we	do	As we do
Do	go	in	Do go in

The words didn't make sense, but Jim never thought about that. He didn't expect them to make sense. They were just words, and he read them in a big, loud voice.

"Well done, my boy," said the master, smiling down at him. "You are a very good scholar, Jim Hastings, a very good scholar."

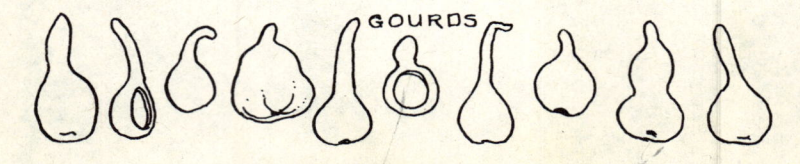

GOURDS

Jim changed his mind. He liked school. Why shouldn't he like school? Wasn't he a very good scholar?

Even being a good scholar didn't keep your feet from going to sleep. But Jim found something that did. That is, it did if you didn't try it too often. You raised your hand and said, "Teacher, teacher, I want a drink!" Then you walked over to the water bucket and drank out of the yellow gourd dipper.

When recess came, the girls bundled up and the boys didn't, and everyone ran outdoors. The other girls wouldn't have a thing to do with Sally and Mary. So the two tomboys went off by themselves to make snow angels. They lay flat down on their backs in the snow and moved their arms up and down to make wings. When they got up again, there, where they had been lying, were two beautiful snow angels.

Tom told Jim to pull his sled up the hill, but Jim wouldn't do it. Jim didn't have to mind Tom. He only had to mind the master. Jim said Tom was too "bossy."

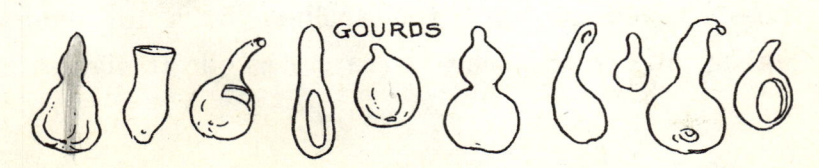

GOURDS

"You think you're smart," said Tom, "just because the master says that you're a good scholar."

I guess Jim did think he was smart. Anyway, he wouldn't pull the sled. He went off with John Gray, who had a sled of his own, and John Gray pulled the sled and Jim, too, up the hill.

By the close of the day the master knew almost all there was to know about every scholar in the school. He knew who were the good readers, which ones needed to start the spelling book all over again, and which ones were no good at figures.

Tom surprised even the master. Would you believe it? He was so good at figures that he even figured out the answer to this problem.

A man added three more sheep to those already in his barn. He then had seven times as many as he would have had if he had sold three instead of buying three. I demand to know how many sheep this man had in the beginning.

Now, if you are as good as Tom, you can figure out the answer to this problem, also. If you can't, maybe you can get your father to help you.

Si wasn't any good at figures, but he could beat Tom when it came to reading. Si could read with expression. Everyone stopped studying when Si began to read. Jim couldn't sit still on his bench. He felt as if he were really skating when Si began,

"Away, away, o'er the slippery ice,
Away, away we go!"

But Jim didn't like it a bit when Si read,

"He's dead and gone,
And he'll play no more,
The boy with the crooked knee."

Jim didn't know who the boy was, but he wished Si would stop reading. Si read with too much expression. He made Jim cry.

Even if Sam did have a "Blue-back Speller," he wasn't the best speller in the school. He was only the second best. He couldn't spell "certainly," and Molly Chase could. Of course, Molly was three years older than Sam, and the biggest girl in the school. Still, Sam wasn't the best speller. It is important for you to remember that.

As for Sally, she wasn't the best at any one thing, but she was good at everything — at reading, writing, and arithmetic, and at sitting still.

"Sally Hastings is the best all-round scholar and the best-behaved girl in the school," said Mr. Hunter at closing time.

Maybe that is why the other girls tried to make up with Sally and Mary on the way home. Sally wouldn't make up with a single girl until that girl promised never to call her tomboy again, or to call Mary Lane that either. In the end every girl promised.

Do you think the boys tried to make up? Well, they didn't. They were worse than ever. They grinned and ran after Sally, calling, "Tomboy! Teacher's pet! Tomboy! Teacher's pet!"

That night Pa told Tom that he knew a good use for the strap on the wall if Tom didn't stop calling Sally names. I guess the news must have spread, and there must have been some more straps on some more walls. Anyway, not one boy called Sally names the next morning.

Days went by, and things in the Hastings Mills school were going along splendidly. Mr. Hunter liked the boys and girls, and they liked him. Then trouble started. It was all the fault of one person, and you can never guess who the troublemaker was. I'm sure you can't.

Of course, Mr. Hunter always had a hickory stick ready for action if he needed it. But he never used it on little boys just because they forgot how to spell a word. He never used it on the big boys except when they came in late from recess or when they laughed out loud in school. The boys didn't want to laugh. They didn't enjoy the sting of the hickory stick. But what could they do with a boy like Sam in the room?

Do you know what Sam could do? He could wiggle his ears. He would be sitting at his desk studying away, with his eyes glued on his book and not a sign of a smile on his face. Yet he could tell as if by magic when a boy was looking at him. Then Sam's ears would begin to wiggle. They kept on wiggling until the other boy laughed right out loud. At once the wiggling stopped as if by magic.

Then, no matter who it was that laughed, the master would say, "Walk right up here! I cannot and will not have laughing in my school."

So Tom or Pierre or Si or some other boy got the hickory stick, and Sam went on studying. But, strange to say, the boys didn't seem to blame Sam, and they never even thought of telling on him. It's a wonderful thing to be able to wiggle your ears. The boys wished they could do it themselves. Sam was doing his best to teach them.

So while Sally was the best-behaved girl, Sam seemed to be the best-behaved boy until one day, and then — .

One morning Tom looked at Sam just as Sam's ears began to wiggle. Today it wasn't only Sam's ears. The skin on his whole head was wiggling. Tom put his hands over his mouth to keep back the laugh, but he was too late. The noise that came out was worse than a laugh. It scared John Gray on his way to the water bucket. It scared him so much that he turned like a flash in Tom's direction. He turned just in time to see the last wiggle. He had never seen ears wiggle before.

"Oh! Oh!" he cried in surprise, pointing his finger at Sam. "That boy does something. He does something with his ears."

Of course, you can't blame a little boy for telling, not a little boy in the primer class. Anyway, the secret was out.

"Tom Hastings, come up here!" called the master. "And Sam White, you come, too."

You know what happened then. When the switching was over, Mr. Hunter told Sam that every time anyone laughed, he'd switch the one who laughed, and Sam, too. Now Sam WAS in a "pile" of trouble. He knew that he could take care of his own ears. But what if the boys found something else to laugh at? What then?

Spelldown

One Friday afternoon the master had a surprising piece of information for every scholar in the school. On the next Friday evening there would be a spelldown. The big girls would be on one team, and the big boys on another. Molly Chase was to be captain of the girls' team, and Sam was to be captain of the boys'. Molly and Sam had been chosen captains because they were the best spellers in the school. All the mothers and fathers were to be there, and there would be a prize for the winner. No boy or girl wanted his ma or pa to be ashamed of him. So every scholar knew what to do. No one needed to tell him.

That night Molly Chase started for home with her spelling book under her arm and a very happy expression on her face. All the girls crowded round her. "We're going to win," they whispered. "We're going to win."

Sam had his spelling book also, but his expression was not happy. As for Tom, he was simply disgusted. Why, he couldn't even spell "does." What could he do in a spelldown? Of course, Ma and Pa would have to be there. Oh, pshaw!

Sally waited until she was sure that Tom was listening before she told Ma about the spelldown.

"We're sure to win," said Sally with a satisfied air. "Molly Chase is the best speller in the school. The boys haven't a chance. Mr. Hunter may as well give Molly the prize right now."

Of course, Tom couldn't stand that. "Molly Chase is not the best speller," he said. "Sam can spell almost as well as she can. When you spell almost as well as someone three years older than you, you are the better speller. Anyway, who cares about an old spelldown? Only girls, that's all!"

Ma put an end to that quarrel in a hurry. She told Sally not to count her chickens before they were hatched. Molly might not win after all. And then, because Ma had a warm spot in her heart for Sam, she talked to Tom after Sally was in bed.

"Did you say that Sam was almost as good a speller as Molly?" she asked.

"She only wins once in a while — only about once a week," said Tom.

"I was thinking," said Ma, "that if Sam knew all the words in his spelling book, he might not win, but there might be a tie. If every boy helped Sam learn a few words —. Well, figure it out for yourself, Tom, and make your own plans."

Figure it out for himself! By the time Tom was out of bed the next morning, he didn't have a plan. He had a plot, a regular plot.

It must have been a good plot because, when Pa heard about it, he chuckled and chuckled and agreed to help. He even gave Tom time off from his work in the barn to run around and see the other boys about it.

"Bring me my share, and I'll start on Sam the minute I lay eyes on him," grinned Pa. Now what do you suppose Pa could have meant by that?

Tom called on Si and Pierre and two other boys, and that was all. You can't let too many people in on a plot. Someone might tell. Later that Saturday morning all the boys met at the smithy. There was Sam, helping his pa. Joe was there, too, working as hard as ever he could.

Tom had some pencils and some small pieces of paper. Paper was scarce in Hastings Mills, but Ma had found the pieces somewhere and had given them to Tom. That was her way to help the plot along.

First Tom made everyone raise his right hand and cross his heart and promise not to tell. Then Tom explained everything.

The blacksmith was to take the "Blue-back Speller," start in the middle where the words began to get hard, and "spell" Sam. Every time Sam missed a word, someone was to write that word the right way on one of the pieces of paper. Then, when there were ten words on each piece of paper, it would be time to stop for that day. There were papers enough for every boy, for Tom's ma and pa, and for the blacksmith and Joe. Then every person in the plot would help Sam learn the words on the papers. And then what? By the end of the week, Sam would know the whole spelling book. He certainly would!

I wish you could have seen the astonished look on Sam's face when he heard about that plot, and I wish you could have heard the blacksmith. He didn't laugh. He simply roared. I am sure the people in the cabins round about heard him.

"Do you think I have nothing to do but to take time from my work to 'spell' Sam?" he asked, when he could stop laughing. "Do you, now?"

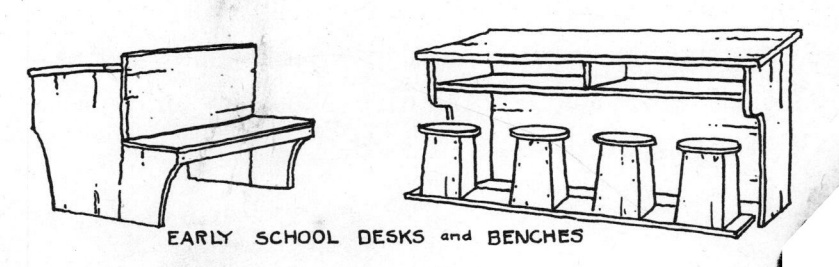

EARLY SCHOOL DESKS and BENCHES

But you remember what I told you. The blacksmith had been a famous speller in his day. He wanted Sam to be one, too. And, of course, there was Joe right at hand to do the work in the smithy. Sam was the only brother Joe had, and Joe declared that he would do the work of two men to help Sam out.

So the blacksmith "spelled" Sam while the boys looked over the blacksmith's shoulder and wrote down the words Sam missed.

Poor Sam! He certainly worked. This plot was no fun for him. But the blacksmith kept telling him how well he was doing and how proud his pa was going to be when Sam won the spelldown. This kept Sam cheered up, and he certainly did his best, his very best.

This Saturday morning was nothing to the days which followed. Sam couldn't sit down to breakfast before his pa would say, "'Yearling,' Sam, how do you spell 'yearling'?"

The minute Sam put his nose in at the smithy, Tom's pa would be there, too.

"Does there happen to be a boy around here by the name of Sam White?" Tom's pa would say, as he took a piece of paper from his pocket. "Oh yes! There he is. Come, now, Sam White, tell me how you spell 'headache.'"

Every now and then Ma would send Jim to tell Sam that she wanted to see him. You know why.

As for the boys, they wouldn't let Sam have one slide down the hill at recess until he had gone off behind some trees and spelled all the words on the papers. The worst of it was that the other boys had found out about the plot, and they had papers, too.

Of course, the girls knew that there was something going on, but they were not worried. Why should they be? Maybe Sam needed help, but Molly didn't. The boys didn't have a chance. They didn't have a chance with Molly.

Then, one afternoon when school was over, Sam made a wild dash for the schoolhouse door. He had stood all a boy could stand. No one was going to walk home with him. No one was going to "spell" him any more that day. He'd go to some place where no one would find him. In a few minutes he was sitting behind some saddles in one corner of the harness shop, telling his troubles to the old harness maker and Shoemaker Dan.

"They won't let me alone," grumbled Sam. "Morning, noon, and night, it's spell, spell, spell. I hate spelling! I do, so there!"

"Come, now," said Shoemaker Dan. "I'm sorry to find you so cross. I was figuring on coming up to hear you win that spelldown. You can't win without work, and you can't win if you're cross."

"I know just how you feel," said the old harness maker, shaking his finger at Sam. "And the worst of it is that all the work you are doing may help some, and then again it may not. I worked my head off once, getting ready for a spelldown. And then, when I knew all the hard words, what did I do? I got caught in a trap — caught in a trap by a rat."

"Caught in a trap by a rat? What do you mean?" asked Sam.

"Just what the words say — caught in a trap by a rat. That's what I mean," said the old harness maker, looking over the top of his spectacles at Sam. "Young man, can you spell 'separate'?"

"Separate?" Of course Sam could spell an easy word like that. "Separate," spelled Sam, with a satisfied air, "sep - er - ate."

"Hum-m-m," nodded the old harness maker, as if to say, "I told you so." "The same rat that caught me caught you, Sam White, smart as you think you are. Now let a smarter man than you are show you something."

The harness maker took Shoemaker Dan's pencil, and on the end of his own bench he wrote "sep - a - rate." "And that's right," he said, shaking his finger at Sam. "Now cover up the 'sep' with one hand and the last 'e' with the other. What have you? A rat — not ten rats or twelve rats, just 'a' rat. There is 'a' rat in 'separate.'"

That was the first time Sam had laughed in almost a week. "Who told you that? Who told you about a rat in 'separate'?" he almost shouted.

"I found it out for myself when it was too late," chuckled the old harness maker. "I found it out when I lost the spelldown to a girl."

"Do you think I might get that word? Do you?" asked Sam between laughs.

"Not a chance in the world," chuckled the old harness maker. "Things like that never happen twice."

"Still, you never can tell," grinned Shoemaker Dan. "A rat might come in handy."

The Friday night of the spelldown came at last. Every family brought a lantern with a burning candle inside. So every nook and corner of the schoolhouse was all lighted up.

Every person in Hastings Mills was there — grandpas and grandmas and babies and all. The boys in the spelldown stood next the wall on one side of the room, and the girls' team stood on the other side. The grownups had the benches.

The master stood by his desk with the spelling book in his hand. Just as the bell of the clock rang for seven, the spelldown began.

It was surprising how well the boys' team did — simply surprising. Every girl on the girls' team except Molly was spelled down, and Tom and Pierre and Si and Sam were still standing.

The master was certainly astonished. He couldn't believe his own ears. Why, these boys had learned more spelling in the last week than in all the weeks before. Spelldowns worked wonders.

Tom spelled "does" and "gentle" and "bucket," and if he finally went down on "heartache," you can't blame him. "Heartache" didn't happen to be on his paper.

At last everyone was down but Sam and Molly. "Measure," called the master, turning to Molly. Molly spelled "measure." "Leather," called the master, and Sam spelled "leather." On went the spelldown — lever, venison, lingering, agreement, and so on, and so on.

"Really," said the master, "this can't go on forever. Four more words, and if no one misses, we'll call it a tie."

So Sam got the word "wonderfully," and Molly got "gentleness." Sam got "whosoever," and then it was time for the last word. It was Molly's turn. Every grownup in the place was sitting on the edge of his bench, he was so much excited.

"Separate," called Mr. Hunter, and Molly spelled, "Separate, sep - er - ate."

"Wrong," called Mr. Hunter, and down went Molly.

"Now, Sam," called the master, "show what you can do."

But it was several minutes before Sam had a chance to show what he could do. Do you know why? The old harness maker laughed right out loud, and he laughed so hard that he could not stop. No matter how hard he tried, he could not stop. Shoemaker Dan kept hitting his desk with his hand, saying, "Upon my word! Upon my word!"

When things quieted down at last, Sam spelled "separate" in a big, loud voice which showed plainly that he was sure of every letter in it.

The spelldown was over, and Sam had won, and oh, was the blacksmith pleased!

Sam walked over to the master's desk to claim the prize while everyone in the schoolhouse, even the babies, clapped and clapped. And right at that minute when Sam was the hero of the hour, what do you suppose he did? I hope you won't blame him too much. I don't believe he really meant to do it. Remember, Sam had had a hard week, and he was very much excited. But whether you forgive him or not, this is what he did. He wiggled his ears.

"Sam White," said the master in a voice so big that everyone in the room could hear, "I ought to give you the hickory stick, but instead I'll give you the prize."

Sam just beamed all over. It is a wonder that he could stop smiling long enough to say, "Thank you." The prize was a book, a reading book called the "McGuffey Fourth Reader."

Of course, Molly was disappointed at the outcome of the spelling bee, and so were her ma and pa. But everyone cheered them up by saying that Molly would win next time. I wouldn't be surprised if that's what happened. Anyway, I question whether Sam won this time. The more I think about it, the more I think it was the old harness maker who won the spelldown. Don't you?

Whittling

Christmas was coming. It was only a week away. Every boy and girl in Hastings Mills was on tiptoe with excitement. Tom and Jim and Sally were certainly careful how they acted these days. Pa said it was surprising how well they minded their P's and Q's.

There wasn't a boy in Hastings Mills as eager for Christmas as Jim was. He hoped that he would get a jackknife. He hoped that he would. He had talked of nothing else for a year.

Jim loved to whittle. He loved the feel of wood in his hands. Sometimes, when Tom let Jim take his knife, Jim would whittle little figures of dogs and horses and deer, and no one had to guess a second time to tell what the figures were.

"You have skillful fingers, son," Pa would say, as he looked at Jim in wonderment. "Someday you'll be my right-hand man in the mill."

As for Ma, she would give Jim her own special smile and put the figures carefully away. Then Jim would tell about the highboy and the lowboy he was going to make for her when he was a man and they all lived together in the house on the hill.

For several days now Jim had been whittling a gift for Ma and another for Pa in the warm corner of the old harness shop. Shoemaker Dan was Jim's special friend, and he let Jim use his knife. No one knew about the gifts except Shoemaker Dan, the old harness maker, and Jim. Ma sometimes wondered where Jim was keeping himself when school was over and he wasn't bringing in wood and water. But she was so busy with other things that she forgot to ask.

And now with Christmas only a week away and with the hopes of a knife of his own growing bigger and bigger, Jim did a terrible thing. It was quite the most terrible thing that had ever been done by anyone in the Hastings family.

The terrible thing would never have happened if it had not been for Grandma Carter. Grandma Carter was very sick. She lived in a big cabin near the general store with her son, the storekeeper. When Grandma was taken sick, Mr. Carter sent for Ma in a hurry.

LOWBOY HIGHBOY

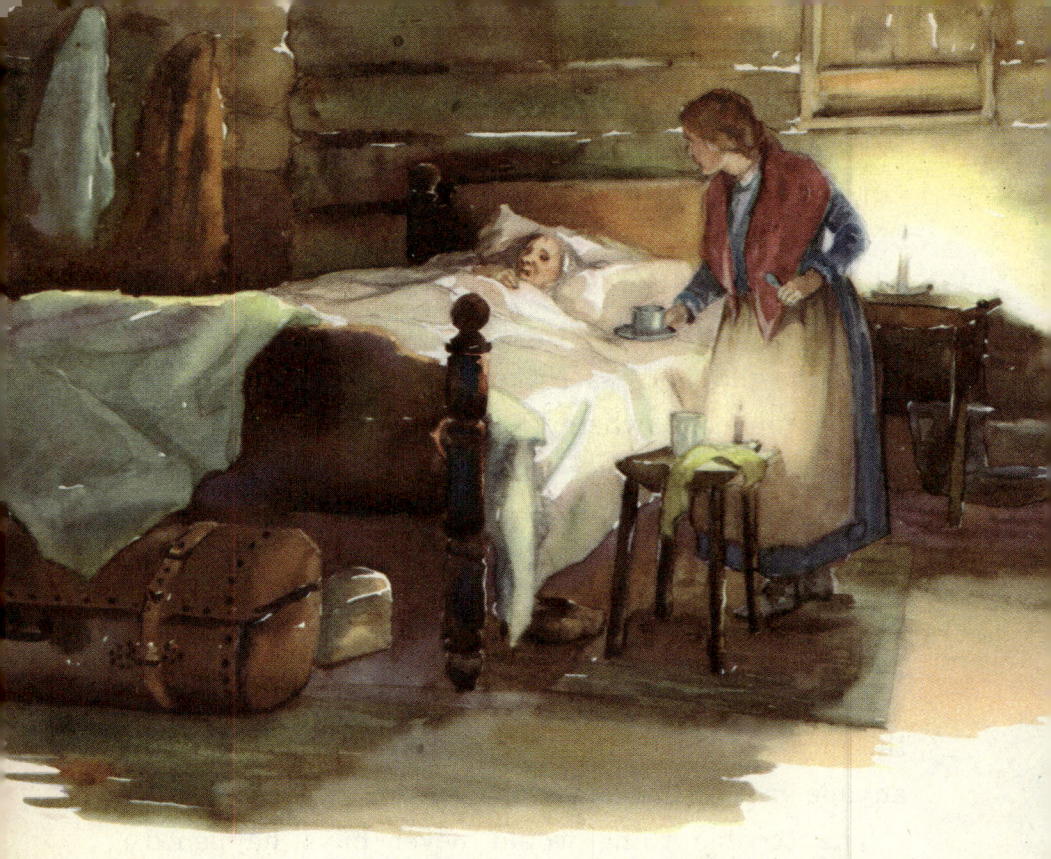

Ma did everything she knew how to do. She put a mustard plaster on Grandma's side, and she made her drink plenty of hot tea made from the dried herbs which she had gathered in her own garden. When that didn't help, Ma put a piece of salt pork around Grandma's neck, and she made her drink more tea made from the bark of the slippery elm tree. Ma stayed up all night, but in the morning Grandma was no better.

"I have done everything I know how to do," said Ma to Pa, when she came home for a few minutes at breakfast time. "You must ride down the river to Yorktown and bring back the doctor."

"Twelve miles down the river in this kind of weather!" said Pa. "There is more snow on the way. I doubt if Thunder can even make it."

"You must make it," said Ma, and her voice showed how worried she was. "Grandma is a very sick woman."

There was no school for Tom and Jim and Sally that day. Tom was to take Pa's place in the mill. Jim and Sally were to do the housework. When they were through, Jim was to watch the fire, and Sally was to come down to the Carter cabin to see whether she could help Ma. Ma made each one of them hang a little bag of sulphur around his neck. If Grandma had something catching, they wouldn't get it — not with sulphur bags around their necks.

Just before Tom left for the mill, Jim asked to take Tom's knife, and Tom let him have it.

Sally and Jim worked with a will. They made the beds together, and they cleaned the house as clean as ever they could. Then Sally hurried into her cloak and hood and was off for the Carter cabin.

Jim was alone in the cabin, alone without a thing to do except to watch the fire. Now he could whittle to his heart's content. He sat on a log stool with a happy feeling deep down inside of him, and picked up the piece of soft wood which he kept for whittling. He reached into his pocket for Tom's knife.

KNIVES

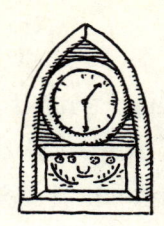

The Christmas Clock

As Jim reached into his pocket for the knife, his eyes happened to travel up, up, up, from one drawer of Ma's chest to the next higher drawer. At last he was not looking at the chest at all. He was staring straight into the face of the Christmas clock, the Christmas clock which Tom and Jim and Sally were NEVER to touch, no matter what happened—NEVER, NEVER, NEVER! Why couldn't Jim have remembered that? Why did a different idea have to flash into his head?

You know a few things about the Christmas clock. You know that it had come from a country across the sea and that it had been in the Hastings family for years and years and years. You know that Ma and Pa thought so much of the clock that they wouldn't think of leaving their old home in the East without bringing the clock with them. But you don't know the most important thing. You don't know why it was called the Christmas clock. So you must hear about that.

Just beneath the clock, and looking as if it were part of the clock itself, was a music box with two beautifully carved wooden doors. In front of the music box and the doors was a wooden shelf with a carved railing around its edge.

On every Christmas Eve, Pa pressed a little gold button on the side of the box. The doors opened, and out onto the shelf slipped some little carved and painted figures. Out they slipped, each into its own place. Then, if you looked, you could see the Three Kings and the shepherds. And in the background, with a bright star overhead to lead the way, was the manger, and Mary and Joseph, and the Child Jesus.

But that was not the most wonderful thing. When Pa turned the little handle just above the button, music began to play, music like little silver bells. "While Shepherds Watched Their Flocks by Night" and "Away in a Manger"—these were two of the songs the bells had played on every Christmas Eve since Jim could remember.

No wonder Pa had said that no one was to touch that clock. It had been made years and years ago by a famous clockmaker. If anything should happen to even one small part, who would be skillful enough to fix it? Certainly no one in these parts! And Christmas Eve without the music of the bells! That was something not to be thought of.

Jim knew all this. Why, then, did he have to remember something else? Why did he have to remember that one of the carved figures, one of the shepherds, was carrying a lamb? Maybe Jim remembered because that was what he was whittling as a gift for Ma—a little wooden lamb.

If he could see the shepherd's lamb for a minute, just ONE minute, his own whittling would be twice as good. He was sure that it would be. He wouldn't turn the handle. He would push the button just once. He would have to climb on top of the chest first, but that was nothing. He could sit up there and look and look. Then, when he was through looking, he would press the second gold button—he knew where to find it—and the doors would close again. He couldn't hurt the clock. How could he hurt it, doing only that? And who would know a thing about it? No one! No one but himself in all the world!

And yet Jim's knees shook as he pulled Pa's chair over to the chest and stepped up on it. The happy feeling was all gone. He turned his head to see whether anyone could possibly be looking. He was alone. The next minute he was sitting on top of the chest with his feet hanging over.

Jim put out his finger to touch the button, then pulled it quickly away again. He heard a noise at the door and was down from the chest like a flash. The noise was only the wind.

Once more Jim was back on the chest. Each minute that passed made him a little braver. This time he did not draw his finger away. He pressed the button, and there on the shelf in front of him, so close that he could touch them, were the Three Kings, and the shepherd with the lamb.

Jim looked and looked. He put out his finger and touched the lamb. Then he felt of it all over. He felt the little up-and-down places in the wood, which the carver's knife had cut to make the wood look like wool. Now he could carve his own lamb. He knew he could. He would start all over again — a new lamb and a better one.

Just as Jim put out his finger to press the second button, he saw the handle. Should he turn it just once to see how it would feel? The handle turned as easily as could be, but nothing happened. Should he turn it again — just enough times so that the silver bells would play one song? Which song would it be? Would it be "Away in a Manger"? That was the song Jim liked best.

Before Jim could really decide that he was going to turn the handle again, he was doing it. To his delight, the first song was "Away in a Manger." Jim seemed to remember that even after the music started, Pa went right on turning. Jim would, too. He might as well hear all the songs. He might as well. But he must hurry.

Maybe if he turned a little faster, the bells would play a little faster, too. So Jim turned faster. The music was just the same, but the handle was harder to turn. Jim guessed he should stop. Just as he thought that, the handle slipped from his hand and started to go backward as fast as ever it could. The music stopped, and from inside the music box came a loud buzzing noise followed by a sudden snap.

From inside the music box came the buzzing and the snapping, and from the door came the angry, astonished voice of Sally, saying,

"Why, Jim Hastings! You've touched the Christmas clock! You've broken it, too, and it will never play again! Wait until Ma and Pa hear about this!"

Wait until Ma and Pa should hear! Jim couldn't wait for a thing like that! The next thing he knew he was out in the barn, lying face down in the fresh straw in the corner. He was shaking all over and sobbing great sobs that would not stop. Tom was bending over him, shaking him by the shoulder and talking to him.

"Come on, Jim, old fellow!" Tom was saying. "You've got to get up. You'll freeze without your coat and cap. Here they are! Put them on, Jim, put them on!"

But Jim could not move. He went on shaking and sobbing. Tom threw the coat over Jim and sat down beside him in the straw.

"Jim, Jim," said Tom. "How could you ever have done it? How could you? I wish I could help you, but I don't know how."

Jim's sobs stopped a little when he felt Tom beside him in the straw. At least Tom didn't hate him because he had broken the Christmas clock. At least Tom didn't.

If Jim felt better, it was only for a minute. Tom was still trying to make him put on his coat when Jim heard the barn door swing open and the stern, decided voice of Ma, saying,

"Get up from here, Jim, and get into the house in a hurry. You have caused enough trouble for one day without staying here to catch cold and get sick. I cannot understand how you could be so thoughtless on this day of all days when I most needed your help. Get up from here this very minute."

Then somehow or other Jim was in the house once more, drinking hot herb tea between his sobs. Ma was rubbing him all over with hot goose grease. Between every rub, she was telling him that she would never have believed that he could do such a thing if she had not seen it with her own eyes. She would never have believed it.

And then Jim was in Sally's bed, all covered up, and there he was to stay until Pa came home. All afternoon he lay there waiting. Tom's knife and his own piece of wood still lay on the floor by the log stool, and from the shelf with the carved railing the shepherd with the lamb looked down at him.

It was late that afternoon, during a heavy snowstorm, that Pa reached home. He looked cold and tired and stiff as he opened the cabin door. He was covered from head to foot with the thickly falling snow.

Of course, Pa had stopped at the Carter cabin to talk to Ma, to tell her that the doctor was on the way, and to ask about Grandma Carter. And, of course, by this time Pa knew. The first thing his eyes turned to was the clock on the wall. The clock was the first thing, and the second was Jim.

Pa didn't excuse Jim a bit. When a boy was eight years old, as Jim was now, he was old enough to mind and to remember that Pa had a good reason for everything he told Jim not to do. Because Jim had not minded, he had broken the Christmas clock and had spoiled Christmas for all of them. And because Jim had done this, he would have to take what was coming to him. He might as well find that out first as last. Of course, you can imagine what happened then.

It was a pretty miserable Jim who crawled into his own trundle bed that night. He would never get a jackknife now. He wouldn't get a thing in his stocking, unless it was a switch. Jim wished that Christmas would NEVER come — NEVER.

The next morning life went on as usual. Grandma was better after the doctor's visit, and Pa and Ma between them could take care of the fire. So Tom, Jim, and Sally were to go back to school.

Jim, on his way into the cabin with the wood, heard Pa talking to Sally. No one was to say a word to Jim about the clock, either now or ever afterwards. What was done was done, and the only thing to do was to forget about it.

For the first time that morning Jim looked at the clock. The doors were closed. It looked just as it always looked, except on Christmas Eve.

Ma herself tied Jim's muffler about his neck when he left for school. Then she lifted his chin, smiled down at him, and sent him on his way. After that Jim felt ever so much better.

Tinkerer

There were times during the day when Jim forgot about the clock and was really happy. One of these times was at recess when he went whizzing downhill on John Gray's sled.

But when school was over and Pa sent him on an errand to the harness shop, of all places, then the terrible feeling was back again.

"Where have you been keeping yourself?" asked Shoemaker Dan the minute he caught sight of Jim. "There are some Christmas gifts that will never be finished if you go on in this way."

At first Jim hung his head and said nothing. Then suddenly the words just poured out. "I'm never going to whittle again, never as long as I live. I hate whittling."

The astonished look on Shoemaker Dan's face went away up to the top of his funny bald head.

"Come, now, lad," he said. "Don't bite my head off. Maybe you aren't going to whittle, but you can't make me believe that you hate it. You'll have to give me a better reason than that."

Now, Shoemaker Dan had been Jim's special friend ever since he had made Jim his first pair of boots. When you have a special friend, you may as well not try to keep your troubles from him. He is bound to find them out, no matter how hard you try. Before many minutes Jim was telling Shoemaker Dan the whole terrible story.

"Laddie, laddie, why did you ever do it?" said Shoemaker Dan, and the kindly ring to his voice showed how sorry he was for Jim. "Did you say that the handle was hard to turn? Did it fly out of your hand and start turning backwards? Was there a buzzing sound and then a snap? Was that all? I declare, it may be only the spring. But what to do about it now is the question."

Shoemaker Dan sat for a few minutes with his head in his hands. Then he slapped his knee and started up from his bench with a faraway look in his eyes, as if he were thinking out loud.

"Not a tinkerer in these parts," he said softly, "or a clockmaker either unless—. Upon my word, I wonder if he could do it?"

"Shoemaker Dan," cried Jim, pulling on the shoemaker's leather apron with all his might. "Do you know someone who can fix the clock? Do you?"

Shoemaker Dan had a hard time quieting Jim.

"Take it easy, lad, take it easy," he said again and again. "There will be time enough to get excited. I don't know whether I know someone or not. But if there is anyone in these parts who can fix that clock, I'll find him. Run along, now, and let me do some thinking."

For several minutes after Jim had left, Shoemaker Dan just sat.

"Too bad to have a boy so miserable at Christmas time," he said to the old harness maker.

"It is indeed," replied Mr. Harding, "and I don't doubt that he is right when he says that he has spoiled Christmas for all of them."

The next minute Shoemaker Dan was not asking — he was begging the old harness maker to let him take his horse for a trip down the river.

"My horse! In this weather!" cried Mr. Harding. "Why, man, you've lost your senses!"

But the more Mr. Harding listened, and the more Shoemaker Dan talked, the more the old harness maker felt like giving in.

"I'm growing old and softhearted," he said at last. "But after all, it's Christmas time. Yes, you may take the horse."

Now, I suppose you are wondering what in the world Shoemaker Dan was thinking of doing. Do you know what a tinkerer is? A tinkerer is not a tinker. A tinker is just a mender of pots and pans. But a good tinkerer is a skillful workman who can mend almost anything. It was a tinkerer that Shoemaker Dan was looking for.

CLOCKMAKER'S TOOLS

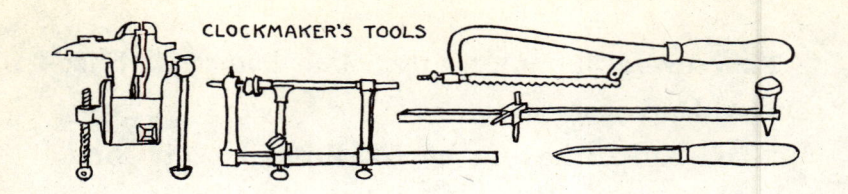

In the days when Shoemaker Dan was "whipping the cat," he often stopped at Hope's Mills on the river below Yorktown. That's why he had suddenly remembered that in Hope's Mills there was a tinkering shop, and in the shop lived —. Why, of course, Joseph Barker was the man Shoemaker Dan was looking for. Even if he wasn't a clockmaker himself, he had come from a family of clockmakers. If anyone in these parts could fix the Christmas clock, he was the man.

That evening the blacksmith sharpshod Mr. Harding's horse, and early the next morning Shoemaker Dan started down the river on horseback.

On his way to school Jim stuck his nose in at the harness shop. He could stand the waiting no longer. Mr. Harding met him at the door, a wide smile of welcome on his face.

"Keep your hopes up, lad," said the old harness maker. "No one can tell what may come of it, but Shoemaker Dan thinks he has found the man. If I were you, I'd say nothing until we really know."

So Jim didn't say a word, not one word.

That afternoon when school was over, Jim saw a man on horseback—on Mr. Harding's horse—ride up to the door of the harness shop. The man was not Shoemaker Dan. Jim stood until he saw the man take a box from the saddlebag and go into the shop.

"It's his toolbox," thought Jim, and there was a lump in his throat as he hurried home to help Pa and Tom with the work in the barn.

A little later, when Ma came to the cabin door and called Pa, the lump in Jim's throat grew so big that he could scarcely talk.

When the work in the barn was over and Tom and Jim went into the house, there were Pa and Ma talking to the stranger and the old harness maker.

"You can understand," Pa was saying, "that the clock has been in the family for years. If you aren't sure that you can fix it, I would rather you would let it alone. Nothing has happened to the clock itself. It keeps time perfectly. It is only the music box which will not work."

SADDLEBAGS

"You can depend upon me," said the stranger. "I am not a clockmaker myself, but my brothers and my father before me were. I myself am only a tinkerer, but not such a bad one at that. If it is only the spring that has snapped, I can shorten it or put in another. If it is anything else, I know enough to keep my hands off."

That seemed to satisfy Pa. Mr. Barker would not think of touching the clock that night. He must have good, strong morning light for work which needed such skillful fingers. He would sleep in the harness shop and be back early the next morning.

Merry Christmas

When Jim left for school the next morning, the Christmas clock was lying on its face on the table before the window. Mr. Barker, with thick spectacles on his nose, was looking it over.

On these days when Ma was so busy with Grandma Carter, Tom and Jim and Sally took their dinner with them and ate it in the schoolhouse. But nothing could make Jim wait for dinner that day.

The minute school was over for the morning, Jim was off for home like a flash. He threw open the cabin door. There was no one at home. The tinkerer had gone. The fire was burning brightly, and from its place on the wall the Christmas clock was ticking away in the stillness.

Jim wondered—oh, how he wondered—but this time he knew better than to try to find out. He made a wild dash for the harness shop, and there good news was waiting for him. The clock was fixed, and the tinkerer, on Mr. Harding's horse, was already on his way down the river.

If Jim sat on his feet and spelled every word wrong and even whistled out loud that afternoon, I'm sure you can't blame him.

Perhaps Jim was the happiest person in the Hastings family that night, but the smile on Pa's face showed that he was the next happiest.

"The clock is fixed, son," he said to Jim, "but we'll wait until Christmas Eve to try it out."

It was still another day before Shoemaker Dan came riding home, tired and stiff from the cold and from the long horseback ride.

"You should never have attempted such a trip in weather like this," said the old harness maker.

But the next minute the look of delight on Jim's face and his happy shouts as he dashed in at the door made Shoemaker Dan forget how tired he was. Even the old harness maker said under his breath, "I guess it was worth it after all."

Two days until Christmas! Every minute Jim could take from school or from his other work, he was sitting by Shoemaker Dan's side, whittling away on a little wooden lamb.

On the day before Christmas, Ma was as busy as a bee. The cabin must be cleaned from top to bottom. There was the goose to get ready and a hundred and one other things not quite so important. All the while Ma was working, the Christmas clock was ticking merrily.

Just before suppertime Tom and Jim brought in one tubful after another of clean white snow.

Ma put the snow into the big kettle over the fire. When supper was over and the water was hot, the tub was put on the floor in the little room next to the warm back of the big chimney. Jim first, and then Sally, and then Tom, each one had a bath in the big tub. Of course, each one had a bath on Saturday nights, but this was a special bath just for Christmas.

When Jim had had his bath, he sat in his red flannel nightdress on Sally's bed all wrapped up in a blanket, and he hung his stocking on the back of Pa's big chair.

When Sally and Tom were ready and Ma could leave her work for a while, Pa pressed the little gold button on the side of the Christmas clock. The doors opened, and out onto the shelf slipped the carved and painted figures. Out they slipped, each into its own place. Then, as Pa carefully turned the handle, there came the music of the bells, just as it had come on every Christmas Eve since Jim could remember.

As the bells were playing Jim's song, "Away in a Manger," the door opened, and in walked the old harness maker and Shoemaker Dan. Jim wasn't surprised. He knew they would come. He knew it all the time. Then Pa had to turn the handle and play the songs all over again.

Jim went to bed with the music of the bells still ringing in his ears. When he awoke, it was Christmas morning, and Tom was shaking him by the shoulder and calling,

"Wake up, Jim, wake up! It's Christmas, and your stocking's plum full of everything."

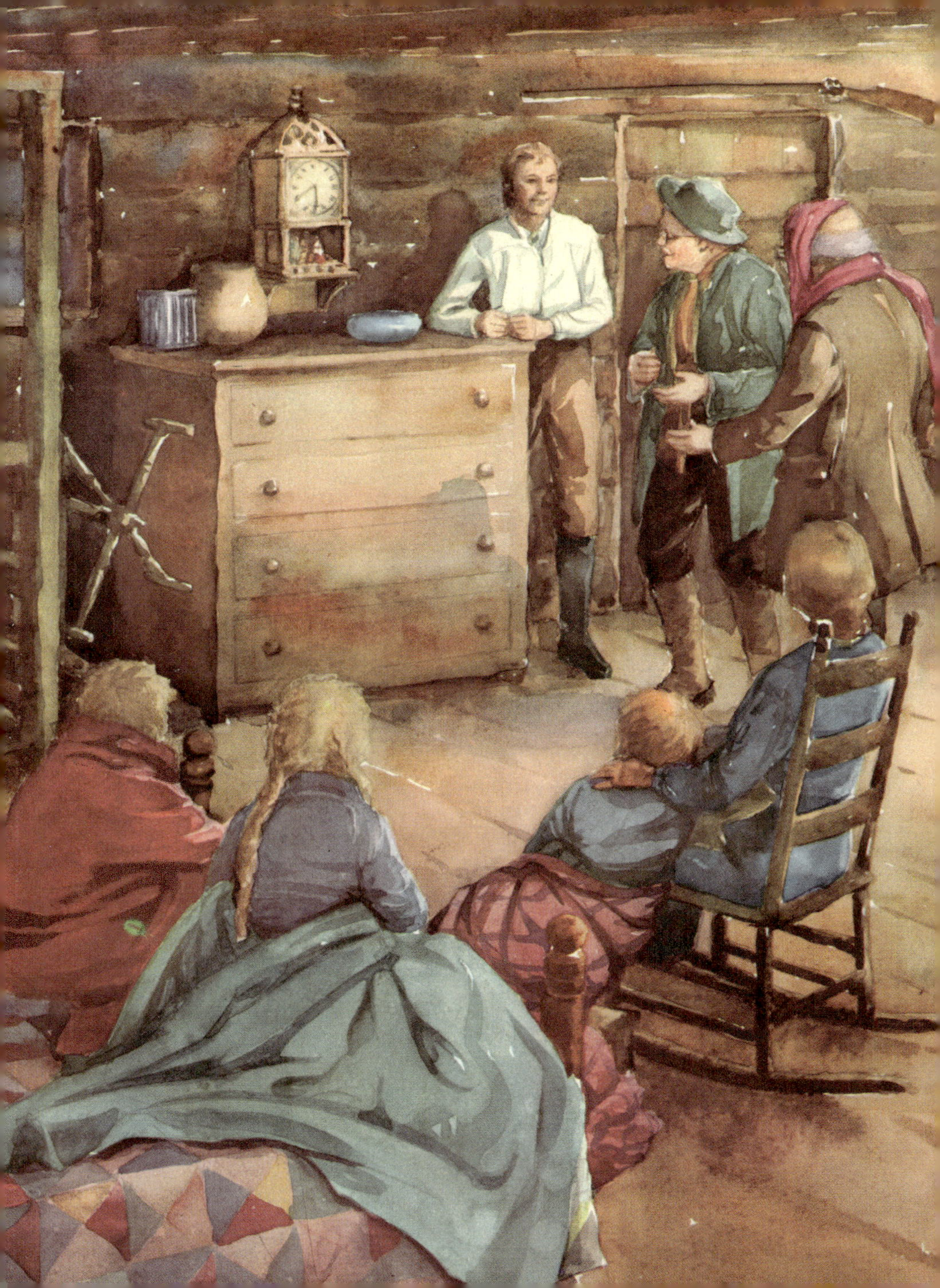

Jim was out of bed with a bound. There on top of his stocking was a big red top. Next he pulled out two sticks of red-and-white peppermint candy. Then came a pair of mittens, some candy hearts, a pair of socks that Ma had knitted, and last of all —away down in the toe—a jackknife. Jim just shouted when he saw that knife.

Sally was as pleased as pleased could be with the sewing basket and needlebook which she found in her stocking. Tom was too much surprised for words when he found a pair of skates with leather straps and iron on the runners. Pa had had the blacksmith and Mr. Harding make those skates for Tom. But after all, Jim was the happiest. He sat and looked at that knife and felt of it all over. He opened it and closed it. He put it into his pocket and took it out again. Then he did the same things all over again. He could scarcely believe that it was really his knife.

Did I say that Jim was the happiest? I don't believe I was right after all. I believe Ma was happiest. Pa had made her a little, low rocking chair, had made it all by himself in his own mill. When Ma sat down in it to try it, Jim put the little wooden lamb in her lap. There were tears in Ma's

BOOTJACKS

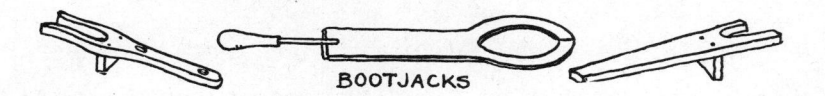

eyes as she looked at it, but the tears came because Ma was so happy. And do you know? It wasn't until then, until that very minute, that Jim told Ma and Pa why he had touched the Christmas clock.

Pa didn't mind a bit that the bootjack which Jim was making to help Pa pull off his boots was only half finished. Pa knew that Jim would have had it done if it had not been for all Jim's troubles. The bootjack could wait, but Pa certainly was pleased that Jim had remembered him. All Jim had to do was to look at Pa's big smile to know how pleased he was.

Of course, Tom and Sally had gifts for Ma and Pa, and Ma hadn't forgotten Pa, not for a single minute.

After the gift-giving was over, Christmas Day went along as usual. There was the Christmas dinner with roast goose and dressing, and six kinds of pie, and a dozen or more other good things. The old harness maker and Shoemaker Dan were right there to enjoy it all.

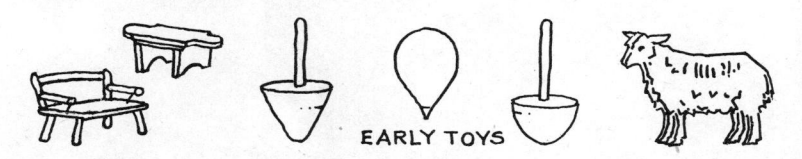

EARLY TOYS

Tom could scarcely wait until dinner was over to try his new skates. And was he surprised when he reached the Big Turtle to find Sam and Si and Pierre there before him! Each of them had wooden skates with leather straps and iron on the runners, too. The days before Christmas must certainly have been busy ones for the blacksmith and Mr. Harding. How do you suppose they ever kept such an important secret as the skates?

Jim and Sally didn't mind a bit that Tom had skates and they didn't. Sally didn't give the skates a thought. Girls were never allowed to skate, anyway, no matter how much they may have wanted to do so. Skating was too unladylike.

So while Sally enjoyed herself with her sewing basket, Jim sat on a stool before the fire, working on Pa's bootjack and whittling to his heart's content. If he whistled softly as he worked, Jim didn't know it. He was too much interested to notice anything.

"When Jim grows up," whispered Ma to Pa, "he'll always remember this as the worst Christmas and the best Christmas he ever had."

"I wouldn't be surprised," answered Pa. "Anyway, it's one Christmas he'll never forget."

SLEDS and SLEIGH BELLS

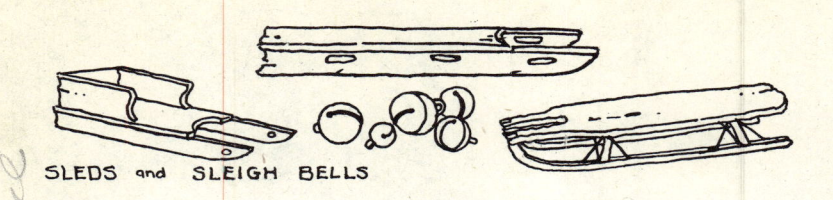

Frozen River

Winter days came and went, and the ice on the river froze thicker and thicker. Now the Big Turtle was used as a highway, and the bells of the horse teams pulling the bobsleds up and down the river jingled gayly in the frosty air.

One Friday afternoon Mr. Lake brought his team to a jingling stop on the riverbank near the general store. When Mr. Lake and Mr. Carter got together, there was no telling how long the talking would continue. They were both too good at driving a bargain.

As Mr. Lake left the store, the sun was going down over the river to the westward. The cold, pink glow of the sunset was spreading over the great whiteness of the snow. The trunks of the trees on the island stood out sharply black against the light of the setting sun.

On this particular afternoon Tom and Pierre had hurried through with their work in the barns. They wanted to save a few minutes for skating on the ice before suppertime.

The boys had just sat down on the riverbank to fasten their skates when they caught sight of Mr. Lake climbing to the seat of the bobsled.

"Come on," shouted Pierre. "We can ride part way down the river and skate back."

Mr. Lake had scarcely time to pull the buffalo robe about his knees before Tom and Pierre had crawled under the buffalo robe, too.

"Well, I declare!" chuckled Mr. Lake. "What does this mean? Looks to me as if we were going to have unexpected company for the night."

"Oh no! Not for the night! Just as far as the bend in the river!" grinned Tom. "We'll be late for supper if we go any farther."

"Giddap, then, giddap!" called Mr. Lake.

The bells on the harness shook out their jingles, the sharpshod feet of the horses stepped safely and surely forward, and the runners of the bobsled slipped along with a smooth, slippery sound all their own.

The full moon was coming up in the sky to the eastward, and the moon and the setting sun together reminded Mr. Lake of something.

"A night like this takes me back to the days when I was a boy," said Mr. Lake with a smile at the corners of his mouth. "Makes me think of one of the best times I ever had in all my life."

"One of the best times you ever had! What was that?" asked Tom and Pierre in one breath.

"A bobsled party that began at sunset and ended by moonlight!" replied Mr. Lake.

"A bobsled party! Could we have one? What do you do at a bobsled party?" With each question the boys bumped up and down on the seat in their eagerness to find out.

"Settle down!" said Mr. Lake quietly, with a sharp ring to his voice. "Do you want to start a runaway on this slippery ice?"

The boys settled down in a hurry. They didn't want to start a runaway or make Mr. Lake angry. They certainly didn't! Not until they found out about the bobsled party!

By the time they reached the bend in the river, the boys hadn't found out a thing, not one thing.

"Tell you about a bobsled party!" said Mr. Lake. "Why, I can't do that. You have to be there to know what a bobsled party really is."

The boys thought that Mr. Lake was trying to be tantalizing, just plain tantalizing. But he really wasn't. He was turning something over in his mind and wondering whether it really could be done. He didn't want to get anyone's hopes up until he was very, very sure. It wasn't until the boys had jumped from the bobsled and were skating toward home that Mr. Lake called after them.

"I reckon if the sun shines tomorrow and if you are smart enough to have your work done by four o'clock, we might try one of those bobsled parties. We'll do all the things I did when I was a boy, and that's aplenty. I don't suppose you'll want to come, will you?"

You can imagine in which direction the boys skated then. In another minute they were hanging onto the wagon box of the bobsled, eagerly talking over plans with Mr. Lake. By the time they started for home a second time, they knew exactly what they were to do.

Every boy and girl in Hastings Mills was to be invited to the party. Mr. Lake was to call for them the next afternoon at four o'clock. If all of them promised to work harder than they had ever worked in their lives before, their mothers and fathers would be sure to let them go and stay long enough to come home by moonlight.

All anyone would need to bring to the party was two hot potatoes to put in his pockets to keep his hands warm. Then he would need a hot brick or a hot tailor's goose wrapped in a piece of an old blanket to put at his feet.

There was twice as much work done in Hastings Mills that Saturday as had ever been done by boys and girls before. Of course, some of it was done in such a hurry that it had to be done over again. Then, too, when Tom tried to give Red and Patch their supper at one o'clock in the afternoon, Pa had to put a stop to that. Ma grew tired of having Sally everlastingly at her heels asking, "Is there anything else I can do to help?" So even the mothers and fathers were happy when Mr. Lake arrived with his bobsled in front of Turtle Rock Inn that afternoon.

The floor of the bobsled was covered thick with fresh straw. On top of the straw were buffalo robes and plenty of bearskins.

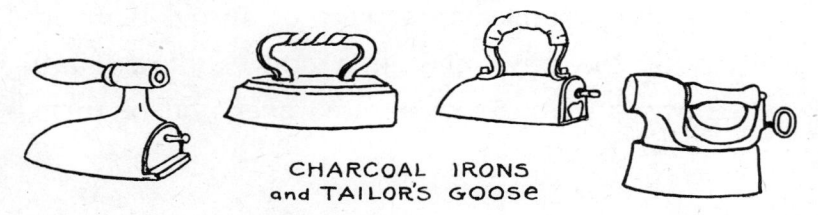

CHARCOAL IRONS
and TAILOR'S GOOSE

I wish you could have seen the boys and girls as they piled into that sled. Most of them had two caps on their heads and two pairs of mittens on their hands. They had two or three mufflers around their necks and as many pairs of thick woolen stockings as they could crowd inside their shoes. Their pockets stuck out with hot potatoes, and if they weren't carrying a brick, they had a tailor's goose wrapped in a piece of an old blanket.

Most of the boys and girls crawled down into the straw, and Mr. Lake covered every bit of them except their faces with the good warm robes. Tom and Pierre, the brave ones, rode their own sleds hitched to the back of the bobsled.

The air was stinging cold and still as ice as the bobsled started down the stage road on its way to the riverbank. The squeak of runners on hard-packed snow, the jingle of bells, and the merry shouts of the bobsled party sounded loud and clear in the frosty air. The breath of the boys and girls was coming in little clouds of steam that quickly turned to frost on their woolen mufflers. But down under the straw everyone was warm and comfortable.

No sooner had the bobsled started down the river than the singing began—"Old Dan Tucker," "Turkey in the Straw," "Wait for the Wagon," and "Yankee-Doodle" with the new words.

It was not long before the two brave ones had enough of riding on their own sleds and crawled down under the warm straw, also.

Down the river went the singing bobsled with the sunset on one side and the full moon coming up on the other. Down the river, one mile, two miles, three miles, and then Mr. Lake turned around. By this time the sun had long since disappeared, but the moonlight on the whiteness of the snow made the world as light as day. Everything that came into the path between the moonlight and the snow had a long black shadow.

Just as arms and legs were getting stiff and the songs were beginning to sound less merry, the bobsled jingled to a stop before Mr. Lake's cabin on the riverbank. There in the cabin, warm with candlelight and firelight, Mrs. Lake was waiting for them. Great cups of warm milk, "rye-an'-Injun" bread, and sausage—would the bobsled riders ever be filled up? Mrs. Lake, looking on in astonishment, really began to wonder.

When supper was over, the real fun began. There were two covered pans in front of the fireplace, and the bottom of each pan was sprinkled with popcorn. When the boys and girls discovered the pans, they were on the floor before the fire in a minute. Faces grew as red from the fire as a short time before they had grown red from the cold. Soon the pop, pop, pop of the corn came faster, faster, faster, faster.

But better than that was the molasses and sugar boiling in the big kettle which hung from a hook above the fire. Si and Sam each brought in a big pan of clean white snow. When the molasses and sugar had boiled long enough, each boy and girl had a cupful, and the molasses poured onto the clean white snow turned into candy.

The boys dropped their candy into every shape they could think of—figure eights and sixes, and twirls of all kinds. The very second the candy was cool enough to pop into their mouths, it disappeared. But the girls didn't do that. They pulled their candy into long ropes until the dark-brown molasses color turned to a lovely tan. Then, when the candy was pulled enough, they cracked it into pieces with Mr. Lake's hammer.

Minutes flew by, and more enjoyable things began to happen. While the bobsled party bundled up again in caps and coats and mufflers, Mr. Lake put some hot coals into a covered pan. Then he picked up the big bundle of sticks waiting for him by the door, and out he went.

By the time the boys and girls could follow him, Mr. Lake had built a fire, and you can never guess where. On the ice in the river—that's where he built it. I suppose you think that the ice melted and that the water came up and put out the fire. That isn't what happened. The night was too cold, and the ice on the river was too thick.

Can you imagine how firelight and moonlight together look when they are shining on white snow and sparkling ice? Can you imagine how they look when they are shining on the faces of boys and girls gathered closely about the fire, but not too close to be in danger? If you can't, I hope you go to a bobsled party like this one someday. I hope you do.

The fire had scarcely begun to shoot out its red and yellow lights before a jingle of bells from up the river announced the arrival of another bobsled. And who do you think was in it? Pa and the old harness maker, the blacksmith and Shoemaker Dan!

"Please, may we come to your party?" grinned Pa, as the four men jumped from the sled.

"We know we weren't invited," chuckled the old harness maker, "but we like parties. It wasn't fair not to invite us."

Now, while the men stood around the fire and warmed their toes, and while most of the girls kept Mrs. Lake company in the cabin, the boys had a grand time on the ice. They played pom-pom-pullaway, run sheep run, and crack-the-whip. If you don't think that you have to be pretty good to play those games on ice, just suppose you try it sometime.

Of course, all good things have to come to an end at last, and so did the bobsled party. Pa was sure that there wouldn't be a boy or girl on time for church the next morning if someone didn't start for home soon. Mrs. Lake called from the cabin door to remind them that every potato and brick and tailor's goose had been hot for more than an hour.

So back into the straw piled the boys and girls, and back into their own sled climbed Pa, the harness maker, the blacksmith, and Shoemaker Dan. Then away up the river went the sleds.

The grand good time was over, but for days and weeks afterwards the boys and girls talked of little else except the bobsled party. Perhaps the reason was that nothing new or exciting seemed to happen in Hastings Mills for weeks and weeks. Snowstorms and blizzards came and went, and the grownups grew tired of the gray days and the cold. Everyone wished that winter would end.

When the second of February came around, the old harness maker kept his weather eye glued to the sky. Not once did the sun shine through the dull, gray clouds.

"The ground hog didn't see his shadow this day," he smiled in glee. "Who knows? Maybe another spring is hiding round the corner."

RIGHT FOREFOOT

RIGHT HIND FOOT

ASLEEP IN BURROW

GROUND HOG

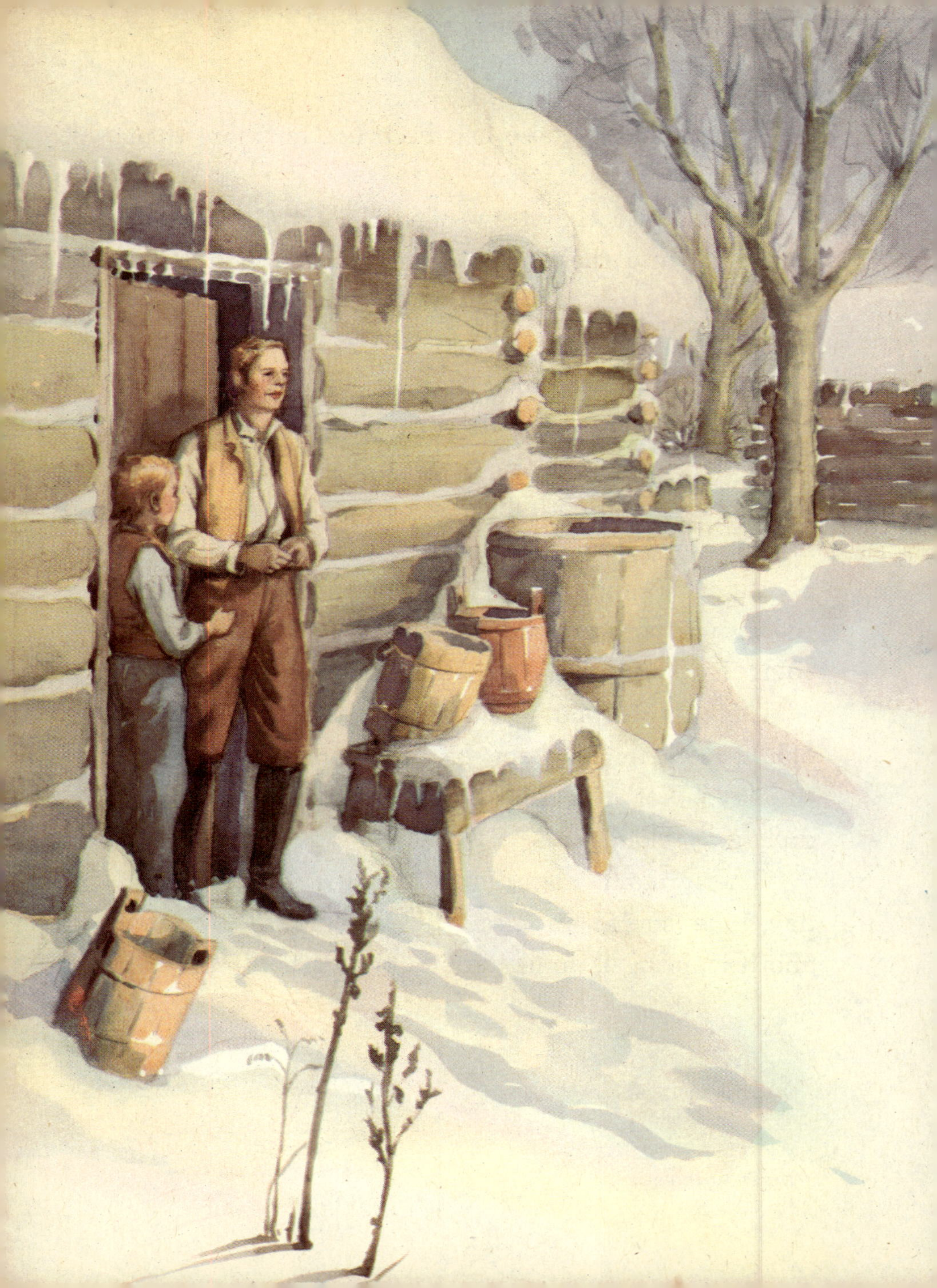

Spring's in the Air

Sap's Running

February passed. Then suddenly and unexpectedly spring was in the air. Tom, climbing down the ladder one morning at sunrise, saw Pa standing in the open door of the cabin, watching the first streaks of color in the sky to the eastward.

"It's March, son," said Pa, as Tom came to stand beside him. "It's March, and it's coming in like a lamb."

As the morning went on, a gentle wind began to blow, the sun shone warm, and the snowbanks on the south side of the cabin softened a little.

By noon the frost had melted from the windows, and the snow had almost disappeared from the wet black branches of the trees. Icicles hanging from cabin roofs dripped continuously, and the snow beneath was peppered with holes where the drops of water fell on the softening snow.

The day following the first of March continued warm and sunny. Little by little the snowbanks were shrinking away, and in a place or two small patches of brown mud were showing through.

"Sap's rising," announced Frenchy, on his return trip from the Big Woods.

At once all thoughts of wood hauling were at an end. Pa and Frenchy, with Tom and Pierre and Jim following close behind, went from one maple tree to another in the Big Woods.

Into each tree the men bored a hole a little larger than a man's finger. Then into each hole they

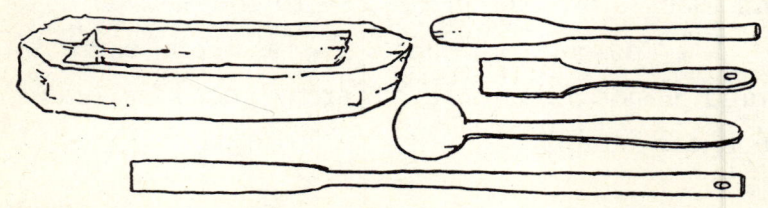

MAPLE SUGAR TROUGH and PADDLES

drove a hollow tube, or spout, the same size as the hole. The spout was about eight inches long and was made from the branch of an ash tree. Pa had hollowed out the soft inside part of the branch with his jackknife. He used an ash branch because ash wood does not give a bad taste to the maple sap.

Into each trunk below the spout the men drove an iron nail with a head on only one side. The nails reminded Tom of tobacco pipes. On these nails the boys hung the wooden sap buckets which Tom had helped Pa to make during the long winter evenings. No sooner were the buckets in place than the sap began to drip from the spouts into the wooden pails.

The boys saw the dripping sap and remembered that they were very thirsty, and what could be better for a thirsty boy than a taste of maple sap? They put their tongues on the ends of the spouts. The sap was thin and icy cold, and very, very sweet. Again and again the boys tasted the sap.

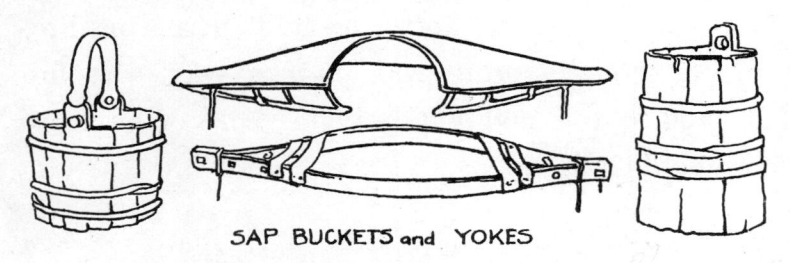

SAP BUCKETS and YOKES

Bright and early the next morning Pa and Tom were on their way to the Big Woods. Each of them was pulling a sled. On Pa's sled were a big iron kettle, some dry wood, and plenty of hot coals in a covered pan. On Tom's sled was a barrel bound round with wooden hoops.

Pa went at once to the place in the woods where the branch of a fallen tree had been placed crosswise between two other trees. He hung the big iron kettle from the fallen branch with an iron chain, and under the kettle he built a roaring fire.

Even though spring was on the way, the fire felt good in the snapping, stinging cold of an early morning in the woods.

Tom, in the meantime, was going from tree to tree emptying the sap from the wooden buckets into the barrel. As soon as the barrel was as full as Tom could pull all by himself, he made his way back to the fire, and Pa emptied the sap into the big kettle.

Tom stood around the roaring fire long enough to warm his hands and face and toes, and to fill his nose with the good smell of sap boiling. Then off he went with his sled again.

By noon all the sap had been emptied into the big iron kettle. Indian Jack, on his way through the woods, agreed to watch the kettle while Pa and Tom went home to dinner.

BEAR ANIMAL TRACKS MUSKRAT MINK

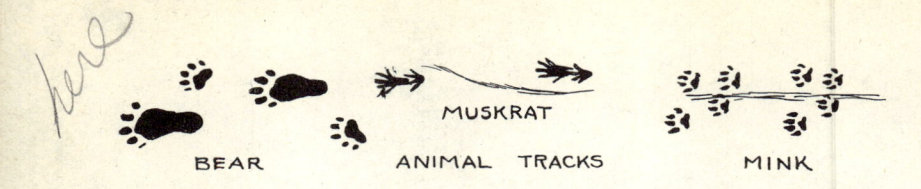

When Pa and Tom came back again, they each had a wooden yoke across their shoulders. Leather straps hung from the ends of the yokes, and at the ends of the straps were big wooden hooks. Hanging from each hook was a large bucket, much larger than a sap bucket.

All afternoon Pa sat with his feet to the fire and watched the sap kettle. When Tom grew tired of sitting, he wandered off by himself, looking for animal tracks in the wild woods.

Every once in a while Pa would take a wooden ladle, skim off the top of the boiling sap, and throw the worthless part upon the ground.

Now and then, when the sap was boiling too quickly, Pa would take a long-handled ladle, lift the sap high above the kettle, and let it fall slowly back. He did this again and again. Pa called this airing the sap. Airing cooled the sap, and kept it from boiling too quickly.

By sundown the sap was sap no longer. It had boiled down until it had become maple syrup. Pa and Tom filled the large wooden buckets with the maple syrup, covered the fire with wet snow, and started for home with the syrup buckets hanging from the yokes across their shoulders. Tom kept his hands on the edges of the buckets to keep them from swinging.

The next day and the next Pa and Tom were busy with the sap gathering. The sun continued to shine and the snow to melt.

"No chance of a long run of sap in weather like this," said Frenchy one afternoon, as he passed by the log where Pa and Tom were sitting. "I'd give my best hat for a sign of 'sugar snow.'"

"'Sugar snow!' What's that?" asked Tom, as Frenchy went on to his own syrup kettle in another part of the woods. "I never heard of 'sugar snow.'"

"You see, Tom," said Pa, "the sap, rising through the trunk and branches of the tree, makes the green leaves grow. If the weather is warm, the sap rises quickly, and the leaves appear in a hurry. But if a snow should come now, not too cold a snow, the sap would take longer to rise, and the trees would be slower in putting out their leaves. Anything which makes the sap rise more slowly gives us more time to fill our sap buckets, and that means more maple sugar for all of us."

A few mornings after this, Tom woke with a start. He felt something wet on his face. He put up his hand to feel. Something wet fell on his hand. He sat up in bed to see what was happening. Snowflakes were coming through a place between the logs where the plaster had broken away.

"'Sugar snow'!" cried Tom in glee, as he hurried down the ladder to dress before the warm fire. "Now Frenchy has his wish."

Outside the cabin everything was covered with snow, soft snow that looked like feathers. Tom whistled all the way to the woods. He liked the "sugar snow." He liked the long days of sap gathering. He wished the sap would rise forever.

Sugaring Off

On the evening of the "sugar snow" Pa had a hungry look in his eye as he put the sap buckets on the cabin floor.

"My mouth is watering," he said to Ma. "You know why. It wants some maple sugar candy."

"I've been expecting this," smiled Ma. "I'm surprised you've waited as long as this. Suppose we ask the neighbors in for a sugaring off. This clean, new-fallen snow won't last forever."

It didn't take long for that news to spread. The minute supper was over, the Hastings cabin was filled with people—Sam and Si and Pierre, the old harness maker and Shoemaker Dan. They were all there.

While the boys and girls played blindman's buff and the men joked and talked and waited for the candy, the women stood around the big kettle over the fire and helped Ma stir the syrup with the long-handled ladle.

Just as blindman's buff had reached an exciting stage, Ma dropped a little of the syrup into a cup of cold water. It held together in a soft ball. Ma could lift it with her fingers.

"Syrup's waxing!" called Ma. "Get your places in a hurry."

Then what a mad rush there was! Everyone took a pan or a bowl from the table and hurried out to fill it with snow. Into each pan or bowl Ma poured a ladleful of golden-brown syrup.

Sometimes the syrup fell straight down into the snow and came out as a long stick of golden-brown candy. Sometimes it stayed on top of the snow and spread out like a big, round penny. But however it dropped, it was always good.

There was plenty of syrup in the kettle and plenty of snow outdoors. Everyone laughed and talked and ate until he could eat no more.

Of course, that wasn't true of Pa. Ma just couldn't fill him up. He liked maple sugar candy too well. At last Ma said that she would open the door and drive him right out into the snow if he asked for another mouthful.

"All right for you, Mrs. Hastings," said Pa. "Just for that, I'll forget to find you that bee tree. Now aren't you sorry for what you said?"

Ma's supply of honey had run short, and Pa had promised to find her a bee tree. But Pa couldn't scare Ma. He liked honey too well himself to go back on his promise.

The games and the merrymaking began again, and the rest of the syrup in the kettle went right on boiling. Every once in a while Ma would pour a little of the syrup into a cup and stir it round and round. Then she would shake her head, and back into the kettle the syrup would go. At last, when she tried it, it turned into little grains of sugar as she stirred.

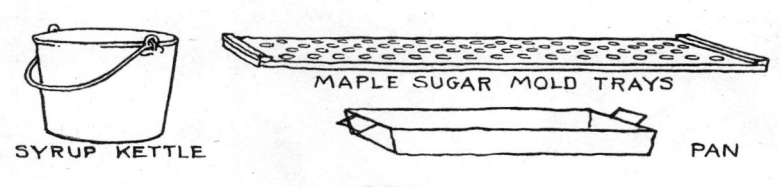

SYRUP KETTLE   MAPLE SUGAR MOLD TRAYS   PAN

"Syrup's graining! Bring the pans!" called Ma.

Then everyone at once reached for the pans which Ma had ready and waiting on top of the chest. When the pans were full of the boiling syrup, they were put away to cool. By morning the syrup would be hardened into golden-brown cakes of maple sugar.

The sugaring off for that night was over. But many evenings after that Ma was busy with her syrup kettle. The "sugar snow" did just what Pa had said it would do. The days that followed were cold, not the sharp, stinging cold of winter days, but cold enough to keep snow from melting and to make the sap rise more slowly. For almost four weeks the sap ran from the tapped trees.

Then one evening when the filled buckets were taken from the shoulder yokes, Pa looked at Ma.

"Run's over," said Pa, "and the sap in these buckets will be no good for graining."

"I'll use it for syrup and molasses," said Ma. "It's been a good year for maple sugaring. I've never seen a better."

Bee Tree

Now March turned to April, and the drumming call of the prairie chickens in the early morning announced to all who listened that spring had come to stay. Pussy willows were in blossom along the banks of Indian Creek. Birds sang in the bushes, and flocks of ducks and geese passed overhead on their way to the north. The prairies were turning green once more, and wild flowers were thick under the trees in the Big Woods.

When April was well on its way, the bees began their humming as they looked about for early flowers. The pussy willows along the creek were the first to be visited.

Pa, watching the bees, remembered his promise. He must find Ma a bee tree. Sally and Jim overheard him as he talked to Tom one morning.

"I know what a bee tree is," said Jim. "It's a tree in which the bees store honey during the summer months so that they will have plenty to eat when there are no flowers."

"You're right, Jim," said Pa, "and I'm going to find that bee tree. Summer is coming, and the prairies will be covered with flowers. The bees can make fresh honey. I am going to help myself to the honey which is left over, now that winter is gone."

"But how can we find the tree?" asked Sally.

"Leave that to me," laughed Pa. "I am going to make a beeline for it. Come to think of it, I have always been alone when I've been searching for a bee tree. This time I'd like company. Suppose all three of you come with me."

You can imagine the excitement that this news caused. The next morning Pa and Tom, with Jim and Sally trailing after, were off for the Big Woods. Each of them carried an empty bucket. Pa had his ax, and Tom had a sap bucket filled with maple syrup. Neither Sally nor Jim nor Tom knew what was going to happen, but they were sure that whatever it was, it was going to be fun.

The first thing Pa did was to choose two tree stumps far apart from each other in different parts of the woods. Jim and Sally covered each stump with maple syrup.

HONEYBEE

LARVA   WORKER   DRONE   QUEEN   EGGS

Before many minutes the bees found the syrup and began buzzing round it. "What great good luck," they seemed to say. "Why should we look for flowers? Here is honey for the taking." In a twinkling they began to carry off the syrup.

"Now," said Pa, as he and Tom and Jim and Sally stood near the second stump to watch the bees. "This stump belongs to Tom and Sally. The first stump is for Jim and me. All you have to do is to watch the bees and see in which direction they are going. Then follow them in a straight line. You'll find that they will make a beeline for their home in the bee tree. If you lose sight of one bee, keep your eyes open for another. Jim and I will start from the other stump and do the same thing. If we have good luck, we'll meet somewhere in the woods. Near the place where we meet, we should be able to find the bee tree."

Then Pa and Jim started off for their own stump.

This sounded like a game to Tom and Sally, and they were eager to begin.

One of the bees, after buzzing about the syrup, rose into the air and flew around in circles as if trying to decide which way to go. Then off it started in a beeline for the bee tree.

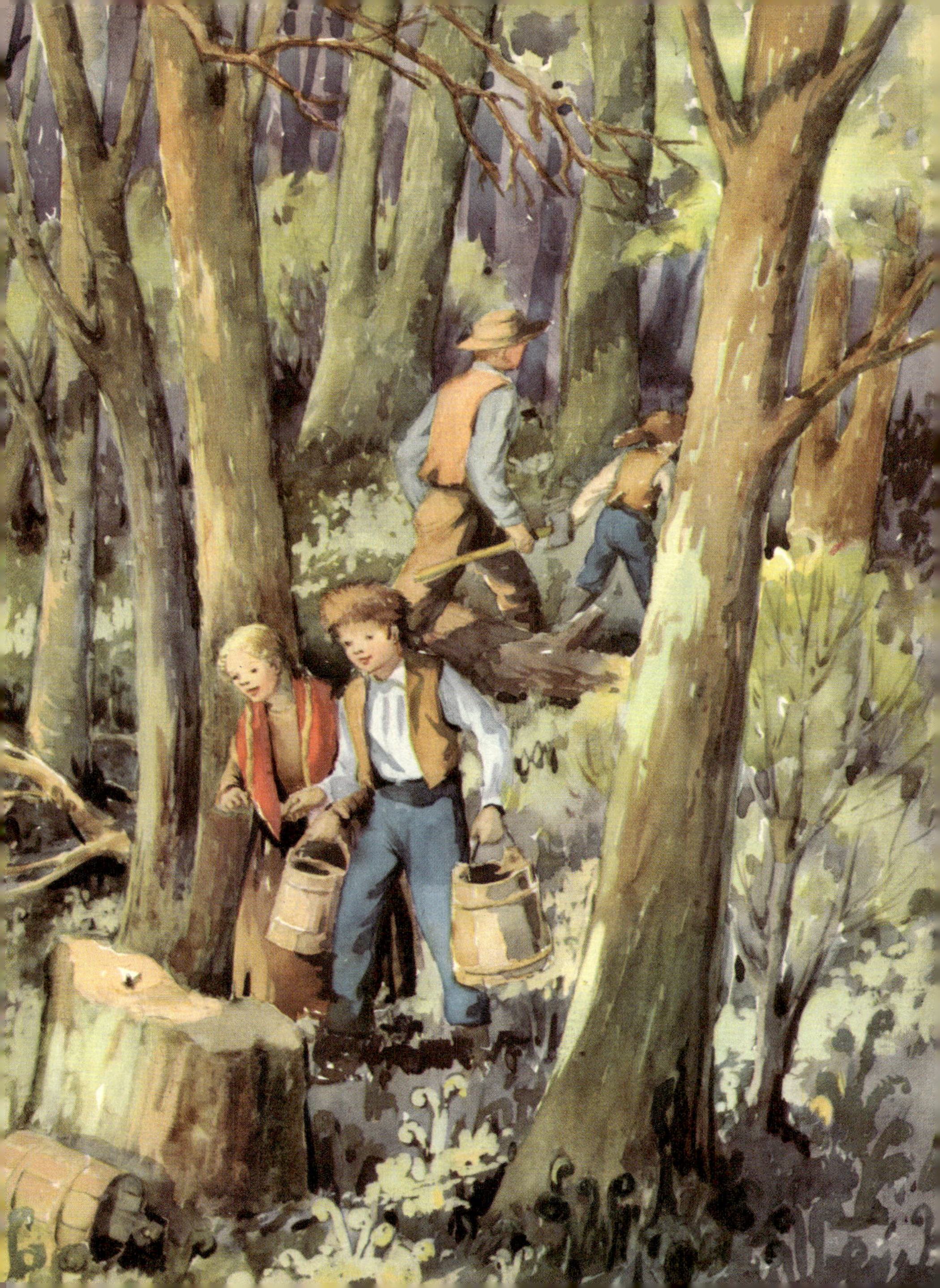

Tom and Sally followed as best they could, but they soon lost sight of the bee among the trees. They stood still for a minute, caught sight of another bee, and followed it. Slowly but surely they followed the bees. After a time they heard a crackling noise in the underbrush, and there were Pa and Jim coming toward them.

When all four were together again, they looked about for the bee tree, and not far away from their meeting place they found it. They could tell that it was a bee tree because bees were hurrying in and out of a hole at the top, and a decayed place near the foot of the tree showed that the trunk was hollow.

"How can we get the honey?" asked Tom and Jim and Sally all in one breath.

"I'll have to chop down the tree," said Pa. "That is the safe and sure way."

"But the bees will sting. They will chase us away," cried Jim and Sally, each one more excited than the other.

"Not if we smoke them out," said Pa. "So suppose Jim and Tom make a beeline for home and bring us some hot coals. In the meantime, Sally and I will watch the tree."

When the boys returned with the coals, Pa built a fire of leaves in the decayed opening at the foot of the tree. The wet leaves smoldered, and the thick smoke filled the hollow trunk to the very top. The bees, overcome with the smoke, could do no stinging.

Then, with his sharp ax, Pa began to cut down the tree. When a tree is hollow, it is not hard to chop. Tom and Jim and Sally, standing far enough away to be safe, had not long to wait. When the tree had fallen, Pa cut open the trunk from end to end with his sharp ax. The trunk was filled from top to bottom with honey.

It was plain to be seen that the tree had been a storehouse for bees for years and years. Some of the honey was old and dark, but the honeycomb near the top of the trunk was clean and good and a lovely golden color.

"Even this honey is not as fresh and yellow as the honey I found in a bee tree last autumn when the bees had just finished their summer's work," said Pa.

"What will the bees do now?" asked Jim, while they were all hard at work filling their buckets with the golden honeycomb.

"Find another hollow tree," answered Pa. "They will carry every bit of this honey, except what we take from them, to the new bee tree. The old honey will be made into fresh honey, and the bees will have a new, clean home."

When the buckets were full to the very top, the four honey gatherers made their way home. Ma could hardly believe her eyes when she saw the buckets.

Pa and Tom and Jim and Sally started back to the woods to fill the pails a second time. As they left, Tom could tell by Ma's smile that she was planning something — something good that had to do with honey.

Though there was honey enough in the hollow tree to fill the buckets again and again, the buckets weren't filled a second time, and you can never guess why. No sooner had Pa's sharp eyes caught sight of the bee tree than the sharper eyes of Jim caught sight of something else.

"Look! Look!" cried Jim, jumping up and down and pulling on Pa's arm. "Someone is taking the honey. Look! Look!"

Sure enough! Someone was taking the honey, not one somebody but three. There, sticking her paw into the bee tree and pulling it out again dripping with honey, was a mother bear. She looked long and thin after her winter's sleep. With her were her two cubs.

Tom had only one idea in his head. He must run home and bring back Jenny. But Pa stopped him by saying sharply, "After all, Tom, it's springtime, and even a bear cub needs a mother."

The bears were so much interested in the bee tree that they paid no attention to anything that was going on around them. Not even the sharp crack of a branch under Tom's foot, as Pa and the children drew nearer, made the bears look up. But Pa kept far enough away to be perfectly safe.

"A bear at this time of year—a hungry bear with her cubs—is no bear to fool with," said Pa.

By this time the cubs had found a better way of eating honey than sticking in their paws. They had crawled down on all fours into the hollow trunk. Those bear cubs were honey all over. Every once in a while, when they got in their mother's way, she would give them a slap with her big paw. The cubs didn't seem to care. They went right on eating honey.

For a long time Pa and Tom and Jim and Sally stood watching the bears. Then home they went with their empty buckets. They were just in time to cover with dripping golden honey the big pile of pancakes which Ma was making for them.

FROW   CLUBS   SHINGLE-HORSE   HAND-SHAVES

The House on the Hill

Tom sat on a shingle-horse in the open door of the mill. A warm May breeze blew lightly through the open window, and the afternoon sunshine floated in upon the floor.

Tom was pulling a sharp tool called a hand-shave across the shingle fastened to the shingle-horse. Pa stood watching Tom at his work. He could have smoothed a dozen shingles while Tom was shaving one. Why didn't he take the hand-shave and send Tom on his way? It was not like Pa to waste time after this fashion.

"Where do you think my shingles will go?" asked Tom as he worked. "I'm marking each one with a cross so that I'll know which are mine."

"Marks won't show long when these shingles begin to weather," said Pa with a slow smile.

"Then maybe we can put all my shingles in one place. Above the front door perhaps! Do you think we can do that? Do you, now?" asked Tom, his blue eyes fairly begging Pa to say "Yes."

"Not a bad idea," replied Pa, as his slow smile turned to an amused grin. "Then if the house is still standing when you are a man, and if you have a boy of your own, another Tom, you can point to those shingles and say, 'See those shingles! I made those shingles in my pa's mill.'"

"And I'll show him the bricks Sam and I are making for the chimney! And I'll tell him that I saw the beams and clapboards of this house when they were nothing but trees in the Big Woods. Won't he be surprised to hear that? Won't he?"

Tom stopped work in his excitement and sat holding the hand-shave and looking up at Pa. Thoughts of great things about to happen crowded thick and fast into his head.

"When WILL the house-raising be?" he asked, his eyes on fire with eagerness to find out.

"I've told you a hundred times," answered Pa. "It's for the farmers along the Big Turtle to set the day — when corn planting is over and the spring work is done. That may be most any day now."

"Most any day now! Maybe it will be tomorrow, and my shingles aren't finished!" cried Tom, setting to work with a will.

Pa's eyes turned from Tom to the pile of finished shingles in one corner of the mill. Then, with a proud and satisfied step, he walked over to the place where great oaken timbers, each a foot square, lay piled one upon another along the side of the mill.

Outside in the mill yard other timbers and piles of clapboards were seasoning in the sunshine. The log bench inside the door was piled high with wooden pegs, and with the iron nails which the blacksmith had made for the house-building. Against the wall were window frames and windows already finished. Three weeks ago Pa had driven an ox team, with a load of lumber, forty miles away to the city by the lake. It had taken Pa a week to make that trip. But what of that? Had he not driven a good bargain when he had traded the lumber for the glass in these same windows?

No wonder Pa had a contented and satisfied feeling! Ever since the day when he had stepped foot from the covered wagon and had chosen the valley of the Big Turtle for his new home, he had been planning something. Planning for the day when a house would rise under the two big maples on the hilltop! His house, the first frame house in Hastings Mills, made from lumber sawed in his own mill! Through all these months he had been choosing the finest trees in the Big Woods and sawing them into great timbers. Through all these months the uprights and the crossbeams and the clapboards had been seasoning little by little under Pa's watchful eye. Now everything was in readiness, and Pa's great day was almost at hand.

He walked over to the open door of the mill and stood watching Bright and Flash as they pulled the heavy stoneboat up the hillside. Frenchy and Indian Jack were walking slowly along beside the big cream-colored oxen. The boat was loaded with great pieces of stone from the riverbank, great pieces of stone to be used as the foundation for the new house.

Silently, without a word to Tom, Pa followed the oxen up the hillside. He helped unload the stone and then sat for a time with Frenchy and Indian Jack on the low brick wall which circled the well that he had dug on the hilltop. Frenchy unfastened the well sweep and let down the wooden bucket. The men drank of the clear, cold water. And always as they sat, the talk was of the house-raising.

Resting time over, the stoneboat started once more for the riverbank. Pa was alone on the hilltop. He stood for a time staring down into the hole near the two big maples.

Pa had dug that hole with the help of Bright and Flash and the big scoop-shovel which the blacksmith had made for him.

Someday the hole would be the cellar for the new house. Tomorrow, thought Pa, he would begin laying the foundation stones, but tonight — . Tonight he would ride down the river to talk to Mr. Lake and set the day for the house-raising.

He turned his steps toward home, and there, coming to meet him, were Ma and Jim and Sally. How lighthearted and gay they all were as they stood under the maples talking over plans!

The new house was to face to the south where the big front windows could keep a welcoming eye on the stage road and strangers who passed that way. Opening from the front door was to be the hall, with a sitting room on one side and a parlor on the other. At the back were to be the kitchen and a bedroom for Ma and Pa at one end. Upstairs there was to be a room for Sally on one side of the hall and a room for the boys on the other. Across the back was to be the storeroom where Ma could keep her spinning wheel and reel and loom.

Yes, it was to be a big house and a grand one, "The House on the Hill." Already Jim was carving the top piece for the corner cupboard, and Sally was helping Ma with the hooked rugs. Everyone who was to live in the house was to have a part in building it. "That's what will make it a home," said Ma, "when everyone has a part in it."

It was long after bedtime that night when Pa returned from his trip down the river. Tom lay stretched out on the attic floor with his ear to the ladder hole. Ma, waiting in her low rocker, had begun to nod over her knitting.

When Pa announced that the house-raising was to be a week from that day, from that very day, Tom came tumbling down the ladder with a shout which waked Sally. Even Jim came crawling from his trundle bed. But Ma and Pa didn't have a cross word to say — not one. How could they? They were just as excited as Tom and Jim and Sally.

The days which followed were crowded with things to be done. Pa had the foundation to lay and the great timbers to haul to the hilltop. When Ma thought of feeding all the neighbors for miles around, she wondered if she could ever do all the work. But Ma didn't have to do it alone. Grandma Carter, the blacksmith's wife, and every other housewife in Hastings Mills remembered the countless times when Ma had helped her. The minute the news spread, each one of them promised that on the morning of the house-raising there would be meat roasting, and bread and pies and puddings baking in every cabin in Hastings Mills.

The morning of the house-raising dawned warm and sunny. On foot, on horseback, in wagons — every man who could leave his work was on his way to the hilltop as soon as the sun was up.

The sun was still low in the sky to the east when ropes were fastened about the first big timber and the first upright for the new house was pulled into place. Every man was proud of his strength and skill and eager to show what he could do. Pa seemed to be everywhere at once, helping this group, giving directions to that.

By noon the uprights were all in position, and many of the crossbeams were pegged into place.

By noon, also, the tables which had been spread under the maples were bending down with the load of good things to eat that the women of Hastings Mills had prepared for the house-raising. The men rested for an hour, ate as only hungry men can eat, and sang and joked and told stories.

It was late afternoon when the rooftree beam was finally in place. A great shout of success went up from every man, woman, and child on the hilltop. The house-raising was over. With the framework in place, Pa could finish the house by himself during the weeks to come.

Now came the time for the blacksmith's fiddle. Everyone joined in a song of good wishes for the health, happiness, and success of the family that was to live in "The House on the Hill."

Then group after group of tired workers made their way toward home until only Pa and Tom were left on the hilltop.

The sun was going down over the prairies to the west. Pa's eyes turned from the great timbered framework of the house and followed the stage road down the hill, past the group of cabins which was Hastings Mills, and on over the corduroy bridge to the west bank of the Big Turtle.

"Someday, when you are a man, there will be a big city in this valley," he said softly to Tom.

"A city!" said Tom in wonderment. "But it will still be Hastings Mills! No one can change that! And we'll still live in 'The House on the Hill.'"

Tom turned his head toward the house under the maples and then gave a shout of excited surprise. "Look, Pa, look! Away off there! Look! Look!"

Pa turned in the direction to which Tom was pointing, and there, coming down the stage road from the east, was a covered wagon — two, three covered wagons traveling together.

"Upon my word! Springtime! Settlers on their way to new homes in the West!" cried Pa. With Tom by his side and with a wide smile of welcome on his face, he hurried forward to meet the strangers. Pa's dreams were coming true.

Word List

The following list includes 521 words in this *Fourth Reader* that were not taught in the preceding books of the basic ALICE AND JERRY SERIES. The word form or the word combination here given is the one in which the word first appears. Since variants of these forms are treated in the *Teacher's Guidebook*, such variants are not counted as new words.

5 stagecoach Lightning bugle Mills	20–21 22 wrinkled reckon sealed wax	36 corduroy possible stuck marked	51 jeans hickory shirt anybody
6 leather straps beneath	23 Sam	37	52
7 dust Tom bonnet	24 25 dash steady	38 shelter sank push	53 acquainted 54 fur satisfied
8 Grandpa escape	26 prairie buffalo	39 boots rear axle lever	55 knitting rush
9	27 fording	40–43	56
10 calico beaver state	28 thundered grumbling	44 cave plum Jenny shot	57 z-z-z-ing 58 magic government haw taller
11 shoot	29		
12	30 toiling oxen	45	59 Frenchy salt
13 fresh pawing	31 feedbox jolting churn	46 build dam harness	60 suggested
14 Maryland		47 gristmill grinding flour lumber	61
15	32 whip		62 iron forge charcoal
16 Sally	33		
17 school	34 grin freckled hunted	48	63 anvil fan burn
18 overflowed roast beans pumpkin		49 shone lark fox telltale	
	35 cloak mud sloping		64 clay mold
19 buttons		50 taught	65

374

66 plaster
limestone
ashes
powder
67 poles
68 wheat
grain
haul
69
70 downstream
sugar
smart
figured
71 general
axheads
barrels
kegs
72–73
74 peppermint
cloth
75 decided
yoke
76–77
78 yearling
forehead
79 speak
quite
rubbing
80 nodded
contented
81 pioneer
82 maples
frame
house-raising
83 latchstring
hinges
spinning
A B C's
84
85 trundle
puncheon
braiding
attic

86 loom
Christmas
87 bullet
pouch
greased
ramrod
88–89
90 wasting
91 spool
thread
needle
weasel
92–93
94 chill
bars
bucket
95 seek
pork
96 half-breed
hitched
bows
carrots
97
98 giddap
gee
honey
99 creek
arrowhead
100
101 disgust
102 dragging
103 walnut
nut
underbrush
104 chop
clearing
105 notch
106
107 pooh
sore
108 ached
starved
109 limping
miserable

110 hit
111 worst
112–113
114 hasty
pudding
115 lead
poured
melted
fingers
116 eleven
complained
no-account
117 Fields
118 Silas
Si
119 folks
carding
machine
120 power
Joseph
scholars
121
122 stake
claims
squat
123 circuit
agreed
124–125
126 torrent
furnish
127 donate
128 formed
lengthwise
129 screech
owl
reeds
woodchucks
130 predicted
terrible
131 staring
teased
rustle
132 scared
133–135

136 sock
announced
mad
silly
137
138 quarrel
curly
combed
139 dye
140 spun
yarn
woven
entered
141 fleece
shear
142
143 bother
144 measure
145 weaver
146 indigo
soap
wire
old-
fashioned
147
148 crackling
149 reel
skeins
knot
150 lye
151 lump
plant
blossom
substance
152
153 squeezed
154 several
155 curiosity
wrapped
paper
156
157 shrink
158 hooks
tenterhooks

375

159	teasel	182	explored Evil Spirit interpreted	202	jacket roosting	229	
160	feathers hood			203	yelping hero streaks	230	wheel-barrow Tucker spectacles bald
161	sewed pressed tailor's	183	stealing banished warned	204	stubborn		
				205		231	bent thumbs
162	muffler drawer usual	184		206	Yankee-Doodle determined tramp		
		185	sickness			232	rather
163		186	leaped decayed phosphorus			233	
164	writing					234	Thomas
165				207	pretend	235	inch
166	coonskin	187	Devil's silently	208	rye-an'-Injun tangled	236	pattern
167	preparations licks prints hoofs					237	prepared stiff
		188	butchering	209		238	vise stitch seams
		189		210	rollicking dandy		
		190	doubled November				
				211	oaken ironbound stew	239	
168	venison sprinkled	191	bawl squeal			240	paste firmly
		192	bristles hind	212–213		241	
169–170				214	tinderbox flint steel spark	242	perfectly
171	smoldered	193	livers lard quarters beef			243–244	
172						245	bolder
173	supply trench cabbages onions			215	growl none	246	neighbor action plans
		194	hams brine spareribs	216–217			
				218	scarcely	247	practiced
174	Waubonsie hazy mists blizzard			219–222		248	signal
		195	seasoned herbs mixed	223	invite twice	249	snarling
						250	protect
175	succotash Shmokoman grunted moccasins			224	jig	251	peace
		196	sausage tallow tubes wicking	225	straw clapping	252	
						253	spells
				226	Virginia partners Irish	254	slate-gray flakes
176	speechless	197	silk			255	hailed teams jingled
177	quiver	198		227	person		
178		199	pigeon Dutch	228	pinched tanned wear Dan	256	whose whizzing
179	tobacco lodges circle						
		200				257	remain arithmetic
		201	exactly prayer				
180–181							

376

258 particular	280–281	311 unless	345
259 single past desks	282 plot regular	312–313	346 ladle skim syrup
	283 roared	314 sharpshod	
260–261	284–286	315 throat	347–349
262 gourd dipper	287 rat separate	316 depend	350 buff
		317	351–353
263–264	288	318 attempted	354 April pussy willows
265 famous ought	289 lantern	319 tubful bath	
	290–291	320 flannel	
266 lessons primer peeking	292 beamed McGuffey	321	355 stumps
		322 lap	356–360
	293	323–325	361 cubs
267 recess behave class	294 whittling P's and Q's skillful special	326 bargain pink	362
		327 robe	363 shingle-horse hand-shave
268 John study swinging		328–332	
	295	333 squeak	
269	296 mustard elm	334	364
270 page		335 molasses	365 timbers
271 drank angels lying bossy	297 doctor	336–337	366
	298 sulphur	338 pom-pom-pullaway games	367 foundation dug sweep scoop-shovel
	299		
	300 carved manger Jesus	339 February dull hog glee	
272			
273 problem demand	301		368
	302 lamb		369 hall parlor upstairs
274 expression o'er Molly	303–304	340	
	305 sobbing bending	341 sap's	
275		342 icicles dripped bored	370
276 sting wiggle blame	306 stern caused		371 dawned strength position success
	307	343 spout thirsty tongues	
277	308 excuse		
278 switching	309 chin		372 health
279 Friday information pshaw	310 tinkerer errand	344 hoops chain	373

377

Glossary

In this glossary you will find the meanings of some of the words used in this book. The glossary will also help you to pronounce the words. Watch the syllables and the accent marks.

a

ac quaint', to get to know someone or something

ac'tion, doing something

a gree', to think the same thing someone else thinks; to say you will do a certain thing; to decide

a larmed', expecting trouble; frightened

a light', to get down

an nounce', to say, or tell; to give news; to give notice

an'vil, a big block of iron, with a flat top pointed at one end, on which hot pieces of iron are hammered into shape

ash, what is left after wood has been burned; a kind of tree

a stir', in the air; moving about

at tempt', to try

ax'le, a bar of wood joining the two front wheels or the two back wheels of a stagecoach, a wagon, or a cart and on which the wheels turn

b

ban'ished, driven away from home

bar'rel, the long, hollow front part of a gun, through which a shot is fired

beam, to smile a big, happy smile; a long, heavy piece of wood made ready for use in building

bear'a ble, not too hard to put up with

bea'ver, a high hat for men, made from the skin of a beaver or from goods that looks like beaver skin

bee'line, the shortest and straightest line from one place to another

bel'lows, a tool worked by hand and used to blow air to make a fire burn faster

bench, a long table to work on, often called a workbench; a seat made from a long board fastened to wooden legs

bold, brave; not afraid

bot'tom, the low land along a river; the part of a thing that is the lowest

bound, wrapped around or held together, as ironbound; kept in, as snowbound; sure or certain

bow, the part of a yoke that goes around the neck of an animal; one of the rounded pieces of wood that held up the covering on top of a covered wagon; a narrow, rounded piece of wood with a string tied to the ends, from which an arrow is shot; a narrow piece of wood with horsehairs tied along one side, which is drawn across the strings of a fiddle to make music

378

brush, thick, low bushes and small trees, also called underbrush; a tool with sharp wire teeth, used to comb wool

c

card, a brush with wire teeth, used to comb and straighten wool threads before spinning; to comb with such a brush

char'coal, wood that has been partly burned in a place from which air has been shut out

cir'cuit, a journey from place to place and back by a different way to the starting point

claim, land chosen by a settler and marked by him to show that he wanted to buy it; to ask to buy such a piece of land; to say that something is yours

clap'boards, narrow boards nailed to the outside walls or roof of a building so that they overlap and throw off rain

clear'ing, an open place in the woods where the trees have been cut down

con tent', satisfied; not wanting more than you have; a feeling of being satisfied

coon, a raccoon, a small animal with gray-brown fur and a bushy tail with rings on it

cor'du roy, made of logs placed side by side, as roads and bridges in early days

crack'ling, making sharp little sounds heard again and again; what is left after that part of fat needed in making lard has been used

cross'cut saw, a long saw with a handle at each end, used by two people to cut logs in two crosswise

cu ri os'i ty, a feeling that you want to find out something that you don't know

d

de cayed', rotten

de pend', to trust or count on

de ter'mine, to make up your mind; to decide

dis gust', a feeling that you have when you dislike something or someone very much

dou'ble, to go back the same way that you came; to fold in two pieces the same length

dull, colorless; not bright

e

earth'en, made of earth, or clay

es cape', a getting away from danger or from something you don't like to do; to get away

ex plore', to look all around; to search

ex pres'sion, to say or talk in such a way as to make something seem real and true to life; the look on a person's face

f

fig′ure, to learn by yourself how to do something; to plan; a number, as in arithmetic; something made in the shape and form of something else, as the figure of a lamb

ford, a place in a river where the water is not deep; to cross a river at such a place

forge, a kind of fireplace used by a blacksmith to heat iron before it is hammered into shape

fresh, not tired; new

g

grist, wheat and corn to be made into flour or that have already been made into flour; a gristmill is the place where the flour is made

ground, to become stuck on; worked down into a fine powder, as grain ground into flour; the earth

h

hail, to welcome

hick′o ry, heavy cloth; a kind of tree that certain nuts grow on; the wood of this tree

high′boy, a high wooden chest of drawers, set on legs

i

in ter′pret, to make someone understand what someone else is saying

j

jack, a tool used to hold in place the thing one is working on; a bootjack is used to hold a boot while the foot is pulled out

jeans, trousers made from heavy cloth, such as is used to make overalls

k

keg, a small barrel

knot, in spinning yarn, twenty threads tied together; a hard, lumpy stick of wood

l

la′dle, a big, deep spoon with a long handle

lead, a blue-gray metal, such as you find in pencils

le′ver, a long piece of wood or metal, one end of which is put under something heavy to make lifting easier when the other end is pushed down

lick, a place where salt is found on the ground

low′boy, a low wooden chest of drawers, set on legs

lum′ber, wood that has been sawed and made into boards; to move along slowly, as when pulling or carrying something heavy

m

meas′ure, a certain amount; to show how much

mill race, an opening left at the end of a dam, through which the water can rush to turn the mill wheel

mis'er a ble, unhappy

mist, drops of water in the air, not so heavy as rain, but making a fog that cannot be seen through easily

mold, a hollow frame in which something you are making is shaped while it is soft and is then left to harden; to shape something

mus'tard plas'ter, a piece of cloth on which wet flour and powder made from mustard seeds are spread

n

nap, the short, raised threads on the surface of woolen cloth that make the cloth feel hairy

notch, a cut place shaped like the letter V; to make such a cut

o

oak'en, made from the wood of an oak tree

oil'skin, cloth that has been oiled so that water will not go through it

or'di nar y, the way that things happen often; something out of the ordinary is something that does not happen very often

p

par tic'u lar, a certain one; special

pass, an opening or a way through; to go by someone or something

paw, to scrape with a foot, or paw; the foot of an animal

per'fect ly, exactly; just as it is supposed to

phos'pho rus, a waxy substance that shines in the dark

pi o neer', one who opens up a new part of the country and settles there first

plot, a secret plan

po si'tion, the place where a thing belongs

pouch, a bag made of leather, in which bullets were kept

pour, to let run, or flow; to speak quickly, telling the whole story; to flow or move steadily

pre dict', to tell what you think is going to happen

prep a ra'tion, what is done to get ready; a getting ready

pre pare', to get ready

press, to iron clothes to make them smooth; to push down

pun'cheon floor, a floor made from logs which have been cut in half and then smoothed off on the flat side

q

quar'ters, the four parts into which the body of an animal is cut for meat, each part having one of the legs

quiv'er, a holder, or covering, in which arrows are kept

r

rail, one of the bars at or around the edge of anything, as a seat or a shelf, often called a railing; one of the small logs laid crosswise between posts to make a rail fence

ram′rod, a round bar that was used to push the bullet and patch down the barrel of a gun to load it

rear, back

reck′on, to believe, think, or suppose

reed, tall grassy plants that grow in wet places

reg′u lar, real; true

rol′lick ing, lively; jolly

roof′tree, the long beam at the top of a sloping roof, to which are fastened the boards making the roof

rye-an′-In′jun bread, bread made with corn meal and rye flour

s

seam, the line of stitches made when two pieces are sewed together

sea′son, to add such things as salt and pepper to food to make it taste better; to dry out, as wood

sharp′shod, put shoes on a horse, with sharp points on the bottom to keep the horse from falling on snow or ice; wearing such sharp-pointed shoes

shear, to cut off the wool of a sheep, with shears; shears are big scissors

skein, a small bundle of yarn

skim, to take off the very top

smol′der, to burn slowly, with no flame but much smoke

snarl, to growl and show the teeth

spe′cial, belonging to some one person or thing and no other

spell, to mean, as to spell trouble; a spelling book or a speller is a book that shows the right letters in many different words; a speller is also a person who knows the right letters in words; to spell a word is to give the right letters in the word; to spell also means to make someone spell a word to find out whether or not he can do it

squat, to settle on a piece of land without first buying it; a squatter was one who squatted on a piece of land; to squat also means to drop and sit on one's heels

stake, to mark off a piece of land by driving pointed sticks into the ground; a pointed stick

stern, sharp; hard

stone′boat, a flat sled without runners, dragged along the ground carrying heavy loads of stone

streak, a line of light

stub′born, not willing to move or change

suc′co tash, beans and corn cooked together

sul′phur, a yellow substance, used in making matches and gunpowder, and also supposed to keep people from getting sick

t

tan, to make leather from the hide of an animal; a light, brownish color

ten′ter hook, one of the sharp hooks to which cloth is fastened on a frame and stretched into the shape wanted

tim′ber, a thick piece of wood with squared edges

tor′rent, a rush of swiftly moving water

trun′dle bed, a low bed that can be pushed under another bed when not in use

try out, to heat a substance to melt out the part you want in a clear state, as to try out lard by heating pork fat

u

up′right, standing so as to point straight up and down; a big timber set on end to make part of the side of a building

u′su al, as always; everyday

v

vise, a tool that holds tightly the thing being worked on

w

warn, to give someone notice of what will happen

wax, a substance which is softened by heat and put on a letter to seal it; a yellow, greasy substance made by bees; to put wax on something; to become thick and soft like wax

wick, the string down the middle of a candle, also called a candlewick and wicking

y

year′ling, a year old; an animal that is a year old

Acknowledgments

The author of *Singing Wheels* is deeply indebted to the following publishers and writers for generous permission to adapt ideas and situations from copyrighted materials:

Harper & Brothers, Publishers for Chapters 1, 7, and 8 from *The Little House in the Big Woods* and for Chapters 22 and 23 from *Farmer Boy*, both by **Laura Ingalls Wilder**, used in "Bringing Home the Deer," in "Butchering Time," in "Whipping the Cat," and in "Sap's Running."

Eric P. Kelly for *Christmas Anvils* used in "The Christmas Clock."

Chas. P. Burton, author of the Bob's Hill books, for suggestions used in "The Screech Owl," "The Wolf Hunt," and "Bee Tree."

The black-and-white line drawings in the book are based on historical materials found by the artists in museums and in published materials, some of which are still in copyright. The publishers wish to express appreciation for the ready co-operation extended by the following:

The Bucks County (Pennsylvania) Historical Society, pages 23, 30, 64, 66, 190, 195, 207, 214, 230, 238, 258, 262, 263, 266, 270, 271, 290, 299, 315, 323, and others.

Chicago Historical Society, pages 71, 74, 75, 99, 123, and others.

The Chronicle of the Early American Industries Association, for many of the stoves shown on pages 126 and 127.

Davis & Furber Machine Co., North Andover, Mass., for photograph of the original wool carding machine, pages 146 and 157.

E. P. Dutton & Co., Inc., Publishers, New York, for certain sketches from the works of Marion Nicholl Rawson: page 75 (horse-poke from page 272 of *Handwrought Ancestors*); page 83 (wooden latch from page 147 of *Sing, Old House*); and page 343 (shoulder yokes from page 11 of *Handwrought Ancestors*).

Evanston (Illinois) Historical Society, page 118.

Memorial Hall, Philadelphia, pages 14, 15, 59, 115, and others.

The Museum of The University of Pennsylvania, pages 174, 175, 179, 182, 183, 187, and others.

The Platt & Munk Co., Inc., Publishers, New York, for certain sketches from *The Book of Cowboys* by H. C. Holling: page 86 (flintlock rifle details); page 98 (horse and ox shoes).

James Spear Stove & Heater Co., Philadelphia, Pa., for photograph of cast-iron stove shown at right on page 127.

University Press, Publishers, Des Moines, Ia., for certain sketches from *Before the Railroad* by Dorothea Tomlinson: page 64 (brick kiln); page 66 (burning limestone); page 119 (loom).

Washington's Headquarters and Valley Forge Museum, pages 6, 7, 18, 19, 22, and others.

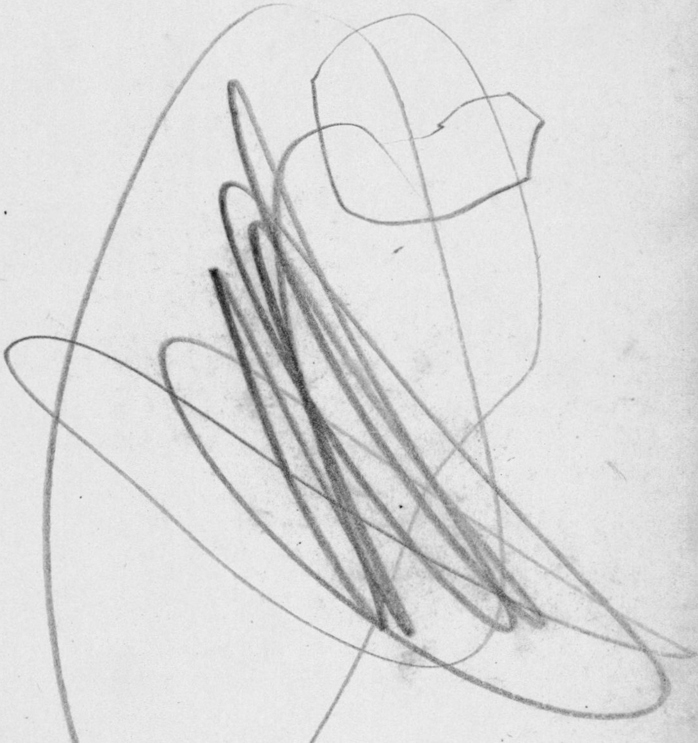

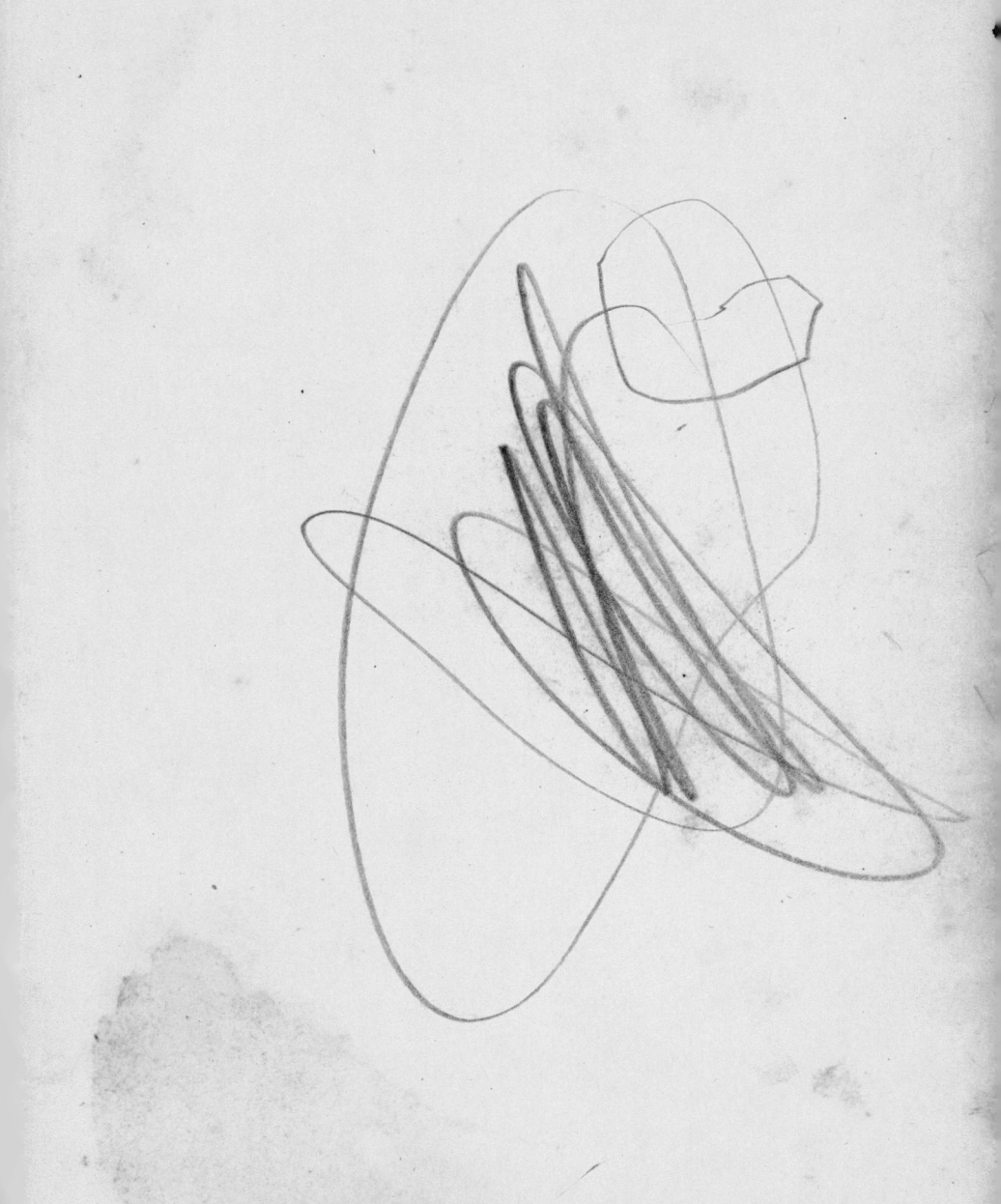